PROXIMA FIVE

What Reviewers Say About Missouri Vaun's Work

Love at Cooper's Creek

"Blown away...how have I not read a book by Missouri Vaun before. What a beautiful love story which, honestly, I wasn't ready to finish. Kate and Shaw's chemistry was instantaneous and as the reader I could feel it radiating off the page."—*Les Reveur*

"*Love at Cooper's Creek* is a gentle, warm hug of a book."—*The Lesbian Review*

Crossing the Wide Forever

"*Crossing the Wide Forever* is a near-heroic love story set in an epic time, told with almost lyrical prose. Words on the page will carry the reader, along with the main characters, back into history and into adventure. It's a tale that's easy to read, with enchanting main characters, despicable villains, and supportive friendships, producing a fascinating account of passion and adventure." —*Lambda Literary Review*

All Things Rise

"The futuristic world that author Missouri Vaun has brought to life is as interesting as it is plausible. The sci-fi aspect, though, is not hard-core which makes for easy reading and understanding of the technology prevalent in the cloud cities. ...[T]he focus was really on the dynamics of the characters especially Cole, Ava and Audrey—whether they were interacting on the ground or above the clouds. From the first page to the last, the writing was just perfect."—*AoBibliosphere*

"This is a lovely little Sci-Fi romance, well worth a read for anyone looking for something different. I will be keeping an eye out for future works by Missouri Vaun."—*The Lesbian Review*

"Simply put, this book is easy to love. Everything about it makes for a wonderful read and re-read. I was able to go on a journey with these characters, an emotional, internal journey where I was able to take a look at the fact that while society and technology can change vastly until almost nothing remains the same, there are some fundamentals that never change, like hope, the raw emotion of human nature, and the far reaching search for the person who is able to soothe the fire in our souls with the love in theirs."—*Roses and Whimsy*

Birthright

"The author develops a world that has a medieval feeling, complete with monasteries and vassal farmers, while also being a place and time where a lesbian relationship is just as legitimate and open as a heterosexual one. This kept pleasantly surprising me throughout my reading of the book. The adventure part of the story was fun, including traveling across kingdoms, on "wind-ships" across deserts, and plenty of sword fighting. ...This book is worth reading for its fantasy world alone. In our world, where those in the LGBTQ communities still often face derision, prejudice, and danger for living and loving openly, being immersed in a world where the Queen can openly love another woman is a refreshing break from reality."
—Amanda Chapman, Librarian, Davisville Free Library (RI)

"*Birthright* by Missouri Vaun is one of the smoothest reads I've had my hands on in a long time."—*The Lesbian Review*

The Time Before Now

"[*The Time Before Now*] is just so good. Vaun's character work in this novel is flawless. She told a compelling story about a person so real you could just about reach out and touch her."—*The Lesbian Review*

The Ground Beneath

"One of my favourite things about Missouri Vaun's writing is her ability to write the attraction between two women. Somehow she

manages to get that twinkle in the stomach just right and she makes me feel it as if I am falling in love with my wife all over again."
—*The Lesbian Review*

Jane's World and the Case of the Mail Order Bride

"This is such a quirky, sweet novel with a cast of memorable characters. It has laugh out loud moments and will leave you feeling charmed."—*The Lesbian Review*

Visit us at www.boldstrokesbooks.com

By the Author

All Things Rise

The Time Before Now

The Ground Beneath

Whiskey Sunrise

Valley of Fire

Death By Cocktail Straw

One More Reason To Leave Orlando

Smothered and Covered

Privacy Glass

Birthright

Crossing The Wide Forever

Love At Cooper's Creek

Take My Hand

Proxima Five

Writing as Paige Braddock:

Jane's World The Case of the Mail Order Bride

PROXIMA FIVE

by

Missouri Vaun

2018

ISBN 13: 978-1-63555-122-8

THIS TRADE PAPERBACK ORIGINAL IS PUBLISHED BY
BOLD STROKES BOOKS, INC.
P.O. BOX 249
VALLEY FALLS, NY 12185

FIRST EDITION: SEPTEMBER 2018

v

CREDITS
EDITOR: CINDY CRESAP
PRODUCTION DESIGN: SUSAN RAMUNDO
COVER DESIGN BY MELODY POND

Acknowledgments

I'd like to thank the team at Bold Strokes Books for all the continued support. Rad, Sandy, Ruth, Stacia, and my editor, Cindy, you guys are really terrific to work with. I continue to be so grateful to all of you for the community of writers and readers you've introduced me to. I'd also like to thank my beta readers, Jenny, Vanessa, Alena, and Deb. A special thank you goes out to Anne Laughlin for reading a very early draft of the first few chapters and offering valuable feedback. Peggy, thanks for talking geology with me. I greatly appreciate our shared love of rocks.

I hope you enjoy reading this adventure as much as I enjoyed writing it.

Dedication

For Evelyn, for always.

CHAPTER ONE

Leah Warren dreamed a landscape of eternal daylight. Wait, not a dream. She squinted at the fierce light from the small oval window. As sharp as a laser, the shaft cut through the dark compartment. Leah tried to lift her arm, but the nerve signal from her brain went unanswered.

Should get up. Need to move. Nothing. Her body refused to respond.

Leah rotated her eyes away from the window toward the spaceship's interior. Emergency lights flickered, but they were no match for the intensity of the light from outside. The long glass access door for the stasis tube hovered above her, open but partially blocking her view of the rest of the ship. *Is the crew awake? Where are the others? Are we on Proxima B?*

Exhaustion.

So sleepy.

She fought the urge to close her eyes.

Her body jerked awake. She hadn't meant to doze off. How much time had passed?

Hazily, Leah realized she was still in the stasis tube. She fought against gravity to sit up. Her thoughts were murky and confused. She covered her face with her hands and exhaled. The interior lights were brighter now. The compartment illumination had risen to normal levels. The floor was cold against her feet as she slid out of the tube and made her first attempt to stand. Dizzy, she dropped back to a seated position.

Where is John? The onboard doctor should be checking her vital signs right about now. There was a list of protocols that should follow extended cryogenic hibernation. Hydration was imperative. Her foggy brain remembered that much.

Leah managed to stumble to a water unit. She pulled a tube free and drank. A fit of coughing followed the first few swallows, but after a minute she was able to drink comfortably.

Her mind was coming back to life. She scanned the hibernation quarters that bordered the cargo bay for the fifty crew members. Her tube was the only one open. A sick feeling threatened to overwhelm her as she viewed the dark, unopened stasis beds from across the large compartment. Swallowing the nausea, she examined the panel readout of the nearest tube. *Inactive. Vital signs, negative.* The doctor, John Reed, was dead in his tube. *Why? What happened?*

All the other panels she checked delivered the same data. She was the only survivor. Her entire crew was dead. She barely made it to the nearest trash receptacle before throwing up.

Leah dropped to the floor, leaned her head against the smooth surface of the wall, and focused on breathing. In and out, in and out. The muscles in her arms and legs began to quiver. *A stress reaction? Or a symptom of extended hibernation?*

First things first, address basic needs.

Sorting through data wouldn't be an option if she passed out from dehydration. There'd be no one to revive her. She was utterly alone. Panic choked her airway. Leah took a deep breath, stood, and braced against the narrow passageway for a moment to settle another wave of nausea that threatened to capsize her.

Life support, water, and food systems seemed to be operational. She drank a protein mix. Waited a minute to make sure her stomach was stable, then took a quick shower and discarded the stasis sleeper suit. The brief spray of cool water helped. She pulled a faded blue shirt and cotton pants from her gear trunk. The softly broken in fabric felt good. It felt familiar. The skin on her arm pebbled. The air was cool but not cold; maybe she was simply fatigued. The lightweight crew jacket she tugged on offered an extra layer. She finger-combed her wet hair, droplets of water soaked into her jacket where damp tendrils brushed her shoulders. She leaned against the console in the galley and searched for something to eat from the store of rations.

Despite the fact that she had no appetite, her body needed food and more fluids.

And she needed energy and nutrition to think.

It was hard to keep food down as she visualized her crewmates, forever asleep in their cryogenic chambers.

Dead. They were all dead.

Her body trembled with silent sobs.

Leah forced herself to concentrate on chewing, then swallowing, then chewing and swallowing again.

CHAPTER TWO

Dust and smoke swirled in small puffs around her boots as Keegan kicked a clump of smoldering black embers. They scattered across the dirt. This particular outpost had been constructed of packed earth and timbers, surrounded by a few open-air shelters with plank siding. Now all that was left of the wood struts was blackened sticks and ash.

This place wasn't continually manned. It was more of a stopover for small squadrons heading north or south along the desert rim. But there had been at least enough supplies here to feed a few troops for several days, and now everything had been taken, the shelves picked clean. But why go so far as to destroy an outpost that would at some point be resupplied? Why not just steal the food?

"Fucking raiders...cowards and thieves." Tiago stepped through the charred struts of the doorframe. The door hung at an angle, one hinge ripped away. He was almost as tall as Keegan, and what he lacked in height he made up for in mass. He was stoutly muscled through the shoulders and chest, swarthy, with dark hair. "Well, this is your mess to clean up. I have to be in Haydn City before lights out."

"I can handle a few raiders." Keegan wondered what was so urgent but was happy to be rid of him.

Tiago made a circle in the air signaling to his two men. The three of them piled into his crawler, leaving Keegan and her two soldiers, Yates and Gage, standing near the smoldering rubble.

"Report back to me with anything you find." Tiago leaned from the crawler's passenger side door. "I want to question the raiders personally."

"Fuck you." Keegan muffled the comment with a cough.

"What did you say?"

"I said, no problem." She smiled thinly. There was no way she was reporting back to him. She and Tiago held the same rank, even though, lately, he acted as if they didn't. She didn't answer to him, and she wasn't about to start now. The dust trailed behind Tiago's crawler as they drove east, toward the green zone.

"There are two sets of tracks." Yates was standing several feet away looking west toward the desert.

Keegan joined her. They stood shoulder to shoulder. Yates was a couple of inches shorter than Keegan, her skin brown, her build slender but fit. Yates's long black hair swirled around her face in the breeze.

"They took every fucking thing." Gage walked over to where they were standing. He was almost as tall as Keegan, but thicker. He was as solid as a tree. His thickly muscled, tanned arms bulged from his sleeveless shirt. He picked up a stone and threw it at nothing.

Keegan studied the horizon.

"We'll have to split up." Yates holstered her weapon. She was practically a sharpshooter with a gun and if possible, even more lethal with a knife.

"Why did they split up? Were they trying to throw us off?" Gage squatted as if examining the tracks might answer his questions.

"We won't know for sure unless we follow." Keegan crossed her arms.

"Well, there goes your two-day furlough." Gage looked up at Keegan.

"Fuck." Keegan turned and walked back toward her two-wheeled rover. She slid her rifle into the sheath mounted at the side and reached for the canteen. After a minute, Yates and Gage joined her. "I was hoping for a drink. All I can taste is dust."

"They never keep the good stuff here anyway." Yates pulled her canteen free.

"You two take the crawler and follow the tracks heading southwest. I'll track the ones that head northwest." The military-issue crawler could carry four. Keegan's rover was really only good for one, two in a pinch.

"I'm starving." Gage was always hungry.

"You two." Yates shook her head. "One of you is always whining about lack of food or drinks."

"We can't all be as self-controlled as you, Yates." Keegan admired Yates. She was glad that at least one of them was professional and disciplined, and was especially happy that it didn't have to be her.

"Don't you mean evolved?"

"Ha. Good one." Keegan shook her head as they walked back toward the vehicles. "If you don't overtake them within twelve hours, turn back for Haydn City. It's not worth the risk for the value of what they found here. Even the liquor." Keegan paused to allow her joke to sink in. Yates shook her head. "Report to Maddox whatever you find if you get back before me." Maddox would likely be at the garrison by the time they returned, and he could share any pertinent intel with Behn, the chieftain of the ruling clan. The three of them had taken an oath to serve under Chief Behn's House, the house of the Tenth Clan.

"You mean we're not going to turn any intel over to Tiago?" Yates smirked.

"Yeah, that's not happening." Tiago was Chief Behn's son, sadly, soon to take the chieftain's chair. But until then, Keegan refused to answer to him.

"Just don't openly piss him off." Gage crossed his arms. "I'd hate to have to step in and save your ass."

"As if." Keegan snorted. She checked the readout on the rover. There was plenty of power left, enough for several more hours of running time, even over rough terrain. The sun was strongest in the desert so she could deploy the solar charger even if she had to stop to sleep.

Gage nodded as he and Yates climbed into the front seats of the all-terrain vehicle.

"I'll see you in twelve hours, or less." Keegan balanced the rover between her legs, her boots planted firmly on the ground, and lowered tinted goggles.

"Last one to Haydn City buys the drinks," Gage shouted. He sped away, not waiting for a reply, a churning dust trail in his wake. Yates gave a single wave from the passenger seat.

Keegan gripped the accelerator and the rover lurched forward. She shifted her position, low over the steering column, keeping her center of gravity fluid as the rover moved across the soft and shifting terrain. After about two hours, the tracks veered due north. They were clearly skirting the boundary of the desert rim, parallel to the green zone. She put the rover in neutral and scanned the horizon with binoculars. Three clicks ahead, she saw smoke. She knew the spot.

Greer had taken over the outpost a few years earlier. It had been a safe place for his son who'd suffered in the city because of his physical limitations. City life was hard for anyone who was perceived to be weak, or for those who tolerated weakness.

Thick black smoke was not a good sign. She hastened, revving the rover, throwing sand as the oversized wheels gained air and bounced over the dunes.

When the structure was in sight, she abandoned the rover and continued on foot. The vehicle was easily hidden from view by a dune. Weapon drawn, Keegan crouched low and moved swiftly toward the earthen structure. Whatever had happened she'd missed it.

Tire tracks moved north again, away from the structure across the sand. One four-wheeled all-terrain vehicle, pulling a trailer from the look of it.

There, on the horizon.

Keegan sighted the dust of their escape through the binoculars. They had a good head start, but she'd catch them. She stowed the glasses and looked back toward the smoking structure.

The small homestead probably hadn't awarded the raiders with much. Anyone choosing to live this close to the desert rim was barely scraping by. In Greer's case, he had a particular reason for being here, and it certainly wasn't the acquisition of wealth. Keegan scanned the surrounding barren land. This outpost was on the frontier border of Chagall's province, a province bound to Behn, the chieftain, but regionally under Chagall's control. Keegan didn't like Chagall. He was weak, lazy, and soft. And those were his good qualities.

Keegan kicked a broken pottery chard with her boot. She exhaled loudly and then surveyed the outpost for Greer's son.

Keegan's tolerance for suffering had grown as thin as the gauze mask that shielded her nose and mouth from dust. And in this world, women and children seemed to suffer more than their share. She'd been luckier than most, because she was physically stronger than most boys, even as a teen. She'd pushed herself in the art of hand-to-hand combat. She was winning cage fights by the time she was in her late teens. Average men would not even consider challenging her. Her reputation and skills with a gun or a knife, and her popularity among the soldiers of the Tenth, garnered her a healthy dose of respect, even from Tiago, and he was tough to impress. He basically respected nothing but his own desires.

There was no movement about the place. She circled the exterior of the adobe building. Smoke still drifted from an open window at the back. A thread of black swirled up and dissipated against the cloudless sky. Greer's body lay near the door. She'd have described his position as facedown, except that his head was missing. She discovered the missing head mounted on a stake in the dirt near the fire pit. Broken cookware was scattered all around the death marker like clay confetti, his gaping mouth and glassy eyes frozen.

Keegan leaned closer to study his lifeless face.

This brutal scene seemed extreme. She knew enough about Greer to know he wouldn't have put up much of a fight. He'd have given the Fain raiders what they wanted, so why had they killed him? The Fain stole food, supplies, and women; murder in this manner was highly unusual. Small hairs tingled up the back of her neck. Were they trying to send a message? And if so, to whom?

The Fain were hunters and scavengers, oath-bound to some shadow leader they called Solas. The Fain were a loosely organized group of disenfranchised citizens. They dwelt in the hollow hills of the lifeless dark, on the night side of the planet, in a world unto themselves. In her opinion, shared by many, the Fain were outcasts and deserters. They lived at the edge of the dark. In recent years, they'd started raiding dwellings along the thin strand of livable space, the green zone.

Lately, there'd been isolated, violent attacks. As if they were becoming more militant. But why? Stealing was bad enough. Killing was just going to piss everyone off even more. The squadron of the Tenth had already been issued a "shoot at will" directive. It was hard to shoot an unarmed person holding a bag of food. But it was another thing to come across someone capable of what had just befallen Greer. This was a different sort of thing altogether.

A sound from behind caught her ear. Keegan swiveled toward the dark doorway of the building. She should have probably checked the interior first. Sloppy. Instinct directed her movements as she edged past the fire pit. She stopped near the entryway and listened. No more sounds.

She crept forward, weapon in hand. Upturned furniture, clothing, broken dishware, and open and emptied drawers were strewn about haphazardly. The raiders had taken everything of value. A streak of blood led her to a storeroom at the back of the dwelling. Shelving was askew, empty now, with the exception of one ruptured bag of flour. The white powder was clumped in spots like miniature snow drifts, splattered with blood.

Tristan, Greer's son, lay at the back of the room. Blood pooled under his head from a single gunshot. Keegan stood over him clenching and unclenching her fist. If only she'd arrived sooner.

He was facing up, as if he was looking at Keegan, but not seeing her. He was still, his slender arms at his side as if he was sleeping, but his eyes were open, seeing nothing. His deformed legs were covered by long trousers, and his crutches were broken and tossed in a corner. Despite his father's efforts to shield him from the cruelties of this world, his had been a short, painful life. If he'd been fit, strong, the raiders would no doubt have taken him, recruited him to fill their ranks. But this child had been neither fit nor strong.

For a fleeting instant, memories flooded Keegan's head. Her childhood, her introduction to the world. She couldn't remember her mother, and she'd never known a father. Life on this rock was hard for a child alone. By force of will, she blocked the memory.

Keegan knelt beside Tristan and closed his eyes, keeping her fingers in light contact with the young boy's face. He was still warm, but he was no more. Keegan holstered the firearm and found a blanket to cover his body. *Fuck all.* A tingle of rage wound through her gut.

She looked out the back window of the thick-walled, dwelling in the direction the raiders had headed. Her heart thumped in her chest. She took a few deep breaths and exhaled slowly. Anger caused mistakes. She looked back at the blanket covering Tristan. Her memories of the past threatened to rise again. She swallowed the lump in her throat and closed her eyes against them.

Keegan thought of the rolling hills to the north. The unsettled lands. Quiet, pristine, and the scent of evergreens in the air. When she opened her eyes, she felt calm, focused.

The main squadron had been heading south along the edge of the Great Desert, in a show of force meant to discourage exactly what had just taken place at this outpost. Six of them had split off, headed back to Haydn to report their findings. But then they came across the first ransacked weigh station. It was dumb luck really. And with a little more luck, Gage and Yates would catch the other half of this Fain raiding party and put them to rest permanently.

Keegan strode back to the rover, still thirsty for something stronger than water.

She would easily be able to overtake those in retreat before nightfall.

CHAPTER THREE

D r. Leah Warren was a geologist, not the flight commander or an engineer. Although each member of the crew had been trained to step into different roles if an emergency called for it, she wasn't as confident about her ability to reboot the ship's navigation system as she should be. Maybe it was hibernation fatigue, but her mind felt sluggish and unclear. She'd managed to choke down another freeze-dried meal while she checked systems and attempted to bring a few of them back online. The data seemed to indicate a solar storm, mid-flight, had damaged certain key functions. She couldn't be absolutely sure just yet, but probably one of the systems affected had been navigation. The computer cycled the data stream while she waited. The data pack was very large, indicating an extended time period, possibly longer than the anticipated two-decade flight time from Earth.

According to the atmospheric readout, the planet's air was breathable, she'd figured out that much. Although carbon levels were lower than Earth's, she wouldn't have trouble breathing if she ventured outside the ship. Well, except for the temperature, which hovered around one hundred and two degrees.

The ship had obviously landed at the edge of the desert region. How far from the habitable zone? Unknown. Could she pilot the shuttle craft if she needed to? Yes, probably. But she wanted to explore outside the ship on foot first, just to get her physical bearings. And to walk on solid ground. The passage from Earth was supposed to take twenty years. It had been far too long since she'd breathed outside air or felt the warmth of the sun on her skin. It seemed impossible to imagine. The scale of space and time was hard to grasp even having experienced it. Or, more accurately, slept through it. She was four light years from home, and there was no return flight. The enormity of it all settled over her, making it hard to breathe. She paused in the corridor and took several deep breaths.

While she waited for the data to collate, she punched in the codes for the other ships.

"This is *Proxima Five*, come in colony central command. This is *Proxima Five*." The communication screen was dark except for a single green thread that rippled and spiked like an EKG readout every time she spoke. She cycled through every ship's emergency call frequency after getting no response from central command. Nothing.

She pulled up the navigation screen on the nearest terminal. A topographic overview of the landing site filled the screen. The only sound in the silent compartment was the humming of the cooling fans in the wall and the clicking of the keypad as she zoomed out.

If the other colony ships had already landed, their beacons would ping on the map. Nothing. The next logical question prompted her to switch to astral charts. She confirmed that she was in the right planetary system; she had landed on Proxima B. The first four ships should have already arrived at the drop site. She exhaled and sank back in the chair, unsure of how to interpret her findings.

The solar charging arm had been deployed, but it would take another few hours to have enough battery to bring more systems online. Leah checked the power reserve and decided to cycle down everything except life support. If she didn't keep the interior of the ship cool, then she'd never survive and she needed to keep food storage and the mainframe cool and operational to figure out what the hell had happened.

The cryo bay was eerily dark and silent. She stood in the doorway for a moment looking over the rows of dormant, failed tubes before she went inside. Kristin's stasis unit was near the center of the compartment. Leah rested her palms on the unit, looking down at Kris, a ghostly sleeping figure beneath the frosted glass. Sleeping beauty, only there would be no kiss that could wake her.

They'd gone through astronaut training together. Kris had been her roommate, and they'd become close. Kris was the best friend Leah had, and they'd dreamed of starting this adventure on a new world together.

Leah laid her cheek against the glass. It was cold. She closed her eyes and let the tears come. *Oh, Kris. I'm so sorry.*

After allowing herself to grieve briefly, she closed the hatch of the dark compartment and walked slowly back to the galley.

There were other ships.

There *were* other ships.

She repeated the phrase, more of a wish than a declaration.

Her ship, *Proxima Five*, had been one of ten colony ships to leave Earth for Proxima B. The Roman numeral V combined with the profile of an eagle had become the ship's insignia on the mission patch, and it was printed on the back of the jacket she was wearing.

Proxima B was an Earth-like exoplanet in the habitable zone of Proxima Centauri, a red dwarf star. The Earth next door. Four light years from home, this planet was supposed to be plan B for humanity as Earth breached its own planetary boundary, the point of no return. The point of looming extinctions because of industrial excesses, overpopulation, and climate collapse. The Earth's demise was the harsh reality of anger politics and the side effects of populism.

The last days on earth would be ugly. She felt a twinge of guilt that she'd escaped the looming collapse, of everything. The Proxima missions represented the last gasp for humanity. Every bit of resources in reserve among the remaining first world countries were gathered to make the ten ships resemble something like the mythical Ark from the ancient great flood.

Leah had been happy to sign up for the mission. A chance to be part of something truly meaningful. A do-over, a chance to do things right. Mankind had learned from its mistakes, right? That was her hope, her belief. All of it was a huge leap of faith. Unfortunately, only a few would be awarded the chance to start over on a new world. She'd been one of the lucky ones, although, at the moment, she didn't feel very lucky.

She spent the next hour prepping a field bag with supplies: water, protein bars, high-powered binoculars, solar charger, a handheld O2 tank, and a locator to track her position in relation to the ship. The locator relied on optics bounced off the atmosphere from a transmitter on the ship. Low-tech, but functional in even the most technologically isolated setting.

Hours had passed, but she had to remind herself that there would be no sunset. Proxima B was tidally locked, like Earth's moon, one side awash in permanent daylight, the other side trapped in an endless cold night. Only a green, habitable zone ringing the central part of the planet from pole to pole had a temperate climate close to that of Earth in the nineteenth century.

That had been the last question in the Proxima B puzzle. Was there an atmosphere? Two decades before the first colony ship left Earth's orbit, the question had been answered. A probe measuring the infrared bounce back from the planet's surface finally determined there was an atmosphere. Enough of an atmosphere to circulate wind to keep the habitable green zone at the perfect temperature for liquid water, possibly even an ocean. Her ship had obviously missed the planned drop in the green zone and come down in the desert. But by how far? Since the other ships hadn't registered on her initial scan, she worried that she was completely in the wrong hemisphere.

Leah needed to see the landscape for herself. She needed to venture out or she was going to lose it. Being confined inside the ship with her dead crewmates was causing the walls to close in. She needed to move. She needed to breathe the outside air and feel a breeze across her skin. She needed to touch the sand.

Leah sealed the door from the cargo compartment to keep the rest of the ship cool once the exterior door opened. The seal on the large bay door gave way with a hiss, and a blast wave of oven-temperature heat flooded the compartment. Leah staggered backward and shielded her eyes. The tinted bay window had obviously softened the sun's intensity. She shucked out of the jacket and pulled dark glasses from the field bag and put them on. She tromped down the cargo ramp and hesitated for just a moment before remotely closing the hatch from a keypad near the bay door.

The surrounding terrain was desert, but a dark line of something undulated through the heat on the distant horizon to the east. Trees? Dwellings? That was her hope. She probably didn't have enough stamina to make it that far, but she could close the distance enough to get a better view using the long-range binoculars from a higher vantage point.

The plan was to walk in a straight line following set coordinates and then return to the ship and regroup. Her body was not acclimated to the extreme heat, and she knew she wouldn't be able to take much exposure to it.

After an hour of walking in the soft sand, she was incredibly winded. More fatigued than she should be, more than she expected to be, but she was sure her strength would return. She obviously needed additional time to rebound after the extended hibernation.

Leah stopped walking and took several deep breaths. Her head throbbed and her head felt heavy, foggy, almost as if she had a hangover. It might have been foolish not to give herself another day to recuperate, but she was anxious to find the other ships. That was assuming her craft had come down anywhere close to the planned colony site.

She knew she would not survive for very long alone.

Leah was only fifteen when the first images of Proxima B reached Earth. Rapid technological advances had opened up the possibility of light-powered space travel at significant speeds in the decade before she was born. Ultralight nanocraft probes—miniature probes attached to lightsails—moving at one hundred million miles an hour, still took twenty years to do a flyby mission near Alpha Centauri to send back the pictures. It took another decade to build and fund the Proxima initiative. She was twenty-five when she finished undergrad and applied for astronaut training.

There were four colony ships ahead of hers and five to follow. The first four ships were tasked with setting up the infrastructure required for long-term habitation. Structures had to be constructed, communities designed, and a power grid established before colonists could begin to arrive. What better place to harness solar power than a world where the sun never set?

The third and fourth ships carried colonists, tradesmen and craftsmen, male and female, and agriculture. And with agriculture came livestock and certain insects for pollination. Truly, each ship was an Ark, carrying pieces of the puzzle that would be used to build a new world order.

Her ship, *Proxima Five*, transported the Earth Science group—physicists, chemists, biologists, cartographers, mathematicians, and geologists. She was hopeful that the ships that preceded hers had rendezvoused at the planned colony site where there should be water. That was assuming the data they received from the probe was accurate. Inevitably, a lot could happen, even an extended drought, in the decades it would take for the colony ships to make the journey from Earth.

Leah chewed on a protein bar and drank a third of her water. She'd turn around soon, but she wanted to get a view from the top of the large dune just ahead.

When she crested the ridge, she realized the dust she'd seen on the horizon earlier hadn't been due to the wind. A vehicle of some kind was below. It was as if her brain was working in slow motion. Her first thought was that these were people from one of the other ships who'd seen her craft go down. But then nothing about the men seemed familiar. Her intuition told her to hide. She moved too quickly, and the crest of the dune collapsed beneath her feet. She half tumbled, half slid down the long slope.

Dark figures filled her vision, backlit from the sun. Two of them grabbed her, and her head bobbed to one side as she was dragged toward the vehicle. The men drug her by her arms so that she couldn't stand and she couldn't break free. They dropped her, and one of them roughly yanked the gear bag away. He rummaged through it, sniffing the half-eaten protein bar before tossing it in the sand. Another man removed her sunglasses and put them on. Hands searched her body invasively, without any care for personal space. She swatted at the man's broad, dust covered fingers. He groped and ripped her shirt open.

Panic constricted her lungs. She focused on breathing. Just breathe. Her mind raced as she tried to grasp what was happening.

She broke free and scuttled away from them, moving into the shade cast by the large tires of the nearby vehicle, but one of the men grabbed her foot and pulled her back. He was above her now. She searched his face for some ounce of kindness and saw none. His muscles were sinewy, and his skin was leathery, sunbaked, with stubble on his face. His clothes were the color of the sand, splattered with dark stains.

"Check for others." One of the men standing beside where she lay spoke to the man standing next to him, and he walked in the direction she'd just come from, but he didn't climb the dune.

The fact that he spoke English gave her a millisecond of hope that almost instantaneously faded. Something wasn't right. These men didn't fit within her framework. Was it possible that they were rogue colonists from the first four ships?

"I don't see anyone else."

"Get up." The man who'd tugged her by the leg yanked her painfully up by her arm and propelled her toward some sort of military looking vehicle connected to a trailer packed full of supplies and gear. The vehicle looked oddly similar to something she'd seen on Earth. Leah felt her limbs giving way from exhaustion. She stumbled and fell to her knees.

The man who'd jerked her to her feet grabbed a handful of hair and shoved her face into the sand. She tried to roll over so that she could breathe, but this only gave him better access. She kicked and fought him, swinging wildly. She managed to kick him before he pinned her legs. He slapped her so hard her head snapped back, thumping hard against the ground. The other two men stood and watched, their faces shadowed, their collective energy aggressive.

If these men were from one of the other colony ships then it was becoming clear why they'd been cast out.

Winded and dizzy, Leah was yanked to her feet and dragged toward the vehicle. The man forced her into some sort of heavy gauge wire cage at the back of the trailer and locked the gate.

Shock and nausea fought for dominance. Leah got to her knees, there was not enough room to stand, and grasped the cage with both hands.

"What are you doing? You can't do this!"

The man ignored her. He took a long drink of something from a flask, and then turned to look out at the open, lifeless landscape.

"Let me go! Let me out of here. You have no right to do this." Leah shook the cage door. It rattled but didn't give way.

The man stowed the flask, and with his arms over the top of the cage, leaned against it. Leah shrank back.

"You better shut up or I'll put something in your mouth to keep you quiet."

Leah drew herself up into the corner, as far as she could move away from him, and made herself as small in the space as was possible.

He smirked at her and then turned to join the other two men as they climbed back into the four-seated crawler. She fell sideways as the trailer lurched forward across the sand. Her heart sank. They were taking her away from her ship.

She tugged the pieces of her torn shirt together and wedged herself into the corner of the small cage. Leah hugged her knees to her chest. She couldn't see the men from where she was at the back of the trailer, but she heard occasional muffled comments. Their words were too unclear over the whine of the engine to make out.

Stupid, stupid, stupid. She'd been careless and cavalier to strike out alone and unarmed. She squinted up at the glaring sun.

CHAPTER FOUR

K eegan stood several feet in front of the rover, its solar panel open and charging. Slowly, she followed the horizon's thin ribbon with binoculars until she saw the dust cloud. She lowered the distance glasses for a minute and then checked again. Although night would not come to the desert, she would still have to sleep, at least for a few hours. And hopefully, so would they.

Damn, how were they still ahead of her?

She'd expected to intercept them by now. They had not altered course; they were definitely heading toward the Black Cliffs. She needed to catch them before they entered the Narrows to make a run for darkness on the far edge of the green zone. She'd never capture them if they made it that far. It would be unsafe to even attempt it without backup or cold weather gear.

The sun's glare on the gauge made it hard to read. Keegan leaned down and shielded the readout with her hand. It would take a few more minutes with the engine off to rebuild the charge. She straightened and looked back toward the horizon. The good news was they had nowhere to hide in this terrain.

The canteen was stowed under rations in the small cargo compartment at the back of the rover. It was two-thirds full. She took measured sips and let the water sit on her tongue before swallowing. Something stronger than water was what she wanted, but water would have to do for now. She closed her eyes, with her back to the sun, and thought of other things.

The coolness of water.

The sound of the wind in the conifers.

The sensual dip of a woman's waist just where it met her hip. And then the velvet skin along the inside of her thigh…

A shadow passed across her face. A bird crossed overhead, flying west out over the endless sand. Keegan sipped more water.

Where could you possibly be going?

Away. Which was exactly where Keegan had wanted to be for her two-day leave. Away and free.

She watched the black bird effortlessly cross the sky. She swept her fingers through the stubble at the back of her head where the tattoo was inked into her scalp. The mark represented comfort and belonging. Knowing the mark was there even though she couldn't see it grounded her. The tattoo meant something.

She leaned against the seat of the rover and tried patience on for size. Not the best fit she decided. Waiting didn't suit her.

Leah squinted through the bars. She swallowed, her throat ached from dust and thirst, and the constant exposure to the sun was sapping what little reserve she'd built up. From inside the cage, she could see her bag near the front of the trailer. It contained water and protein bars, but there was no way for her to reach it.

She wasn't sure how long they'd been driving. At some point she dozed off despite her best efforts not too. Exhaustion and heat were working against her already overwrought system.

The vehicle stopped, and the man circled to the back and unlatched the gate. Leah couldn't decide if she was more afraid to be inside the cage or out of it. Either option seemed perilous.

"Get out."

She tried, but she fumbled her first attempt because her ankle was stiff, her foot an uncoordinated ball of pins and needles from resting for too long at a strange angle. He grabbed her arm as she stepped from the cage. Leah worried that once she stood she'd feel the urge to relieve herself, but no doubt the lack of water she'd consumed made that unnecessary.

Her head felt too heavy as she was tugged away from the cage toward the shaded side of the crawler. The man wrapped dark cord around her wrists several times. He yanked it tight, too tight, and lashed the cord to an exposed roll bar. He pulled it taut so that Leah's arms where above her head.

Her fingers began to tingle. She pulled her knees underneath her body in an attempt to lessen the vertical stretch of her arms. Feeling began to return to her hands. Leah flexed her fingers and tried to slow her rapid breathing. She needed to stay calm and keep her wits about her.

One of the men began to set up a canvas tent while one of the other men worked to start a small fire. He mounted a large pot low over the gradually increasing flame and sat back. He was watching her now, and his scrutiny made her skin crawl. She rotated so that he couldn't see her face.

A shadow fell over her. It was the man who'd tied her hands. He knelt and with a finger on her chin, forced her to look at him.

"Which House do you belong to?"

She didn't understand his question. Dizziness threatened her again. She blinked, trying to clear the fog, but didn't answer.

"Who do you belong to?" he asked again and pushed her sleeve past her elbow as if he needed to examine her arm for some reason.

Who did she belong to? No one. What was he looking for? If he thought she was alone would that be better or worse?

"It doesn't matter." He stood.

The sun never waned. She squinted as he stood, backlit, and moved away from her. This sun was so much larger than Earth's sun, which made sense because Proxima B rotated around a red dwarf star, from a much closer orbit. Luckily, because it was technically a dying star, despite the heat, the sun didn't emit enough ultraviolet rays for Leah to sustain too much of a sunburn from the exposure.

But what time was it? It must be late. In a normal twenty-four-hour day it would have to have been dark by now, nightfall, but not here.

Maybe her ship had landed near the drop zone after all, but if that was true, then who were these men? Whoever they were, they didn't know her, and they didn't seem like any of the men she'd met from the crews of the other colony ships. Not that she'd have known them by name, some of the crews were rather large, but she might have recognized them. Their aggression had surprised her.

Could it be that she'd missed the scheduled landing window? Timeframe was one of the things she hadn't sorted out. Even if she could be certain of where she was, she had no idea of when. Maybe these men were part of the first crew. That ship had departed almost five years ahead of hers, charged with setting up the initial infrastructure for a settlement. Maybe that's why they'd asked about others. Maybe they knew she came from one of the other ships. Somehow, she doubted that to be true based on the questions they'd asked. What had they meant by house? What had he asked, what house was she from? Facts were not adding up; her head pounded from need of food and water.

Leah felt an unwanted tear trail slowly down her cheek. She squeezed her eyes shut and clinched her bound fists.

CHAPTER FIVE

A blast reverberated through the desert camp.

One of the men sitting near the cook fire rocked backward. Blood splattered across his torn shirt from the wound in the center of his chest. He sank back to the ground and didn't move. Before the second man could take cover, another gunshot. Half his face was gone when his body hit the sand.

The third man, the one who'd tied her up, scrambled to his feet. Leah squeezed against the smooth metal of the vehicle, trying to make herself invisible. The last man standing rested his hand on the weapon clipped to his belt, but he didn't remove it from the clasp. The look on his face was one of surprise. Leah followed his gaze until she too saw the figure approaching.

Leah shivered either from nerves or shock or dehydration or all three. The air was hot, but she began to tremble. She pulled her knees to her chest and huddled next to the metal frame. She prepared to hear another blast. She squeezed her eyes shut, covering her face as much as she could with her upstretched arms. When she heard nothing, she opened her eyes. The gunman had walked to the fire and nonchalantly lifted the lid on the cook pot. The man stood like a statue, never taking his eyes off the shooter.

At first glance, Leah had assumed the gunman was a man. The gunman definitely had a masculine physique, and nearly shaved head, but the smoothness of the neck, the shape of the jawline, these details told Leah the shooter was a woman. She had the build of a professional athlete or collegiate swimmer. Her shoulders were broad and her biceps were well-defined even though she wasn't flexing them. She wore a sleeveless shirt so that Leah could see some sort of markings on her shoulder, a tattoo of some kind perhaps. Wide leather straps crisscrossed her chest. The pants she wore looked like part of a military uniform. Green-gray cargo pants stretched snuggly over muscled thighs, riding low on narrow hips.

The shooter straightened and looked at the man. She was taller and oozed confidence. The man took a few steps back but still made no move to pull his weapon.

"I don't want any trouble with you." It seemed he knew the shooter, and he was clearly intimidated by her.

The woman took a step toward the man. Her eyes were shadowed, her expression unreadable; the strange looking rifle was at her side. Her stance was relaxed, but energy pulsed off her as if her entire body was a weapon, cocked, loaded, ready to fire.

"You can take the woman." He took a step backward. "I'll take the supplies and leave you the woman. She's worth more than all of it."

"I have a better idea. I'll take everything, including the woman, and drop you right here with your friends. I sort of prefer that plan. It's cleaner…Simpler." The shooter glanced at Leah, then took another step forward as she raised the rifle.

"Keegan, I don't want any trouble with you—"

"Too late." His words were cut short by the blunt force of the rifle blast to his midsection. The close-range discharge of the weapon threw him back several feet where he hit the ground with a solid thump. His arms twitched, and blood splattered from his mouth as he tried to speak. Keegan stood over him for a few seconds before she discharged another round into his chest. "That was for Tristan."

Leah shivered as Keegan strode in her direction. Keegan knelt and set the rifle aside. When she made a move to reach for Leah, she flinched. She did not want to be touched.

"Hey, I'm not gonna hurt you." Keegan held her palms up as if to signal that she meant no harm. She pulled a knife from a sheath at her waist and cut the cord, releasing Leah's hands. They dropped to her lap, aching from loss of blood flow, and at first her thick fingers wouldn't move.

Leah's muscles twitched and her face ached from being struck earlier. Her head felt as if it weighed a hundred pounds, and she was having difficulty remaining upright.

She needed to get back to the ship. That was the only thought she had as she struggled to her feet, using the side of the vehicle for balance. She took a few steps. Could she walk that far? How far had they traveled?

Keegan stepped in her path. Leah tried to move around her, but Keegan caught her by the arms. Her grip was painfully strong.

"Let me go." She'd meant for the words to sound commanding, but her voice cracked because her throat was so dry.

Keegan held her fast.

"Are you going to kill me?" Her words sounded small and far away.

Keegan was twice Leah's size, pure muscle mass, and tanned from the sun. Dark-eyed, sensual, and recent empirical evidence suggested, violent. She was probably six feet tall, towering above Leah by six inches. She leaned very close as if she were sampling Leah's scent. Like some predator memorizing the fragrance of the prey it was about to devour.

"Are you going to kill me too?" Leah repeated the question.

"I hadn't planned on it." There was teasing in her voice, but she didn't release Leah.

"Let me go." The request was barely more than a whisper. Barely more than a wishful thought. Where the earlier command had no effect, the whispered request seemed to hold power.

Keegan let her hands fall away. No longer anchored, Leah swayed on her feet. She shifted her stance in an effort to stabilize.

"What's your name?" Keegan asked.

She blinked, surprised by the mundane question in such an extreme context. "Leah."

Whoever this warrior was, the man had known her by name and he'd been afraid of her. Keegan reached for Leah again. "I'm thinking you're not too stable on your feet."

Leah was mesmerized by Keegan's intense gaze. And because of it, she made no move away from Keegan. As if she was in some sort of trance, she stood there and allowed Keegan to capture her again.

Keegan was standing so close now, too close, so that Leah could feel the warmth of her skin. She smelled of leather and fresh air with the faintest hint of something…juniper perhaps?

"You're hurting my arm."

"Am I?" Keegan didn't release her. She brushed the back of her fingers over Leah's cheek where she'd been struck. In contrast to what Leah expected, Keegan's touch was gentle.

"I need to get back."

"Back where?"

"To my…" Leah's head began to swim. Her vision shrank as if she were at the end of a very long, dark tunnel, and the air rushed from her lungs. *No, no, no.* She sank against Keegan's chest, the world swallowed up in darkness.

❖

Keegan eased Leah to the ground. For a few moments, she stood silently and studied Leah's limp form.

Keegan knelt down, pushed strands of hair off Leah's face, and studied her delicate features. Her cheeks were flushed, but otherwise her skin was pale. Keegan had never seen someone so pale, as if she'd been living underground, protected from the elements. Leah's hair was dark, and Keegan had noticed her gray eyes the minute she'd gotten close enough to see their color. Gray eyes were rare. Everything about Leah seemed rare and otherworldly. Keegan rocked back on her heels and tried to imagine what this woman could possibly have been doing in the desert to come in contact with these men. Her body had no markings of ownership. Her pale skin implied she'd spent time in the Dark Hills. But she'd been tied up, so these men were not her family or her friends. Leah had been with them against her will.

She held Leah's hand up and examined her slender, tapered fingers. Soft, smooth, no calluses anywhere. Her breasts, where they showed above the torn front of her shirt, were unblemished and full, the sensual curve of her stomach was exposed at the hem of her shirt. Leah was exquisite.

Keegan stood and surveyed the camp. She would claim everything, including Leah, and take it all back to Haydn City.

It was near midnight and she was tired. The men had set up a large canvas tent to shield them from the unrelenting sun. Keegan decided to take advantage of the camp. It had been a long hard day of riding. There was a cook fire smoldering in front of the canvas tent, open at the front. Keegan scooped Leah up in her arms and carried her to the shade of it. She retrieved a bedroll from her rover, spread it out, and then gently moved Leah on top of it. She returned to the cook fire and served herself some food. She sampled from the spoon. A stew of some sort, probably made with the stolen provisions. It had the flat taste of a soldier's rations. She rummaged in the cases at the back of the raider's crawler until she found a flask of whiskey. She took long draws letting the warm liquor settle her system. She glanced sideways at the man who'd called her by name.

Something felt wrong.

He'd known her name, but she didn't recognize him. She rolled him onto his side so that she could examine the back of his scalp. His hair was in a shaggy, short cut. But when she separated the dark hair at the base of his skull, she saw the mark. He had the same mark she did, designating him as a soldier of the Tenth.

She unsnapped the holster at his belt and pulled the sidearm free. It was military issue, not refurbished or bootlegged. She kept the gun in her hand as she stood up.

Why would a soldier of the Tenth be raiding outposts with the Fain? Other garrisons had suffered from deserters in the past, but not the Tenth. The Tenth was in power, they answered only to Chief Behn, they were the favored legion. In that position, they were well compensated with housing, food, and women.

And why had he tried to disguise who he was?

He'd let his hair grow, and his shabby, ill-fitting clothing was clearly meant to disguise his station and training. All of these details puzzled Keegan and she had no idea what they meant, but she had the distinct feeling there was something much bigger than petty theft behind it.

His wrist bore the branded F signaling his allegiance to the Fain, as did the other two, but the tattoo on his scalp settled in the back of her brain uneasily. Before the fire died completely, Keegan dragged the bodies of the dead men away from camp. Unfortunately, she'd shot one of them in the head so it was impossible to check for markings on his scalp. The other man bore no such marks.

She returned and stood over Leah considering what to do next. She entwined her fingers and pressed them at the back of her head, elbows out, and paced in front of the tent.

She wasn't supposed to be in the fucking desert. She should be making camp at the edge of the great wood, with the scruffy green hills cresting on the distant horizon to the north on two days of leave away from the stifling city. But she wasn't. There'd been no option but to alter course and track the raiders. Their incursion had to be dealt with swiftly.

She looked back at Leah, her frail beauty tugging at Keegan's insides like an insistent whisper. *Save me.*

Fuck it all.

Could anyone truly be saved? The world was cruel and all Keegan had ever known was struggle for the sake of self-preservation. Her choices had been to fight for her place in the world or suffer at the hands of others. Fighting was all she knew. But Leah was so beautiful and Keegan felt an instant attraction. She shook the thoughts from her head. She needed sleep. Her brain was too tired to figure it all out just now.

If they rested now then started driving, she could reach Haydn City before she needed sleep again. She decided to cast off the cage and load her two-wheeled rover into the trailer. Tethers would hold the rover upright, and then she repacked all the stolen supplies and gear into the open spaces around it. Now she was truly exhausted.

Leah was still out when she returned to the tent. Keegan took a small cup of water and pressed it to Leah's mouth. She tilted Leah's head up and forced liquid between her lips. Leah coughed. Her eyes fluttered for a moment. She swung at Keegan knocking the cup out of her hand.

"Hey, I'm not going to hurt you. You need to drink some water."
Keegan tried to still Leah's arms.

"I need to get back."

"Wherever it is you want to go, you're too weak to get there.
And you're far from anywhere right now."

Leah looked at her, as if she was seeing Keegan for the first
time. She felt the intensity of Leah's gaze deep in her chest, like
fingers closing around her heart. The sensation caught her by
surprise. After only a moment, Leah went limp in her hands. She
was out again. Keegan eased her head to the bedroll.

Keegan wasn't sure she was good at caretaking. She might be
terrible at it. And yet, something about Leah tugged at protective
impulses she didn't even know she had. Leah was like some fragile,
beautiful being lost in the wild, waiting to be rescued.

The air temperature was high, but Leah had begun to chill.
Although still asleep, she shuddered. Maybe this was the first sign
of heat exhaustion. The desert was an intense environment, even
in short doses. Keegan drew Leah's body against hers to still her
tremors. She wasn't sure what else to do. Intimacy with a stranger
normally felt very different from this. Intimacy usually involved
some exchange of money or favors. There was no exchange for this
and yet, oddly, it felt okay.

Sex was readily available in Haydn City. Affection, on the
other hand, was hard to come by. Possibly the only time she'd felt
genuine affection had been with Esther, when she was a teen. Esther
was a few years older and had always been kind to her. Keegan
allowed herself to remember the warmth of that embrace. She
imagined Esther's arms holding her must be what it was like to feel
a mother's love, although she couldn't be sure because she had no
memory of hers.

Holding Leah now was very different from the chaste memory
of Esther's comforting hug. Some deep longing stirred inside
Keegan, and she tamped it down. She forced herself not to notice
the soft press of Leah's body against hers. Or the smell of her skin.

Chapter Six

L eah gradually became aware of the light. Immense brightness as if it were midday, but surely she hadn't been asleep for long. The truth was she had no sense of what time it was since the sun's position never changed. Why hadn't she thought to wear a watch? Shafts of light filtered through the thin tears in the tarp overhead. Only as her brain began to fully wake did she realize she'd slept, under an open-air tent, cradled against Keegan's shoulder. The shock of this discovery hastened her waking.

Her first inclination was to push out of Keegan's arms, to rush away from her, to gain the safety of distance. But she hesitated, realizing she was soothed by a sense of warmth and shelter. How could someone she feared make her feel safe at the same time? How long had they slept this way? She shifted her arm draped across Keegan's stomach and Keegan stirred. Then Keegan regarded Leah as if she too were surprised by the coziness of their embrace. Keegan smiled awkwardly and then abruptly left her and strode away from the tent.

Leah assumed Keegan was seeking privacy to relieve herself, and she looked around for a spot to do the same. The barren landscape didn't offer much visual buffer for discretion.

She didn't venture far, just far enough to sink behind a small dune near the camp. She stood and scanned the desert. The ship, where was it from here? Time since leaving the ship felt like a fog of blended images she wasn't sure were memories or dreams. She closed her eyes and placed her palm on her forehead. Her head began to swim so she opened her eyes, hoping the horizon would help her stabilize.

"You should eat something."

She turned to see that Keegan had brought her a bowl of steaming food. How long had she been standing there looking away from camp? Ever since she'd landed here this planet had been stealing time from her.

Minutes.

Hours.

How long ago was it that she woke in the stasis tube? Twenty-four hours? Now she wasn't sure.

Keegan motioned with the bowl, an indication for Leah to take it.

"Thank you."

Leah followed Keegan back and sat on the ground next to the small cook fire that she hadn't even noticed Keegan stoke. She shook her head, hoping to reset her fuzzy brain. The food was simple but savory. Some mixture of legumes with bits of dried meat. As she chewed a second spoonful and then a third, she realized it had been quite some time since she'd had any real food.

"This is good. I think I was very hungry." Leah tried to sound gracious. She looked down, swiftly aware her torn shirt was revealing much more cleavage than she felt comfortable showing.

Keegan nodded and only made brief eye contact, as if suddenly shy. Leah had to remind herself that this was the same woman she'd watched shoot three people. She was grateful for the food and thankful that Keegan had liberated her from those men, but she needed to get back to her ship, otherwise she'd never figure out where the mission had gone off track.

Leah studied Keegan as she ate.

"Are you from the colony?" It hadn't occurred to Leah to just ask Keegan until now. Maybe Keegan knew the answers to at least some of her questions, but there'd been other, more urgent distractions, and she'd been in no condition to ask.

"What colony? You mean clan?"

Clan? Leah didn't know a better way to ask the question. Could the colony be referred to as a clan? That word had become so heavy with negative connotations on Earth that no one used it.

"Which settlement are you from?" She tried a different approach.

"I'm a soldier for the Tenth."

"The tenth what?"

"Clan. The Tenth House." Keegan scowled at her as if she was annoyed by the question.

"Is it a clan or a house?"

"Both." Keegan frowned. "You ask strange questions."

"Forget it." Leah stood and brushed small bits of debris from her pants. She walked to the trailer and pulled her gear bag free. She rummaged inside for the locator device. She was ignoring Keegan now as she held the mechanism hoping to locate the radio signal from her downed ship.

There. The device pinged, and a small blue dot appeared to the southwest.

"What is that?" Keegan stood beside her.

"Nothing."

Keegan clearly didn't like that response. She ripped the device from Leah's hand, and when Leah grabbed for it, Keegan, with a hand at the base of Leah's throat, held her at arm's length like some juvenile game of keep-away. Leah felt her cheeks flame.

She again tried to reach for the device.

"I'm not sure what this is, but I think I should hold on to it for you." Keegan blocked her, then took the entire satchel out of her hand and put the small console back inside. "We should get going." Keegan motioned with her head toward the vehicle.

"I'm not going with you." Leah took a few steps away from Keegan. "I appreciate what you've done for me so far, but I must return to my…I'm traveling in a different direction."

"We'll be in Haydn City before noon. Haydn City is that way." Keegan pointed east, away from Leah's ship.

This was the most infuriating conversation. It was as if they were speaking a different language.

"I said, I'm not going with you."

Keegan scowled. She reached for Leah's arm and tugged her toward the vehicle. Leah did her best to resist. She tried to pry Keegan's fingers from her arm, but Keegan's grip was as hard and unmoving as stone.

Keegan tossed Leah's bag in the cargo area and then reached to open the cropped door of the crawler. Now Leah was frantically swinging at Keegan with her free arm, but she might as well have raged at air for all the difference it was making.

"Stop fighting me. I'm trying to help you." Keegan held her by both arms, her voice low and commanding, as if she were used to getting her way.

"Let go of me." Leah wasn't giving in.

"Stop." Keegan pinned her arms and pressed her against the side of the vehicle.

"You're hurting me." Leah wriggled but was unable to free herself.

Keegan's body was full against hers now, their faces only inches apart. Leah met Keegan's intense stare. Keegan's lips parted, and for an instant Leah thought Keegan might actually kiss her. She wasn't in the mood to be bullied into a kiss, no matter how attractive Keegan was.

"I don't know who you are, or where you came from, but you are the most confounding woman I've ever met." Keegan looked down at Leah's exposed cleavage. She exhaled slowly and returned her gaze to Leah's face. "You're coming with me. End of discussion."

"No, I'm not." Leah resumed her useless struggle.

Keegan was so much taller and stronger than she was. Self-defense classes rose to the surface in her foggy brain, and suddenly, she knew what to do. She stomped over the arch of Keegan's foot, then kneed her in the crotch. That didn't have the desired effect, but when Keegan glanced down, Leah struck Keegan in the nose with her forehead.

"Fuck." Keegan released her and covered her face. She leaned over with one hand on her knee and the other pinching her nose. A thin trail of blood trickled from her fingers.

Leah felt a twinge of guilt but used the opening to back away, out of Keegan's reach.

"No one forces me to do what I don't want to do. No one controls me." Defiance was probably the wrong course of action, but Leah's temper had gotten the better of her. She'd suffered the indignation of being confined, tied up, transported against her will, and with her strength returning, she was no longer in the mood to fulfill the role of the victim.

"So, you like to play rough?" Keegan wiped at the blood with her fingers and grinned.

Oh, no, this had not gone at all the way Leah wanted. She wasn't trying to flirt, but clearly that's the way Keegan was choosing to interpret things.

"I'm not playing. This is not a game." Infuriated, Leah continued to back away.

Keegan took a cloth from her pocket and wiped at her aching nose. She acted as if Leah's rebuff was some sort of amusing game, ratcheting up Leah's annoyance.

"There's nowhere to go." Keegan followed Leah as she continued to back away. "Seriously, you're in the middle of nowhere here. Look around."

Afraid to take her eyes off Keegan, Leah failed to notice the uneven sand that took a dip just behind her. She stumbled and fell, sitting down with a thump.

Leah was exasperated by her clumsiness, and Keegan's expression of smug victory as she towered over her was further insult. But Leah wasn't ready to give up. She kicked the side of Keegan's knee, causing her to crumple beneath a stream of expletives. Leah scrambled to her feet and ran, expecting Keegan to follow. The soft sand slowed her escape. She was sure Keegan would catch her, but when she didn't, Leah glanced over her shoulder. Keegan hadn't moved from where she'd fallen. Leah stopped and turned completely, watching for any sign of movement. What if Keegan was really hurt? What if she'd hit her head on a stone beneath the sand when she fell? *Dammit.* Leah couldn't leave without knowing for sure.

Slowly, she approached. Keegan was deathly still, on her back, with her arms at forty-five degree angles to her body. Leah edged closer. She saw no sign of blood on the ground beneath Keegan's head. She stepped closer.

As quick as a coiled snake's strike, Keegan grabbed her ankle and pulled hard. Once again, Leah hit the dirt, and this time Keegan was on her before she could get up. She pressed Leah against the ground with the weight of her body. Leah braced open palms against Keegan's chest and tried to shove her off, but Keegan was too strong.

Keegan could see the anger in Leah's eyes. If possible, Leah was even sexier when she was angry. Leah writhed beneath her but couldn't break free. She managed to pin Leah's arms above her head with one hand. She ran her thumb over Leah's cheek.

"I knew you cared about me."

"What?"

Oh, yes, Leah was definitely angry.

"I knew if I just lay there you'd come back to check on me." Keegan swept her hand down over Leah's ribs until she reached the curve of her hip. "Your actions give you away."

Keegan wanted so badly to sweep her palm up across Leah's partially exposed breast, but she held back.

Keegan knew enough about women to read the signs when a woman found her attractive. Leah was definitely drawn to her, despite the cold shoulder, despite the anger. Leah relaxed a little beneath her weight, but her expression didn't soften. Keegan slid her thigh between Leah's legs, and she applied subtle pressure.

Keegan wanted Leah to know that she would not pressure her into sex as much as she wanted it right now. Overpowering Leah was too easy. This was a dance and the melody between them had only just begun.

"If you force me to go with you, I'll only run away the first chance I get."

Keegan smiled. "Maybe you'll change your mind about that." She stood up and offered Leah her hand. Her libido was humming, but she chose to ignore it for the sake of future possibilities.

Leah hesitated, but finally accepted Keegan's assistance and allowed herself to be tugged from the ground. Keegan didn't release Leah's hand as they walked back to the crawler. She reached around Leah and opened the door.

"You'll regret this." Leah began to wriggle in Keegan's arms, but her defensive movements were less volatile than before. Keegan hoisted Leah through the open door and closed it.

"Probably." And truthfully, Keegan wondered if she would, but she wasn't ready to let Leah go. Not yet.

Clearly still angry and breathing hard, Leah reached for the handle as Keegan looked away. Before she could unlatch the door and open it herself, Keegan bound her hands and used the remaining cord to lash her wrists to the roll cage around the passenger compartment.

"Sorry, but this is for your own safety." Keegan's tender nose reminded her that maybe it was for her safety too.

Leah kicked at the door as Keegan walked away. It rattled loudly. Keegan started breaking camp, ignoring her. Leah kicked the door again. Keegan admired Leah's spunk.

Leah fumed in the passenger seat as she watched Keegan gather things and stow them in the trailer. She'd woken up cradled in Keegan's arms, and now she was tied up and held against her will. Leah's mind couldn't make sense of any of Keegan's actions. Helplessly, she watched as Keegan packed the bedroll and cooking pot. Keegan climbed into the driver's seat next to her, smiled, and then they were moving again, continuing east farther away from her downed ship. Keegan's cockiness, no, her arrogance, her arrogant self-confidence was driving Leah crazy.

Leah studied Keegan's sculpted jaw as she drove. Her feelings about Keegan were so damn confusing. Warring urges collided in her chest. She wanted to be as far away from Keegan as she could but was also inexplicably drawn to her. Keegan's powerful body excited her and at the same time frightened her a little. She'd never known anyone like Keegan, man or woman. Keegan gave the impression of wildness, untamed, raw, sensual. For an instant, Leah visualized giving herself to Keegan, and her entire body began to warm and vibrate. She looked away. Shifting her focus to studying the passing desert landscape. Intent on thinking of anything but Keegan on top of her, pressing her muscled thigh against Leah's sex.

Things could have gone differently just now. Keegan could easily have done more than overpower her, but she hadn't. Leah had felt Keegan's desire and was grateful that Keegan hadn't acted on it. Emotionally, she didn't think she could handle that. An immigrant and an exile, overwhelmed by a place she didn't fully understand, Leah was struggling not to lose herself. Maybe Keegan was right on some level. Maybe she was safer with Keegan than on her own. At least for the time being. Maybe this Haydn City was the colony site. Possibly traveling with Keegan would help her find some answers.

CHAPTER SEVEN

After what seemed like an hour, Keegan stopped and retrieved the canteen which she held for Leah to drink. Leah's heart pounded loudly in her ears, and if she could've reached Keegan, if her hands weren't tied, she'd have lunged and knocked the canteen from her hand just to make a point. But thirst won out over frustration when Keegan held the canteen out to her, and she drank, soothing her burning throat. A canvas half top was covering the passenger seats, offering some small respite from the glaring sun, but no real buffer for the heat.

The first sip resulted in a coughing fit. Keegan held onto the canteen to keep it from spilling. After the coughing subsided, she held it again for Leah, and their fingers touched.

"I need to go back." Leah's voice was raspy. She took another drink.

"Look where you are. There's nowhere for you to go."

The sun was intense. Leah was grateful for the cockpit covering; her skin felt tender even from the limited exposure to the sun.

"Where are you taking me?" Not knowing frightened her.

"I told you...We're going to the city. You'll like it there." Keegan sipped from the canteen too. "It's noisy, it smells, and it's full of people...you'll love it."

"Is that a joke?"

"Why, was it funny?"

"Look, I'm sure your friends find you amusing, but I have another agenda."

"Agenda? That sounds so…official." Keegan screwed the top back on the canteen. "I'm not crazy about going back to the city either. I'm supposed to be on a two-day leave right now and—"

"Then why go back?" Leah cut her off.

"All my stuff is there."

She really couldn't tell if Keegan was joking or serious. None of this felt like a joke to Leah, and her sense of humor had long since evaporated.

Keegan stowed the canteen and restarted the crawler. It resumed its pitch and roll, moving again across the uneven ground. She studied Keegan as she turned her head, as the road veered. For the first time she was close enough to notice the tattoo on her scalp at the base of her skull. It was either an X or the Roman numeral for ten. That detail settled in her mind uneasily.

It wasn't long before the air underneath the covering began to feel too warm. The waxed canvas tarp was heavy and cumbersome. Despite her efforts not to succumb to fatigue, Leah felt herself fading. She'd close her eyes for just a moment.

The crawler jostled and her head banged the headrest. She blinked.

How long had they been driving? A half hour? An hour?

"Do you need more water?" Keegan looked over. "We're almost to Haydn City."

"As if I care." If Keegan thought Leah would willingly or happily submit to such treatment, she was mistaken.

"You can rest there. There will be food and even a hot bath." Keegan continued to be annoyingly oblivious to Leah's displeasure.

A bath sounded luxurious, but she wasn't about to let Keegan know that.

The farther away they drove from the desert, the more the terrain changed. At first to striated rock cliffs bathed in orange from the light of the sun. She longed to gather rock and soil samples and take them back for evaluation in the lab aboard ship. There were more plants now. The foliage of the trees was not lush, but they were tall, with plumes of broad leaves at their crowns. The landscape reminded Leah of artist renderings she'd seen of prehistoric habitats. She half expected to see a dinosaur run past the vehicle at any moment.

Dwellings began to appear in small clusters. Simple, square structures with earthen walls and small, high windows with wooden shutters. And people. There were people milling about. Leah craned her neck for a better view, but they were too far away to gather details about clothing or language or anything else. Structures became more tightly packed and the roadway narrowed. The buildings were no longer single-story, but instead, stacked on top of each other like ancient cliff dwellings in the desert southwest of America. They didn't seem to be laid out along any sort of uniform grid, their rise asymmetrical and off center, as if second and third levels had been unplanned and only added as an afterthought.

This settlement was well established. If this was the colony site, then it seemed plausible that years had passed since it had first been settled. There were so many signs that hinted at the passage of time, one of them being the sheer number of structures. Also, the people. Each colony ship carried a varied number of passengers and crew, but none more than one hundred. There were multiple generations represented in the populace that Leah saw as they passed. She filed all these details away as she struggled to piece together not only where she was, but when.

Noise and dust filled the dry air as Keegan drove along the barely two-lane throughway. Carts and kiosks were set along the road haphazardly so that from time to time they had to wait for another small vehicle to pass. Man-powered pull carts, two-wheeled rovers, and other strange looking small vehicles clogged the dusty street as they neared what looked to be the city's center. They stopped near an arched opening at the edge of a plaza, paved with a stone mosaic pattern. From her vantage point, Leah couldn't identify the shape. The structures that surrounded the plaza seemed more formal in design than the casual dwellings they'd passed earlier. These buildings had sculpted details near the windows and along their tiled roofline.

Pedestrians milled through the plaza on their way to elsewhere. They wore clothing as if from a reenactment of ancient times, browns, tans, draped cloth mixed with modern devices like belts and satchels. Leah tried to take in specifics, to file them away so that she could sort through them later.

The door swung wide, and she realized Keegan had opened it. Keegan freed the cord lashed to the roll bar, but left her hands tied at her wrists. She took Leah's arm and helped her step down where she faced a man dressed similarly to Keegan. He was probably in his late twenties, clean-cut, shaved head. He seemed to be waiting for directions.

"Take my supplies and gear to the staging room. Then see that all the rest of this is taken to the cutter for auction. Not my rover, but everything else. The proceeds should be put in the treasury for the Tenth." Keegan reached for Leah's bag and held it loosely in one hand, sending a spiderweb of panic through Leah's system.

Leah needed that bag. She didn't want to lose sight of it. And she certainly didn't want it to be auctioned off with everything else they'd brought from the desert to God knows where.

"Including the crawler?" he asked.

"No, park the vehicle in the armory too, but take the trailer and its contents, minus my rover, to be auctioned."

"Yes, Commander."

Commander? Leah looked sideways at Keegan.

"Should I take her to the cages for auction as well?"

Keegan met Leah's gaze and held it for what seemed like minutes, but was probably only seconds. A silent challenge? Or a question? Keegan turned back to address the man.

"No, take her to my quarters." Keegan handed him Leah's bag and the other end of the cord that held her wrists. "And ask Esther to get her whatever she needs."

"Yes, Commander."

Keegan turned to Leah. "I'll be back later. Esther will get you settled."

Leah was suddenly afraid. She didn't want Keegan to leave her, tied and about to be led away by some strange soldier. She watched over her shoulder as Keegan took the rifle from the crawler and slipped the strap across her chest. She strode through the plaza without looking back.

❖

The chamber outside the forum was packed. The crowd parted for Keegan, and she nodded but didn't speak to anyone as she passed. She wanted to see Chief Behn, bathe, and eat, in that order. Voices echoed off the thick clay walls and then bounced up again from the stone tile on the floor creating a deafening clatter. Two soldiers stationed at the heavy dark wooden door pushed it open for Keegan as she drew close and then had to shove others back as they crowded the entry hoping to get inside. In the forum, Behn heard appeals and various complaints, for which he was to pass judgment. Clearly, he'd not been able to keep up with the number of citizens hoping to gain an audience.

Malcontents and whiners. As resources thinned, the populous restlessly complained and clambered for the council of elders to fix things. Good luck with that. Keegan had gotten close enough to the inner circle to know that the elders, one chosen from each Great House, only really cared for themselves and their own holdings. They used rhetoric and outright lies to soothe the people they were supposed to represent. And the populace at large swallowed it whole. Keegan wondered what it was like to still have faith. She'd lost hers a long time ago. Not because Behn, the chieftain, was dishonest, but because one man against the tide could change nothing. Humans were petty and selfish. This had been proven to her over and over and over since she was old enough to understand what the words meant.

A shouting match was in progress near the front of the chamber. Of course, it was Tiago and he seemed to be winning. He excelled at being the loudest voice in the room.

Tiago hadn't noticed Keegan yet, but others had. They stepped back away from the center of the room, giving Tiago the floor and Keegan space to confront him, but she had no intention of stepping into his ring of fire. She'd been driving and camping in the open for nearly a week before rescuing Leah. She was tired, thirsty, and in no mood to debate with an arrogant bully.

A long table bordered one side of the large, open room. She took a seat, and a server, a young boy, brought her a cup of water.

"Got anything stronger?"

He nodded. After a minute, he returned with a stein of beer. Keegan reclined and watched the show. After a few minutes, Yates slid into the seat next to her.

"When did you get back?" Yates whispered.

"Just now." Keegan leaned close so that she could speak softly and be heard. "Did you and Gage find the second group of raiders?"

"Yes. There were two men. They started shooting before we even reached them so we had no choice but to fire back."

"Dead?"

Yates nodded. "They had some food and other supplies from the weigh station. We brought everything back to Maddox at the garrison. You?"

"Same." Keegan thought of the men she'd shot, about how one of them had the insignia of the Tenth tattooed on his scalp. She wanted to share this detail with Yates and find out if she'd noticed anything odd about the others, but now was not the time.

"Did you bring back anything else of interest?" Yates quirked an eyebrow as if she already knew the answer.

"Maybe." How could Yates know about Leah?

Keegan hated that Yates seemed to know things almost before they happened. It was a freakish gift. Either that, or she had spies everywhere. Not for the first time, Keegan was glad Yates was an ally.

"What's her name?"

"Leah." Keegan didn't look at Yates; she was watching Tiago continue his rant. "She's feisty and she's already bloodied my nose once."

"I like her already."

"I say we can't send a squadron into the Hollow Hills to route them out of their dark caves. It would be a trap. We'd be going in blind." Tiago shouted near where Behn was seated on the raised platform, and several men standing around him voiced agreement. "The Fain have grown too large in number. And the popularity of this Solas, this rogue leader of theirs, only continues to grow. Now is not the time to strike."

Did this Solas person even really exist? No one had seen him. He was like a ghost. Keegan wasn't afraid of ghosts. In fact, she didn't believe in them. A shadow leader was no leader at all in her opinion, but rather a coward, too afraid to show his face.

The collective energy in the room was edgy. Tiago was skilled at exploiting that. He was quick to suggest a fight even when unnecessary and just as quick to avoid one if it meant he had any skin to lose. He was aggressive by nature and could be unpredictably ruthless, like a viper backed into a corner.

She hated to agree with him, but for now, he was right. There was no need to send more soldiers into the dark lands to track down a few starving, straggling raiders. Embellishing the threat and reach of the Fain was a favored scare tactic from the elders. It also shored up public support for the ever-expanding reach of the military, which Keegan had no complaints about.

Keegan stood, loudly scraping the stone floor with the heavy wooden chair as she got up. The noise broke Tiago's train of thought. He paused and looked in her direction, annoyed by the interruption. Her ability to ripple his smooth surface pleased her. She rounded the table and deliberately cut through the cluster of mostly men loosely gathered around Tiago. Chief Behn shifted in his chair and greeted her with a nod.

"Commander Keegan, what say you?" Behn's words were raspy, as if he were winded, from only sitting.

Tiago was silent, but his body language showed his displeasure for the connection she had with his father. She turned toward Tiago and nodded soberly, as if she respected him, which she didn't.

"I do not claim to know all that Tiago knows, but we discovered two outposts ransacked, and we dealt with those who caused the injury." Keegan clasped her hands behind her back, in a passive stance. She had no intention of doing anything that would cause

Tiago to feel threatened. Offering a viewpoint of any kind, openly, was threat enough for his fragile ego. "We brought the stolen goods back with us, part restored to the garrison's stores and the rest delivered to the cutter for auction."

Tiago stiffened. She knew he was pissed that he hadn't gotten the first look at the loot, especially Leah. She'd had no intention of honoring that request. Two seconds after he'd given that directive in front of the burned outpost, she'd already decided to ignore it.

"The matter has been dealt with then?" Behn met her gaze. His eyes cloudy and tired.

"Yes, Chief Behn." Keegan dipped her head in respect.

"The forum is adjourned for today." Behn slowly got to his feet, with the aid of a steward standing at his elbow.

"So, you agree with me about the raiders we know are hiding in the Hollow Hills, and this Solas—"

Chief Behn raised his hand, cutting Tiago off. "No more talk today."

Keegan's heart sank as the chieftain struggled to walk. Behn was a shadow of the man he'd once been. He was becoming more fragile with each passing month. For the moment, he was respected, and no one challenged him, but surely everyone sensed Tiago's impatience as he watched Behn's decline. He wanted to be in control, and Keegan dreaded the day he claimed the chieftain's chair.

Once Chief Behn left the chamber, the room filled with the murmur of men's voices. Keegan turned to leave, but Tiago blocked her exit.

"Why didn't you leave the raiders for Chagall to dispense?"

A stupid question given the fact that Chagall had the military prowess of a toddler.

"Chagall has no skill or stomach for tracking or killing."

Tiago's eyes darkened and his mouth became a tight, thin line. Intensity pulsed off him as he leaned forward, his broad, muscled forearms across his chest. His gaze bored into Keegan.

"You killed them?"

Why did he care?

"Of course."

"And the supplies they took?"

"We brought everything back." She'd plainly said the same thing to Chief Behn. Why was he asking her these questions? Did he think she'd give him a different account of the story if they were alone?

"I thought I asked you to bring the stolen goods directly to me?"

"Did you?" Keegan played dumb.

Yates joined Keegan, standing at her right shoulder.

"Did the Fain raiders know anything of Solas?" He glanced at Yates.

"No." There was no point telling him that she'd shot them before they'd had much of a chance to speak.

"Hmm, why do you have no interest in finding out who Solas is?"

"I didn't say that." He was becoming obsessed with Solas, and his obsession was only inflating the shadowy leader's reputation. If they simply acted as if Solas had no real power, then he wouldn't.

"And yet you've made no effort to find him." There was a challenge in his voice.

He'd taken a half step back when Yates walked up, but Keegan claimed the space. She didn't answer to Tiago, and she wanted to remind him of that. Beside her, Yates tensed.

"I don't know what you're trying to say. Why don't you say it plainly for everyone present to hear?" Conversation nearby ceased as those standing near the raised platform turned toward them. If Tiago wanted an audience, he had one now.

"I just find it curious that you show no interest in finding this Solas character." Tiago glanced around. He loved to hold the floor. "One might begin to think you were in support of the Fain—"

Keegan lunged for him, cutting him off. He deflected her hands and they circled, switching positions. Yates tugged at Keegan's forearm. Keegan shucked her off, but Yates would not relent.

"I do not support the Fain…Outcasts and deserters…they dishonor the clans and themselves." Yates shoved Keegan toward the door. Tiago smiled smugly.

She lived in the same Great House as Tiago, but there the similarity ended. They were not related by blood, and she felt no kinship for him. When the chieftain, Tiago's father, died, Tiago would claim his throne. Sometimes he acted as if he'd already unseated his father. The power Tiago would inherit through no merit except birth seemed more and more to reveal what sort of man he truly was.

"You can't let him pull you into a fight in the forum." Yates pushed Keegan away from the entrance and into the busy market around the square. "Don't let him get to you."

"Let go." Keegan shrugged Yates's hand off her arm and circled, heart pounding, face flaming. She'd wanted to punch his smug face so badly, but Yates was right. He'd baited her and she'd fallen right into it. "Fuck."

"Stay away from him." Yates shifted to make eye contact with Keegan.

"Easy for you to say. We live on opposite sides of the same Great House."

"And if…when Chief Behn passes, you need to find another place to live." Yates tried to soften her words, but the truth was a painful reality.

Keegan swallowed and stared at the ground with her hands braced on her hips. Yates was right, intellectually she knew that, but in her heart, she wasn't ready to give the chief up.

"Keegan, I know you like to live in the moment, but you need to plan for the future. You'll need somewhere to be when leadership changes." Yates laid a hand on Keegan's shoulder. "And you need to take Esther with you."

Keegan looked up and met Yates's gaze. Her dark eyes were like sharp sticks piercing Keegan's stubborn brain. Technically, she outranked Yates, but in this case, Yates was acting more like the seasoned officer and she was playing the role of hotheaded rookie.

Keegan stiffened. Esther was a servant in the Great House, the chieftain's favored companion, but as Behn's health had waned, Tiago had begun to hint that Esther would be his. She knew this, but Tiago had not acted on this claim, and in some part of her mind she'd convinced herself that she had more time to figure something out that would stop him. The visual of him, with Esther, turned her stomach. It wasn't his looks that soured her insides, he wasn't an unattractive man, what she disliked about him was his unnecessary cruelty. He had no respect for women.

"And now you've brought a woman into your quarters, into your life…"

"I know, I know." Keegan slid her hand over her face in frustration. "I had to bring her back and I had to keep her. I can't explain it."

"You don't have to explain it to me. I only want you to prepare yourself for what's coming."

Prepare yourself and anyone you care about. That was the implication.

Chapter Eight

The young soldier led Leah through the entryway, down a long, narrow hallway with an arched roof. Heavy beams at even intervals cut across the curved ceiling. The floor was tiled with deep red squares crossing the space at a forty-five-degree angle. Every few feet a pattern of small blue tiles interrupted the red. Leah was mesmerized by the intricate pattern as the man tugged her down the corridor.

They skirted a large room filled with women and a few children who were washing, carrying, cleaning, sweeping, and doing other tasks she didn't recognize. The entire scene was an odd combination of ancient and modern. There did seem to be machines here. She'd ridden in one, but inside the house, the technology for cooking was rudimentary, including a large brick oven with an open wood fire. The smell of baked bread filled the space. Leah tried to capture the details of the scene before she was led through another doorway and up shallow stone stairs to a higher level of the house. She followed the man into an open room where a woman greeted them.

Her skin was a warm brown, and her long wavy black hair fell several inches past her shoulders. She had dark eyes and features that reminded Leah of someone from a Persian lineage. Leah would have described the woman as elegant, maybe even regal. Her clothing draped loosely over the swell of her breasts and clung a little more tightly over the curve of her hips. The dress she wore came within a few inches of the floor, cinched with an intricately woven belt at the waist.

"Who is this?" The woman spoke to the man, not to Leah.

Leah was suddenly aware of her disheveled condition. With her dusty, torn clothing, she was a mess from her ordeal. She probably looked as if she'd walked all the way from the desert and slept in the street.

"Keegan asked that I bring her to you so that you could see to her."

"Keegan asked this?"

"Yes." The man dutifully handed Leah's bag and the end of the tether to the woman, who Leah now realized must be Esther.

He left them alone, and for a moment, neither of them moved or spoke. The woman seemed as surprised by the situation as Leah, and Leah couldn't help wondering what Esther's relationship to Keegan was.

"What is your name?"

"Leah." She felt dingy and exposed under this elegant woman's appraisal.

"I'm Esther." Her voice was soft, melodic even, and her eyes were now as gentle as her touch. She untied Leah's wrists and tenderly rubbed the reddened skin where the cord had been with her thumb. "Let's get you cleaned up." She called for Anna, and a young woman who looked to be no more than thirteen, with light brown shoulder-length hair and twig thin limbs protruding from her simple cotton dress, scurried into the room. "Run a bath and bring fresh towels." Anna nodded and quickly left the room.

Esther offered Leah water. Her hands trembled from fatigue so that she had to hold the earthen cup with both hands to drink. Esther refilled it for her twice before the dryness finally left her throat.

Anna appeared in the doorway across the room and announced that the bath was ready. Esther motioned for Leah to walk with her in that direction. They'd said nothing to each other as they'd waited, although Leah's mind was crowded with a million questions.

"Leave your soiled clothing and I'll bring you something to wear. I think I might have something that will fit you." Esther was a few inches taller than Leah. She seemed to be measuring Leah with her eyes before she turned to leave.

Privacy was a welcomed luxury. Leah discarded her clothes and sank into the deep soaking tub of steaming soapy water. She closed her eyes and dropped under the surface, enjoying the aquatic silence for a moment. The tension in her neck and shoulders eased a bit, and she imagined herself in her old apartment back on Earth. Although there'd have been no water for a soak. A bath was an extravagance that'd been chased away by drought and lack of fresh water. This... this felt like heaven.

She looked around the room. There was a basin and a toilet with a tank suspended a few feet above it over the wall. Despite the rustic setting, there was obviously running water and lights, although after further study she realized the light was not electric, but rather from some sort of candlelit lantern mounted on the wall. It made sense that only occasionally would indoor light be needed on a planet of eternal sunshine. One only needed to be near a window to have all the illumination of midday at any hour. The window in this room was shuttered, probably to provide privacy.

Esther was standing in the door watching her. She'd closed her eyes and had not heard Esther's approach. How long had she been standing there? Leah sloshed water as she sat up and covered her breasts with her arms.

"I've left clothing on the bed in the next room." Her voice was soothing. "And a small plate of food on the table near the bed."

"Thank you."

"You're welcome." Ester dipped her head and receded into the dimly lit adjoining room, leaving Leah to sink again into the warm depths of the bath.

Keegan had tried not to openly care, for Esther's sake. For everyone's sake. But Yates was right. She needed to prepare herself for the worst, because change was inevitable. And she wanted no part of the change that Tiago would undoubtedly bring when he assumed power.

By the time she climbed the stone stairs to her quarters, the main room was empty. The smell of something savory hung in the air, but she didn't examine the pot simmering over the fire at the far end of the space.

The room adjacent the living area was dark except for slim bands of light that seeped in along the edges of the closed wooden shutters. Leah was asleep on the bed. Her hair was damp and her strange clothing had been replaced with a white gown. The fabric draped across her figure and gathered at the waist creating a deep V that showed a teasing view of cleavage. Keegan cocked her head and studied Leah's face, so innocent, so unblemished, and no longer angry.

Keegan brushed the back of her fingers across Leah's cheekbone, but she didn't stir.

"She's very beautiful."

Keegan hadn't realized Esther was standing behind her. She looked over at Esther, for a moment not caring whether her emotions were masked or not.

"I can see why you wanted to keep her."

"Did I make a mistake bringing her here?" Keegan stepped away from the bed, not taking her eyes off Leah.

"Come. Sit with me." Esther reached for Keegan's hand.

Keegan allowed herself to be led to the other room. After she'd taken a seat at the table, Esther held her face in her hands.

"Let me look at you." Esther tilted Keegan's face toward the light. "There's dried blood on your cheek."

"It's from my nose."

"Who hit you?"

Keegan nodded toward the darkened bedroom.

"Really?" Esther cocked an eyebrow in disbelief.

"She's smart and stubborn and she caught me by surprise."

"Will you keep her then?"

"I'm not sure she'll stay." Keegan looked toward the dark rectangle of the bedroom door. "She pretty much told me she'll run away the first chance she gets."

"Run away where?"

"I have no idea, but she keeps saying there's somewhere she needs to be." Keegan accepted a bowl of food from Esther. "She's... she seems as if she's from somewhere else."

"Somewhere else?"

"Somewhere far from here."

"The Hollow Hills?"

Keegan shrugged. She chewed slowly and studied Esther from across the table. She wanted to talk to Esther about the future. Did Esther want to leave? If Keegan offered an escape would she take it?

When Esther had first come to live in the Great House, she had taken Keegan under her wing. Esther had whispered things to her. Esther saw things, Esther knew things, and for some reason, she'd confided them to Keegan probably hoping Keegan would eventually rise to a position of power. As a commander of the northern squadron of the Tenth, she did have power, but the kind of power Esther wanted for Keegan was the last thing she aspired to. All Keegan had ever wanted was freedom to do as she pleased. Her position allowed for just that, except lately, things nagged at her insides.

Their friendship had grown over the years. Esther had not asked anything of Keegan beyond friendship, but Keegan knew the request was still there, unspoken. Take her away from this place. Keegan wanted more than anything to help Esther, but short of killing Tiago she wasn't sure what she could do.

"Is something wrong?" Esther reached across the space between them and touched her hand.

Keegan shook her head, but she wasn't sure Esther believed her. Now was not the time to talk about any of it. Maybe later.

"I'll leave you for the night then." Esther stood and smoothed the front of her dress.

"Thank you for taking care of Leah."

Esther nodded and left Keegan to her thoughts. The fire crackled on the hearth, and the air in the room smelled of wood smoke. Keegan finished off the serving of stew and slid the bowl away. The day had been too long. She shuttered the window and relaxed into the shadows of the darkened room.

She poured wine from a cask at the far end of the table and drank it as she watched the glowing embers pulse yellow and orange.

Tired and dusty from travel, Keegan pulled the door to the bath area closed and filled the tub. She soaked until the water cooled to the temperature of the air. She toweled off and stood at the end of the bed looking at Leah. The shutters had been closed earlier so the room was dark, cool, and quiet. Leah still had not stirred.

Keegan discarded the damp towel and stretched out next to Leah. She rested on her elbow, watching Leah sleep. She considered waking Leah up, kissing her, losing herself in Leah, and forgetting the world for a while. But Leah was so deeply asleep that she decided not to.

"Good night," she whispered.

Keegan rolled onto her back with her arm beneath her head. Her body hummed with desire as she lay restlessly near Leah. She closed her eyes and took slow, deep breaths. The bed, the air, the dampness of her freshly bathed skin, everything felt like a caress, only making her desire for Leah more heightened.

Finally, she tugged the light blanket up from the foot of the bed and rolled onto her side away from Leah.

CHAPTER NINE

Leah took in a deep breath as if she'd been underwater and had just broken the surface. She blinked, trying to remember where she was. When she moved, her arms met with no resistance. She held her hands closer to her face and examined them. *Don't panic. Breathe.*

She forced her thoughts to work backward.

I left the ship. Those men attacked me after I slid down the dune. Then the woman...the woman who looked like some sort of warrior, Keegan, she killed them. I need to get back to the spacecraft.

Leah squinted into the light. It burst into the dim room like so many lasers past the uneven edges of the heavy shutters. The room was fairly large with smooth clay walls. Not much else was in the room except the sleeping platform, a wardrobe, a small table, and two chairs set against opposite walls of the space. She rubbed her fingers over her wrists where she'd been tied. She'd forgotten to be angry, but remembering how Keegan had forced her to travel away from her ship brought it all back, and with it, fear. She now had no idea where she was or even how long she'd been in this place. And yet, somehow, she'd managed to fall asleep. She felt rested, for the first time since waking in the stasis tube.

Tentatively, she stood, keeping one hand on the bed until she was sure she was stable. She was comforted by the sight of her bag on the floor near the wall. When she opened the door she saw the woman, what was her name? Oh yes, Esther. She was busy preparing food. She was cutting what looked like small potatoes and dropping them into a pot over an open fire.

Keegan's quarters were rustic but comfortable. The large brick oven and hearth took up a third of the space of this room. Leah paused in the doorway, unsure of what to do.

"Are you hungry?"

Leah nodded.

"Come, sit." Esther placed a bowl in front of Leah along with a spoon.

The contents of the bowl looked similar to porridge.

Leah gratefully ate, letting each mouthful settle before taking another. Her stomach was on edge. She hadn't had very much food since coming out of stasis. A slice of bread the previous night and now oatmeal, or whatever this was, probably was as complex as her system could handle.

"Thank you." After a few swallows, Leah found her voice.

"Are you feeling better?"

Leah nodded. She knew she'd probably been very dehydrated and exhausted.

"How long did I sleep?"

"About fourteen hours."

Leah swallowed. She'd slept in a strange, potentially dangerous place for fourteen hours. Anything could have happened. She shivered, feeling vulnerable and alone, despite the fact that Esther had been nothing but kind to her. Keegan had, at times, been a different story.

"Keegan said you were with Fain raiders when she found you."

Leah didn't know who the men were, but the memory of being attacked and dragged across the sand by them came rushing back. She nodded, chewed slowly, and forced herself to swallow.

"You were lucky that Keegan found you."

Leah wasn't feeling particularly lucky. She'd crash-landed, her entire crew was dead, she'd nearly been assaulted, and now she was probably far away from her ship with no idea how to get back.

"Is Keegan here?" Leah wondered if she'd finally be free to leave.

"Not at the moment."

The clothing Esther had given her felt odd. She wasn't wearing any underwear, and the draped garment was held together by only the doubled sash at the waist. This was not the sort of attire that would allow for a quick getaway, especially without shoes. She should never have offered up her own clothing so easily, but she'd been utterly worn out and beyond arguing about keeping them.

"Where are we?"

"In Haydn City." Esther furrowed her brow like a worried nurse. She poured each of them water and sat down, leaving the cook pot to simmer.

Right. Haydn City. That's what Keegan had said the previous day. Leah felt a headache hovering behind her eyes. Drinking more water would probably help.

"Your skin is so fair. You must be from the border lands near the darkness. I've never really traveled there."

Leah stared at her. The darkness? What was she talking about? Oh wait, of course, one side of the planet was always in sunlight, the other in darkness. Leah wasn't about to tell Esther where she was really from so she simply nodded.

"I'm grateful for the food and rest, but I need to leave. I need to return to my...place." Leah pushed the empty bowl aside.

"This could be your place." Esther studied her thoughtfully. "Keegan has brought you here. You should stay with her."

Anger rose again. She clinched her fists in her lap.

"You could do far worse. Keegan is strong, young, handsome, and kind." Esther had a wistful look. Leah wondered for a moment if Keegan and Esther were lovers. Keegan looked several years younger than Esther, not that age mattered as far as Leah was concerned. But she took note of it nonetheless.

More bothersome than the idea of age difference or Keegan keeping multiple lovers was the notion that in this place she could be kept against her will, that Keegan could lay some claim to her just because she'd stumbled across Leah in the desert. But she tabled her anger for the moment, determined to try to get more information from Esther while she had the opportunity.

"Do you live here?"

"In this house? Yes. But not in Keegan's quarters. I am bound to Chief Behn as his companion. His quarters are across the courtyard."

Companion rather than wife. Leah made a mental note of Esther's word choice.

"He is older and not well these days." Esther's entire demeanor had darkened as she spoke. She looked down at her hands, folded in her lap. "I suppose soon he will pass leadership to his son, Tiago, and I will then belong to him."

"Don't you belong yourself?"

"You say very strange things."

"Keegan said the same thing to me."

They were quiet for a moment. The smell of something savory wafted across the room from the large brick oven.

"How did you get here?" asked Leah.

"I don't understand your question." Esther furrowed her brow and leaned forward as if she felt the need to examine Leah more closely.

"In the very beginning. Where did you come from? Are you from one of the colonies?" Leah rephrased the question.

"I'm from Pylos."

"Where is Pylos?"

"It's a three-hour journey to the south." Ester looked at her as if she were crazy. "Where is it that you come from that you do not know these things?"

"Far from here." That was the understatement of the century, but explaining further seemed useless.

Leah considered making a dash for the door since Keegan wasn't around to stop her. But she had only now regained her strength and she had no idea where she actually was. Biding her time seemed the smartest decision. Esther seemed to pose no threat.

The food made her feel drowsy again, and the thought of returning to the darkened room to rest was appealing. She needed to regain some stamina if she was going to walk all the way back to her ship. But Keegan appeared, suddenly, a hulking shadow in the open doorway, before Leah had time to leave the room. She flinched at Keegan's sudden presence.

Keegan was wearing clean clothing too, but similar to the attire she'd worn previously. A tight fitting black shirt with cropped sleeves that strained across her biceps. And she had the same military style pants on, with pockets down the outside of each leg. Her boots were dusty. Leah was annoyed at herself for noticing Keegan's sculpted arms, and she vowed not to do it again.

She wondered where Keegan had spent the night. The fact that the thought had even swept through her brain also annoyed her. The less she thought of Keegan, the better.

Esther scooped food into a bowl and served it to Keegan who'd taken Esther's seat across from Leah. The idea that Keegan couldn't serve her own food further agitated Leah, but she tried not to show it. She sat quietly as Keegan spooned a few mouthfuls. Keegan gave the impression the lumpy mass of porridge was more interesting than anything else in the room, especially her. She hardly looked up as she ate. Was she avoiding looking at Leah?

The thought that Leah somehow made Keegan uncomfortable would have been cause for joy if she'd believed there was any chance it was true. Given the fact that Keegan exuded confidence, Leah knew intimidation was a tactic not likely to gain her the upper hand. Keegan must have sensed that Leah was watching her. She slowed her culinary assault; she'd been eating as if any moment she'd be required to rush from the room. Keegan leaned back and jutted her square jaw up ever so slightly, enabling her to look down at Leah from a slightly elevated view.

Was she arrogant or just cocky? Leah was undecided.

Esther walked behind Keegan, brushing her fingers lightly across Keegan's shoulder as she passed. "I'll leave the two of you to talk." Keegan kept her gaze fixed on Leah, never acknowledging that Esther had left the room.

They regarded each other across the table, the silence between them churning with unsaid things.

"You look rested." Keegan spoke first.

Leah didn't know how to respond. It wasn't a question, but rather an observation, and since Leah hadn't seen a mirror, she had no idea how she looked.

"I'm glad I didn't disturb you." Keegan cleared her throat and slid the empty bowl aside.

"When?" *When you tied me up? Or when you brought me here against my will?*

"When I came to bed last night…I was afraid I would wake you. I knew you needed to sleep."

"Wait…you mean…wait…we slept in the same bed last night?" They'd slept in the same bed?

"These are my quarters." Keegan tipped her head toward the doorway leading to the bed chamber. "That is where I sleep."

"I should have slept somewhere else then. I didn't know."

"Why would you sleep somewhere else?"

This was like having a conversation with an unstable person. The circular trajectory of it all was making her feel nauseous. The lump of porridge in her stomach suddenly turned to stone.

Maybe she was jumping to conclusions. Maybe in this place, in this culture, people shared quarters. Maybe this was customary and sharing a bed meant nothing.

"Tonight, I will sleep somewhere else." Across from her, she swore Keegan was undressing her with her eyes. Leah tugged self-consciously at the fabric of the gown, closing the V farther to conceal any glimpse of cleavage.

"You will sleep here, Leah." That didn't sound like a request but rather a non-negotiable statement of fact. A foregone conclusion. "I have things to deal with this afternoon, but I'll return earlier than last night."

"Listen, I don't want you to think I'm not grateful for what you've done for me." That was partially true. Leah was grateful for the rescue part, but the rest of this was becoming more troubling. "But I can't stay here. I have my own things to deal with." She used Keegan's words, hoping to make her understand.

"You seem very confused by where you are, and it would not be safe for you to leave without an escort. Especially until you are fully recovered."

Now she felt bad for getting angry. Keegan was trying to look out for her; maybe she just had an odd way of showing it. She was, after all, a soldier of some kind, not a nursemaid and certainly not one given to over communication. But then again, this whole thing of sleeping in the same bed didn't seem like a good idea.

Keegan stood and walked around the table, taking a seat on the bench next to her. Keegan straddled the plank seat, perpendicular to her. Leah turned in Keegan's direction until her knee bumped Keegan's. She readjusted so they were no longer in contact. Keegan's elbow was on the edge of the table, and she leaned uncomfortably into Leah's personal space. She surprised Leah by brushing a wisp of hair off her cheek.

"I don't think you know how beautiful you are, Leah. Haydn City…no city…would be safe for you." Keegan paused and traced the contours of Leah's body with her eyes before redirecting her gaze to Leah's face. "I will try not to pressure you and I will not hurt you, but you must listen to me. For your own safety, you need to stay here."

Leah's flesh tingled, either from anger or fear or something else. Keegan was beautiful too, strong and sensual and dangerous. Her heart thumped against her ribs as if it were trying to escape.

"Am I a prisoner?"

"No." Keegan looked confused and maybe a little frustrated.

Keegan sat back, shifting her weight to her elbow on the table. Then she reached in her pocket and withdrew a silver band about two inches wide, with curious markings, curved and open at one side. Without a word, she placed the silver cuff around Leah's right arm, just above her elbow and, using both hands, bent the metal band until it was snug.

"What are you doing? What is that?"

"This is to mark you as taken. To show others that if they touch you, if they hurt you, they will answer to me."

"What?" This pitch of Leah's voice notched up with alarm.

Keegan stood up. "Rest and I'll be back later. We can talk more then, if you want."

Leah's mouth was ajar. She stared at Keegan's retreating figure in shock. She tugged at the silver cuff, but she was unable to expand it or remove it with one hand. She angled her elbow up to get a better look at the engraved markings. Some intricate pattern with the outline of a bird. And some letters too small for her to read without removing the cuff. What the hell? This was going too far. She needed to leave, and she needed to figure out how to do that as soon as possible.

She reached for the door, but it didn't give way. She pressed her shoulder against it, but still it wouldn't open. Keegan must have locked the door as she left. Leah had been so distracted by the silver armband that she'd failed to hear the sound of the bolt sliding into the lock.

CHAPTER TEN

K eegan took the steps from her quarters slowly. Time with Leah unsettled her, made her doubt her decision to bring Leah back to Haydn City. But how could she have left her behind? Surely Leah would not have survived on her own. How she came to be in the desert remained a mystery that Keegan still intended to solve.

She skirted the edge of the large main room downstairs. The air vibrated with the murmur of female voices as those that worked in the Great House busied themselves with the tasks of maintaining the household. Keegan looked for Esther but didn't see her.

"Keegan."

"Hello, Kayla."

Kayla fell in step beside Keegan. Kayla was a petite wisp of a girl with long straight brown hair. She was Tiago's cousin and now resided in the Great House under the chieftain's protection. Kayla had a terribly inconvenient crush on Keegan.

"Take me with you."

"Where is it you think I'm going?" Keegan glanced sideways at Kayla.

"I don't care. Wherever it is it's more exciting than anything happening here."

They walked side by side down the narrow walkway that bordered the large dining hall only used for special gatherings. As they neared a darkened corner, Kayla flung her arms around Keegan's neck, causing her to stumble into the shadows.

"Kayla, I'm too old for you." Keegan tried to gently untangle herself from Kayla's slender arms.

"I'll be eighteen tomorrow."

"Oh, that's right. The big day." Keegan had forgotten, but she wasn't about to admit the lapse of memory to Kayla.

"You'll be at the party, won't you?"

"Of course." Kayla was a sweet girl, but a family party was the last thing she felt like attending. Tiago would no doubt be in rare, obnoxious form. "Okay, be a good girl and let me get to work."

Kayla bounced on her tiptoes and kissed Keegan on the cheek before Keegan could escape out into the courtyard. Kayla would no doubt make someone a very happy mate, but it wasn't going to be Keegan. She hoped for Kayla's sake and hers that Kayla soon found someone else to distract her.

The garrison was a ten-minute walk from the Great House. She passed in front of the forum and strode along the wide stone steps of the temple. Her head was down. She didn't feel like interacting with the street vendors or the ragged that hung at the edges hoping for scraps of work or food. Her mind was on Leah.

Why had she brought Leah to her place? She could have saved Leah from the raiders and simply brought her back to Haydn City. Keegan could think of any number of men in the city, well-off men who'd have no doubt gotten into a bidding war with each other for the chance to have Leah. The Fain raider had been right. Leah was worth more than the entire lot of everything else she'd reclaimed. And the thought of Leah with anyone else made her crazy. Hell, she was crazy. Still mulling over her own behavior, she was distracted when she entered the garrison.

"Commander on deck!"

Men and a few women at arms stopped what they were doing and stood as Keegan walked amongst them toward the officer's quarters. "As you were." The soldiers quickly relaxed back into their former positions, chatting casually, cleaning weapons, and lounging about.

Maddox looked up when Keegan stepped through the door. He was a serious man and senior to her by about ten years. He commanded half of the Tenth and she the other. The Tenth was divided into two squadrons, one responsible for the southern region surrounding and including the southern precincts of Haydn City. Keegan was responsible for the North. They worked well together. Keegan had learned a lot from Maddox, including discipline and self-control. The latter was still a work in progress for Keegan, but she did her best to follow his example.

"What news if any?" Keegan took a chair opposite the desk where Maddox was reading a duty roster.

"Quiet today." Maddox pushed the roster aside and leaned back in his chair. "I deployed a small unit about two hours ago. They haven't returned, but I also haven't had any distress signals from any of the borders."

Keegan nodded.

"I heard from Gage and Yates that you were able to track the second group of raiders that hit the western outposts."

"Yes. We came across them right after we split off from the main squadron."

"I thought you were on two days of leave?" Maddox quirked an eyebrow.

"Yeah, I heard that rumor also."

"Why don't you take off then? You're not on the command roster until tomorrow. If I were you, this is the last place I'd be."

She knew that wasn't true. Maddox loved his work and rarely took leave, but he was right. What was she doing except hiding? She should be out having fun, letting off steam. She could head back to her quarters, but then Leah would be there and that was scary for other reasons. Besides, the last thing she was in the mood for was another bloody nose for making a pass.

"You're right." Keegan stood. "I'll see you later."

Keegan left the garrison and headed toward the outer edge of the city. The streets became narrower and no sunlight reached ground level because of the height of the buildings that crowded against the dusty alleys. She turned into a darkened arched doorway and followed steps down to a subterranean room. The air was smoky, the room only lit with lantern light giving patrons the privacy of near darkness. One couple, tucked into a corner table looked up as Keegan stepped up to the bar. She recognized the woman but not her male companion. She turned away from them as she leaned against the bar. It wasn't long before the matron of the establishment joined her. Brooke had dark skin, and a sensual tangle of black curls framed her elegant cheekbones. But Brooke rarely, if ever, took clients herself. Too bad, because she was gorgeous. At least she was always available for flirtation. Brooke entwined her fingers with Keegan's, swept the bottle of liquor off the bar, and led her to a table at the back of the room.

"Share a drink with me." Brooke poured two glasses and slid one across the table to Keegan.

"I have no choice when you steal the bottle." Keegan joked and tossed back the shot. It warmed her throat as it traveled south.

"My bar, my bottle." Brooke sipped from the shot glass. "So, Commander, what is your pleasure this fine day?"

CHAPTER ELEVEN

L eah walked aimlessly from room to room. She took breaks from her rounds to lean out the open window. Keegan's quarters were at least three floors from the ground. Too far to jump, although she'd seriously considered it more than once.

The silver cuff lay in the center of the bedside table. It had taken her a half hour of struggle to pry the band apart enough to work it slowly over her elbow and off. She'd opened it enough to wedge it in a crevice of the doorframe and then pried it open farther. The joint of her elbow was red, the skin aggravated from fighting to remove the cuff.

Esther had not returned, nor had Keegan. Leah walked into the bedroom and opened the wardrobe. Keegan's clothes hung on one side, with pants neatly folded on shelves to the right. Inspiration struck.

She tugged a shirt from one of the hangers and held it up to her chest. Of course, it was too large, but she didn't care. Anything would be better than this flimsy wrap she'd been wearing. She slipped into a pair of Keegan's pants, then used the sash from the gown she'd worn as a belt to cinch the pants above her hips. She'd tucked the tail of the shirt in and cuffed the sleeves so that they came to her wrists. Shoes would be more complicated.

A pair of boots were next to a chair across the room, but she had to improvise by stuffing cloths from the bathroom into the toes to keep them from sliding off. Now that she was dressed, she sat on the edge of the bed in the dimly lit room and waited.

At some point later, Leah thought maybe an hour had passed since she'd donned the stolen clothes, Anna, the young girl who'd run her bath the previous day, opened the main door. Leah could see her from the doorway of the bedroom as she set a basin of vegetables on the far end of the long table nearest the hearth. Leah thought Anna might come into the bedroom looking for her, but she seemed to have forgotten that Leah was there, or assumed Leah was sleeping. Anna shuffled around the hearth, stoking the fire and adding water to a cooking pot. Then she left and didn't close the door behind her. Leah seized the opportunity to make her escape, scooping up her satchel from the floor as she made for the doorway. But then she had a thought.

It was going to be a long walk back to her ship. She decided to take time to fill her water bottle from a pitcher on the table. She added a couple of apples to the remaining protein bar in her bag for provisions.

She tried to retrace her steps from the previous day, but her memory was fuzzy and she'd been distracted trying to take in everything as the soldier led her to Keegan's quarters. As she passed the large kitchen on the first floor, she noticed a cloak hanging on a peg along the wall. She took it and quickly draped it around her shoulders and placed the hood over her head. Walking at a quick pace, she proceeded down the long corridor with the intricate tile pattern and then burst into the glaring sunlight of the courtyard. The cloak turned out to be just as useful a buffer against the intense sunlight as it was for disguise. But now that she was out and in the street, where was she going? She wasn't sure which route she should take.

Leah walked in the direction she thought they'd come from, but it wasn't long before she felt as if she was circling back toward her point of origin. The streets didn't seem to be laid out on any sort of grid that she could discern and there were no street names. What had been the methodology of those who'd planned the design of this place? It seemed to be a maze that made no logical sense.

It was difficult to focus on the map she was attempting to construct in her head because scenes on the street kept capturing her attention. Many people lived in poverty, or very close to it. People looked weathered, gaunt, even the children. They seemed to live a very different life from those she'd seen in the dwelling where Keegan resided.

Some streets were thick with vendors and smelled of smoke from small cook fires. She spotted food she didn't recognize, bolts of cloth, tools and pottery. But everything had a dingy pallor, as if even the structures themselves struggled to survive in this environment. Leah did her best to make herself invisible, to make herself small under the cloak. She met no one's gaze nor did she respond when a woman reached for her with an outstretched hand. Leah's sense of fairness and charity made her want to help in some way, but she had nothing to give. She'd be lucky if she managed to save herself. She adjusted the strap of her bag across her shoulder and pressed on.

Occasionally, in the narrow alleys she saw graffiti on the walls, white chalk or paint contrasted against the dark, reddish brown clay. Some of them undecipherable, using symbols and iconography that had no meaning for her. But one word she could actually read: Solas. Was Solas some sort of political leader in this place? Whoever or whatever Solas was, the worse the condition of the area, the more likely she was to see the name.

After walking for what seemed like an hour, she began to notice that some of the corners of the buildings had markers approximately ten feet above the street. Unfortunately, by the time she noticed them she also saw the towers that bordered the courtyard where she'd started. She could see them just above the roof line and knew she'd circled back unintentionally. Frustrated, she was about to turn around and walk in the opposite direction when she heard someone speak in a gruff voice.

She turned, and when she did, the cloak fell back.

"You there!" A gruff looking soldier spoke. Was he speaking to her?

The sunlight blinded her so that she couldn't see. She squinted and shielded her eyes with her hand. She focused on the boy running seconds before he careened into her. They both tumbled, and some potatoes and what looked like squash dropped to the dirt. He scurried to put them into a cloth sack as two soldiers bore down on them. He was hollow-eyed and skeleton thin.

"Stop!" A man, possibly a soldier or policeman, grabbed for the boy.

Still on her backside on the ground, Leah kicked the man in the knee, causing him to falter. The boy slipped from his grasp, darted left, right, and then was swallowed up by the crowd. A second soldier gave chase while the man she'd kicked grabbed the front of her clothing and yanked her from the ground.

Leah struggled to break free. She'd meant to follow the boy's lead, to lose herself in the throng of street vendors and pedestrians. She wanted to disappear. The man held her fast, gripping her by the arm.

Before she could free herself, the second soldier returned. He stepped in front of her, blocking her path. At least she assumed these men were soldiers or some other figures of authority. They were dressed similarly to Keegan, but the uniforms were a different color, and they both carried guns, but upon further inspection, she saw that they weren't clean shaven and carried an air of meanness about them.

"What do we have here?" He used the side of the rifle to shove her. She stumbled back into the first man. She pushed off him, not liking the contact.

"I've done nothing wrong." Leah tried to break free of them again.

"Show your face." He yanked the cloak away so that Leah was now in plain view.

She wasn't sure if they'd assumed she was a man because of the way she was dressed. But now they would plainly see that she was a woman. They seemed to be sizing her up, and she didn't like the expressions on their faces. She began to back away from them but had nowhere to go.

"To what house to you belong?"

Leah didn't know how to answer the question. She looked back and forth between the two soldiers. Should she mention Keegan's name?

"Why are you wearing military clothing?" One of the men shoved her again. Now her back was against the wall. "You helped that kid escape with stolen goods."

A small crowd was gathering, but no one came to her aid. She should have stayed in Keegan's quarters. She'd rushed to escape and now she'd been caught. Leah had no understanding of what was expected of her or what sort of information these men were looking for.

"I wasn't—"

The second man struck her across the face with the back of his hand, cutting her off. "Move." He shoved her in front of him. The two men, one on each side, held her arms and marched her away, in the opposite direction to the towers, farther into the spiderweb of narrow alleys. She planted her feet, stirring dust as they forced her forward, but her resistance had no effect.

Leah tasted blood from her lip. Her jaw felt hot where he'd slapped her.

A face she recognized caught her eye as she was dragged by the men. It was Esther. Just for the briefest moment, she and Esther made eye contact. Esther followed Leah with wide eyes, as if she'd just seen a ghost, but made no move to try to intervene on her behalf. Maybe that wasn't an option. Even the quick glance had revealed that Esther had her own escort and in all likelihood, was not free to act on impulse. A serious looking young man walked just behind Esther, shoving aside anyone who drew too close to her. Esther looked back, and Leah hoped that Esther had understood her silent plea for help.

There were square tarps tethered between structures, casting the street below in shadows. They entered an open area bordered on all sides by holding cells, cages. Some with men and in some, women, with a few children interspersed. One of the soldiers unlocked a door using a combination and shoved Leah inside. There were cots along the back wall of the approximately ten-foot square cage, and straw strewn across the dirt floor. Two women sat on one of the cots arm in arm. Another woman leaned against the far side of the cage staring off into the central part of the large open space.

Leah grasped the bars with both hands and surveyed the place. In the center of the open area was a raised platform, and in the middle of that a wooden structure that looked like something from the witch trials of Salem or some medieval torture device designed to hold its victim in chains while on display. Her hands began to shake. She released the bars and sank into the shadows of the cage until the back of her legs hit the nearest cot. She sat down and covered her face with her hands.

Leah felt utterly alone. She didn't understand any of this place. Those in the military seemed to control everything. And civilians seemed to fear them, based on the fact that no one came to her aid and the expressions on the faces of those who'd watched her be taken. Where she was from, it was a civilian's right to challenge authority. In fact, it was expected.

The woman standing shifted to the other side of the cell. She seemed to be looking for someone or something.

"How long have you been in here?" Leah stood beside the woman. She was rail thin, her clothing dusty and torn in places. Her long brown hair was tangled into a loose braid; straw-dry strands broke free and swirled about her neck and shoulders.

"Two days." The woman had a hollow-eyed expression, her voice emotionless. She studied Leah. "Those are not your clothes."

"No." Leah assumed that was obvious. Everything she was wearing was four sizes too tall.

"Impersonating an officer." The woman smirked. "You're either brave or stupid."

"Stupid." Leah muttered under her breath. Stupid and desperate, and look where that had gotten her. Not very far.

Male voices caught her attention. Several men approached from the alley, their voices a garble of conversations she couldn't quite make out. They glanced in Leah's direction, and she slunk away from the outer bars, into partial shadow.

"Don't worry, they'll take someone from the lower caste."

Leah was horrified that even incarcerated there was a caste system. She had no idea how she'd ended up in this particular holding cell or what caste she was considered to be part of.

One of the soldiers who'd dragged her from the alley opened a cage on the other side of the large open area and pulled a reluctant woman from inside.

"That one too." One of the men pointed and another woman was wrenched from a cluster of women inside the cell.

The two women were swallowed up by the group of men as they walked toward a small gate past the soldier's station.

"What's happening? Where are they taking them?" Leah moved from the shadows and grasped the bars of the cell.

The woman didn't answer, but the look on her face told Leah everything. She began to tremble, so that she was forced to sit down. She hugged herself and squeezed her eyes shut. She should have listened to Keegan. Maybe she was the arrogant one after all. Arrogant and foolish.

CHAPTER TWELVE

After several drinks, Keegan finally felt the knots in her shoulders lessen. Keegan had put Brooke off initially. She wasn't sure she was up for the sort of companionship that Brooke's personnel provided, not tonight. She'd intended to only drink. But in the end, with a slight buzz to dull the ache for what she really wanted, she'd relented.

A woman named Ren, who looked a little like Leah, had been her choice and they'd slipped from the bar to a private room. Keegan lounged in an oversized chair, sipping whiskey. Ren made a slow, sensual display of undressing. Ren was pretty, but not as beautiful as Leah. Keegan couldn't help the comparison. Ever since the first night she'd held Leah in her arms she'd hardly been able to think of anything else. She wanted to bed Leah in the worst way. But considering the bloody nose Leah had given her, patience would work in her favor.

Ren, completely nude, knelt in front of Keegan. She slid her palms up Keegan's thighs subtly insinuating herself between them. Her breasts brushed over Keegan's crotch, and Keegan shifted, spreading her legs farther.

Ren was working the buttons of her trousers free when a rapid, light knock sounded at the door. Whoever it was, they had the wrong room. Keegan ignored the knocking until she heard the door open.

A familiar figure entered Keegan's peripheral vision, Yates.

"Yates, what the fuck?" Her fly was open, and Ren was teasingly tugging the last button free.

"I'm sorry, Commander, but I need to see you."

Yates never called her Commander during off hours unless she was in trouble or unless there was a problem. There must be a big problem for Yates to barge in. She didn't feel like dealing with any problems tonight.

"Whatever it is can wait." She motioned with her half-filled glass for Yates to leave.

"This can't wait."

Keegan's pleasant alcohol buzz evaporated at the sound of Yates's serious tone.

"Fucking hell." Keegan signaled for Ren to stop. Ren rocked back on her heels, bracing her hands against Keegan's legs. "What is so damn important?"

"Your package...the one you brought back with you from the desert?"

"Package?" Keegan's buzzed brain struggled to follow.

"The package—"

"Oh, the package...yeah." Keegan relaxed back against the high, overstuffed chair back. "What about it?"

"Let's just say we need to pay a visit to the cages."

"What?" Keegan came to attention.

"Yeah...and we should go, like now."

"Sorry, Ren, another time." Keegan stood, refastened her pants, and handed Ren's dress to her. She apologized to Brooke for the abrupt departure, tossed a few notes on the table, and followed Yates to the exit. This was not how she'd seen the night ending. Once they were at street level, Keegan pressed Yates for more.

"What happened?"

"I don't know, but I received an urgent message from Esther via courier that she'd seen Leah in the custody of one of Tiago's patrol teams. Two men. And they were headed toward the cages with Leah." Yates skirted the crowd, moving quickly, Keegan was hustling to keep up. "I'm not positive that's where she ended up, but that's a good place to start looking if she got picked up. I came to get you as soon as I heard."

"Dammit, I told her to stay put."

"And you thought she'd listen to you because...?"

"Because...because...well, I thought I was pretty damn convincing." Keegan caught up to Yates and matched her pace. "I told her it wouldn't be safe for her here in the city. It's as if she has no idea what this place is like."

"I'm guessing she's beginning to figure it out."

"If they hurt her—"

"Wow, Esther was right. You really like her." Yates grinned.

"What did Esther say?"

Yates pulled ahead, weaving through the crowded pedestrian corridor.

"Hey, wait up...what did Esther tell you?"

Leah's eyes burned from lack of sleep. How did everyone not go insane on this crazy planet where the sun never set? Humans were wired to match the celestial rotation of the sun, day to night. Without that rhythm, Leah was struggling. Two of the women shared one of the cots. They'd lain down an hour earlier and seemed to be sleeping. Even if Leah could bring herself to recline on the remaining empty bed she knew sleep would elude her. There was no way she'd relax enough to doze off. She pressed the palm of her hands over her eyes, savoring the darkness.

When she'd been a child she was afraid of the dark. Her father always kept a tiny night light burning for her in her room, even when electricity was at a premium. And now, after a few days in this place, she craved darkness.

Her eyes were still covered when she heard a voice she recognized. Her heart sped up. She stood and moved to the front of the cage. Was that Keegan's voice or just wishful thinking? She strained to get a glimpse of the source of raised voices, but she couldn't see them. After a moment, the voices became clearer, and finally, she saw Keegan approach. The two soldiers who'd caught her were with Keegan, along with a striking woman she didn't recognize. It was obvious from tone and body language that Keegan wasn't pleased with the soldiers. She stepped away from the bars as they approached.

"Tiago gave specific orders that he was to examine every captive before release or auction." The soldier stepped between Keegan and the cage door.

"This woman is not a captive and is not eligible for auction. I already told you this. It's been filed with the registrar and she's been banded. Check for yourself." Keegan swept her arm in Leah's direction.

"I'm telling you that we checked and this one is clean. She's not bound to anyone and couldn't even tell us which House she belonged to." He wasn't giving an inch.

Keegan sidestepped and he blocked her. He held his weapon in front of his chest. His continued resistance obviously was a tipping point for Keegan because the instant he blocked her path she shoved the rifle up and out of his grasp and struck his jaw with the butt of the gun.

"I outrank you and I'm about thirty seconds from kicking your ass." The rifle was pointed at his chest. "Open it. Now."

The other woman, dark-haired and intense, stood protectively between the second soldier and Keegan. Reluctantly, the soldier turned and unlocked the cage gate. Keegan made eye contact with Leah for the first time, brief and searing. She tipped her head toward the door, and that was the only invitation Leah needed to move quickly out from behind the bars. She stood behind Keegan, clutching the strap of her bag across her chest tightly.

Keegan used the side of the rifle to shove the soldier back. She faced off with him for a few seconds, then tossed the gun to the dirt and propelled Leah along in front of her. Keegan didn't look back, but the other woman, her very focused companion, never took her eyes off the two soldiers as they followed the alley past the other cages back into the main concourse of pedestrian traffic.

Keegan's fingers were like a vise grip on Leah's arm. She'd have been angry about being handled so roughly if she weren't so relieved to see Keegan. She wanted to cry, but not now, not in front of Keegan and her silent cohort. Leah wasn't sure how long they walked, she was exhausted from lack of sleep and food, but eventually the towers with the red tiled roofs came into view and she knew they were close to the Great House.

Within another fifteen minutes, they were back in Keegan's quarters. Leah could feel Keegan's displeasure, although she hadn't spoken the entire time they'd been walking. Once in the large room that adjoined the bedroom, Keegan began to silently pace. The muscle along her jawline rippled as she clenched and unclenched. Leah waited for the tirade to erupt. She dropped to a seat and covered her face with her hands. Someone touched her shoulder and she realized it was the dark-haired woman offering her a glass of water.

"Thank you." She smiled weakly.

"I'm Yates." Yates extended her hand. Her fingers were long and tapered, and her grip was firm.

"I'm Leah."

Yates wasn't as tall as Keegan or as muscled through the arms and shoulders, but she gave the impression of svelte power, like some sort of distance runner. She exuded intensity of purpose. She smiled at Leah. Yates crossed the room to Keegan, put her hand on Keegan's shoulder, and whispered something to her before turning to leave. She closed the door, leaving Keegan and Leah to face each other alone.

Keegan had stopped pacing and stood looking at Leah like some peeved parent unsure of the appropriate punishment for an errant child. Leah couldn't hold her gaze, and after a moment looked away.

Keegan left the room and returned with the silver cuff, which she slammed down in the center of the table in front of Leah. Then she resumed the pacing. After a few minutes, Leah couldn't stand it any longer. The angry silence was like some sort of drip water torture.

"I'm sorry."

"What?" Keegan practically shouted. She stopped abruptly and stared at Leah.

"I said I'm sorry. I know that you're angry and I'm sorry." Keegan was so angry that it scared her a little.

"Which part are you sorry for? Not listening to me? Not believing me? Not trusting me?" Keegan leaned forward, across from Leah, with her palms on the table. "Or are you only sorry for getting caught?"

"All of it." She *was* sorry for getting caught. This whole situation was incredibly maddening. Now she was getting angry too. She never asked to be brought here. Keegan was the one who put her in this situation in the first place.

"All of it?" There was an empty wooden bowl nearby and Keegan flung it across the room. It bounced loudly from the wall to the tile floor. "That silver cuff was for your own protection. If you'd been wearing it when they picked you up none of this would have happened." Keegan swept her hand across her forehead and took a deep breath. "Do you even understand what almost happened tonight?"

There was a moment of silence.

"No." The truth was Leah didn't know. The experience had scared her badly, but she really had no idea what Keegan and Yates had saved her from.

"Tiago would have gotten to you first. I can promise you that would not have been pleasant. Then either he'd have kept you until he was bored with you, or he'd have auctioned you as a companion to someone else." Keegan's tone softened. "And once that happened I would have had no claim to you. You'd be…"

"I don't want any part of this. I do not belong here. And I will not participate in this…this…societal mechanism obviously built to commodify women."

Keegan frowned and shook her head.

"That sort of thinking has no place here. That sort of thinking will get you killed. This is the way things are. This is the world we live in…end of story." Keegan tapped the table's surface with her forefinger to make the point. "Only physical strength ensures order. Strength is all that matters here."

"A republic run by bullies." A tear slid down Leah's cheek, and she wiped at it with the sleeve of her shirt, Keegan's shirt she was still wearing. It was an angry tear, not a sign of weakness.

Keegan couldn't make out what Leah muttered as she got up and walked toward the bedroom. Keegan followed her. "What did you say?" For the life of her she couldn't figure Leah out. She seemed simultaneously frightened, angry, and defiant.

"I said, I hate this place." Leah spun defiantly. She'd unbuttoned the shirt, and it hung open and loose as she untied the sash to slip out of Keegan's oversized trousers.

Keegan watched as Leah proceeded to strip completely. Leah never took her eyes off Keegan as she slid backward onto the bed. She was propped on her elbows, completely nude. Keegan was speechless, dumbfounded.

"This is what you wanted isn't it?" Leah sounded so calm now. "Sex in return for protection...Isn't that how this system works?"

Keegan clenched her jaw tightly. Despite best efforts, her heart rate had increased and her breath quickened. Leah's skin was smooth, the rise of her breasts cast in soft highlight and shadow from the bedside lantern, and the triangle of stiff dark curls at the apex of her thighs contrasted against the paleness of her skin. As she lay there, her hip was rotated a little so that Leah's thigh hid her sex. Even still, this view was sending a cascading electrical storm through Keegan's system. Leah was the most beautiful woman she'd ever seen, and she was lying there challenging Keegan to take her. And fuck it all, Keegan wanted to, badly.

"Well?" Leah's calm question was unnerving.

Regardless of her alluring display, Keegan knew that this was not really an invitation. At least not one she had any intention of accepting. She wouldn't be played like some archaic board game. Unfortunately, an image of Leah, undressed and in her bed, would be seared in her brain forever. She stood at the foot of the bed for a moment, and then left the room without a word.

No one had ever made her so irrationally angry in her entire life. Leah could stay or go; she didn't fucking care anymore.

❖

Keegan's boots pounded loudly across the tile floor. Leah could hear her footfalls descend the stone stairs and then nothing. Silence. She wiped at another tear and then pulled a blanket up to her chin.

On an angry impulse, she'd undressed in front of Keegan. The entire display was so out of character. She'd never done anything like that before, but Keegan was so infuriatingly controlling that she, well, she wanted to control one thing. The only thing that she could control.

Leah wasn't sure what she'd expected to happen but it hadn't been that Keegan would leave. She'd left without saying a word. Was Leah free to go? Had she finally crossed some point of no return with Keegan and now Keegan wanted nothing to do with her? Leah had no idea. After her failed attempt at escape she must consider that she might actually need Keegan's help to return to her ship. She probably wouldn't make it on foot.

She'd never met anyone like Keegan before and she was ill equipped to understand Keegan's actions.

On some level, was she disappointed that Keegan hadn't called her bluff? Anger quickly replaced disappointment. She tugged the blanket with her as she rolled onto her side, exhaling loudly.

Leah was smart, she had the PhD to prove it, but in difficult social situations she'd sometimes fall back on her looks to win someone over. It had worked in undergrad and graduate school. She hadn't wanted to be defined by her appearance, but she wasn't above using whatever leverage she could to win. Of course, she'd never gone as far as to sleep with someone that she didn't genuinely care for, but flirtation was mostly harmless. Flirtation made everyone feel liked.

She'd anticipated a different sort of reaction from Keegan and Keegan had proved her wrong. Leah hated to be wrong.

She rolled onto her other side, facing the door, and waited, but Keegan didn't return and eventually fatigue pulled her under. Sleep came and she could no longer beat it back.

CHAPTER THIRTEEN

Leah's eyes fluttered and she saw movement near the bed. Her eyes gained focus in the dim light, and she realized it was Esther. Her brief visual contact with Esther in the crowded street the previous day had probably been what saved her. At least that was her assumption.

"I brought you some clothes." Esther's voice was soft, soothing.

"Thank you."

"After you bathe, whenever you're ready, I can show you how the bodice works."

Leah nodded. She pulled the covering over her breasts as she sat up. She did want to take a bath. She wanted to wash yesterday and last night's restless sleep completely away.

"Is Keegan here?" She was almost afraid to ask.

"No, I haven't seen her today."

Leah had expected as much. She nodded again and got out of bed, dragging the blanket with her as she made her way to the bathroom. After bathing Leah felt more awake, more human. She put on the clothing Esther had left at the foot of the bed. There were two dresses that were more like gowns that draped almost to the floor. Both were cerulean blue, with a woven bodice that was darker sapphire blue. She couldn't quite figure out the bodice. She carried it in front of her as she walked into the dining area.

"How does this...oh..." She was surprised to discover that a young man was stationed at the door. It took a moment for her to recognize him as the soldier who'd shown her to Keegan's quarters when she first arrived.

"This is Hardy." Esther motioned toward him.

She wondered if, based on her escape, she was now under house arrest. Leah studied him for a moment, still holding the bodice out in front of her.

He almost looked too be young to be a soldier, but his attire suggested otherwise. He wore the same military style cargo pants and boots as Keegan, although his lanky frame did not fill out the shirt in the same way. The long sleeves were cuffed at the elbows to reveal sinewy forearms. His nearly shaved head gave a hint of sandy brown hair.

"Are you a soldier like Keegan?"

"I'm a private, first class." He straightened to his full height, which was near the high end of five feet. He was probably in his early twenties, but could have passed for eighteen. Leah couldn't help smiling at him. And with a charmingly boyish grin, he smiled back. As far as bodyguards went, he wasn't very intimidating.

As if he'd read her thoughts, his expression grew serious. "I'm to stay with you at all times. Commander's orders."

"I see." So, Keegan didn't want to see her, but at least cared enough to send a protector in her place. That revelation warmed her insides.

"Here, let me help you with that." Esther left the cook fire and took the bodice from Leah.

She signaled for Leah to turn around. Esther reached around, placing the widest part of the woven bodice at the front. Then she showed Leah how the straps went around her shoulders and fastened at the back. The bodice functioned as both belt and bra, holding the flowing garment tight against her waist while also supporting her breasts, pushing them together and upward just enough to show a tasteful bit of cleavage above the V of the gown. Leah swept her hands across the front of the dress. She liked the fit and the color, and for the first time in days, she felt pretty.

Leah returned to the dresser in the bedroom where Esther had placed a rectangular mirror. Keegan obviously didn't need more than the small mirror over the sink near the bath. Leah moved in front of the mirror, checking as many angles of the dress as she could.

"Here, I thought you might also like this." Esther held a hairbrush in her hand.

"I don't know how to thank you." Leah took the brush and leaned closer to examine her hair. It didn't look horrible, but several days of washing and finger combing were not presenting her in the best manner for sure.

"Sit...Let me." Esther pulled a chair over.

Leah sat and Esther began to brush her hair. She used one hand to pull a handful aside and then swept the brush through it until it was smooth enough to catch the light from the window. And then another handful, and another. Leah closed her eyes. Having her hair brushed was heavenly. Leah exhaled and let her back sink into the chair.

"You have beautiful hair."

"Thank you." Leah opened her eyes and smiled into the mirror. "Do you...do you often do things, like cook for Keegan?" Leah was still struggling to decipher how everyone in this large, sprawling house was connected to each other.

"I enjoy cooking. Chief Behn has a cook and Keegan has no one...or, has had no one...so I sometimes do things for her."

Keegan had no one. Until now?

"Do I have you to thank for my rescue last night?"

Esther nodded and smiled thinly. Leah imagined that there was more Esther wanted to say, an admonition perhaps, but she held back. So far, Esther was a model of polite self-control.

"Thank you." The chance sighting in the street, the brief eye contact with Esther as the men had hauled her toward the cages, had probably saved her from something terrible. She wasn't sure exactly what, but Keegan's words echoed inside her head, and given her initial run-in with the Fain raiders, her imagination didn't need much of a boost to picture the worst.

"There's a birthday celebration tonight in the great hall for Kayla, Tiago's cousin. I thought you might like something to wear. That's why I brought the clothing and the bodice." Esther continued to brush her hair without making eye contact in the mirror.

"Do you think I'm invited to attend?" Leah wasn't so sure after the way Keegan had left the previous night.

"Everyone in the house will be expected to attend." Esther looked up and met her gaze.

There was something unspoken in Esther's expression. Leah couldn't quite decipher it, but she was fairly certain it wasn't joy about the upcoming celebration. Dread was more the feeling she got.

❖

Keegan accelerated and rose up off the seat with bent knees to absorb the bounce as the two-wheeled rover climbed the rocky rise and crested the ridge. At the top, she paused to enjoy the view. A plateau lay before them, and beyond the drop-off to the north, a conifer forest and a lake. Keegan loved the scent of pine and inhaled deeply. Yates followed, pulled alongside, and allowed her rover to idle.

They'd followed the boundary of the green zone north from the city, skirting the edge of perpetual sunset with the dark lands just to the east of their position.

"How far north are we going?" Yates sipped from her canteen.

"How far is too far?"

"That depends on what you're running away from."

"Who's running?"

Yates quirked an eyebrow but didn't respond.

"I'm not running." Keegan took the canteen from Yates.

"Whatever you say, Commander."

Keegan spent the night in the officers' quarters at the garrison after leaving Leah. She'd been so angry that sleep had eluded her, and this morning she'd set out with the single goal of finding someone, or something, to punch. So far, she'd gotten no satisfaction. The rough northern route had proved physically challenging, which helped alleviate some of the adrenaline in her system, but anger still simmered just beneath the surface.

The patrol had thus far netted nothing new or undiscovered. Previously sacked outposts had remained uninhabited, and they'd seen no signs of new activity from the Fain. Maybe Gage was having more luck on his route to the west. If he got to punch someone before she did then Keegan was going to be really pissed.

"We should return soon." Yates stowed the canteen. "Don't you have that gathering to attend this evening?"

"Oh, fucking hell." Keegan closed her eyes and white-knuckled the handlebars.

"Yeah, that one. Kayla's turning eighteen, right?"

Keegan nodded.

The last thing she was in the mood for was some family birthday celebration for Kayla. But there was no way she could get out of it. And it wasn't Kayla's fault that Keegan had decided to bring the most infuriating woman back from the desert to live in her quarters. No, that was no one's fault but hers. The distraction had caused her to forget the party, but Yates was right. They would have to turn around soon and head back to Haydn City.

Leah offered a drink to Hardy. He'd been the picture of professionalism all day, refusing to sit except briefly while he ate at midday. Having someone silently loiter about was beginning to unnerve Leah a little. She'd decided to engage with him and see what information she might glean about this place called Haydn City.

"Is there some rule that says we can't talk while you're here?"

"Um, no, not that I'm aware of." He seemed to consider the question further. "Unless talking causes me to be unable to perform my duties." He straightened his shoulders.

"Can I ask you some questions then? And if the questions become too tasking we'll stop."

"What sort of questions?" He sounded a bit suspicious.

"Well, I tried to walk around yesterday…"

"Alone?"

"Yes, I'll admit now that was a mistake."

He nodded in agreement.

"Anyway, I was unable to figure out the layout of this city. I felt as if I were walking in circles."

"That's because the city is a circle."

His confirmation made her feel a little less annoyed with herself.

"Would you be able to draw me a diagram?" She looked around for some way to do that. She opened a drawer in a cabinet near the far end of the table, finding nothing useful she tried the next drawer down, she discovered loose sheets of rough paper. The paper looked handmade. After rummaging around further, she found something to write with, a fat, oblong piece of graphite sharpened at one end. She held the paper and graphite up to Hardy. He nodded.

He drew a single circle in the middle of the paper and then several circles farther out, connected by straight lines. The arrangement looked like the spokes of a wheel with a hub at the center.

"This is the Temple of the Nine." He pointed at the central hub. "And these are the Great Houses."

"What do you mean by Great Houses?"

He looked confused by her question.

"Do you know what amnesia is?"

Hardy shook his head.

"Amnesia is a condition where someone has lost their memory."

"Lost their memory?"

"Yes, imagine if you couldn't remember your name, or where your home was, or who your family was." She sat across from where he stood. The truth of what she'd said struck her. She'd never stopped to imagine what it would feel like to leave the place where all her memories resided. To be forever separated from anything familiar. She swallowed the lump rising in her throat. "Pretend I have amnesia and I need your help to restore my memories."

"Is that true?" He was suddenly concerned.

"Yes, in a way it is true. I have no memory of this place or anyone who lives here. So, tell me, what do you mean by Great Houses?"

"The Great Houses represent the original clans."

"And this house we're in?" She'd heard Keegan refer to the Tenth Clan more than once. Didn't that mean there were ten clans? If so, what was the significance of the Temple of the Nine?

"This is the Great House of the Tenth Clan, the ruling clan, all descendants of the Behn family."

"Are you saying Keegan, sorry, I mean, the commander...is she a Behn descendant also?"

Hardy hesitated, as if by explaining further he would be revealing some secret not meant for him to share.

"I'm only asking for myself. I will not share what you tell me."

"Commander Keegan resides in the house of Chief Behn, but she is not a member of the family."

Was she adopted then? When Esther had described Keegan as alone, was that what she meant? Alone in the world.

"And Commander Keegan is in...the military?"

"The Tenth Clan controls the military."

"So, the Tenth Clan is the ruling clan. That's what you said, right?"

Hardy nodded.

"Does that mean that at other times one of the other Great Houses might be in the lead position? That one of them might represent the ruling clan at a different time?"

"No."

"Really?"

"The Tenth Clan has always ruled."

Leah suspected that the other Great Houses must be involved in some form of government as a ruling body, but she was more interested in the rest of Hardy's map of the city. As she continued to talk with him, he added details to the map—the market, the forum, the cages, the auction square, the arena, and then communities outside the city boundaries. By the time they finished he'd practically filled the paper to its margins.

"And what happens in the arena?" Some aspects of the city design reminded her of ancient Rome from her college studies in history.

"Games, competitions...death matches."

"Death matches?"

"Combat to the death." His voice was so calm he might as well have been describing what he'd had for breakfast.

Leah shivered at the barbaric nature of a fight to the death. She wondered what had to transpire to bring two people to such a place that they would literally try to kill each other for sport.

She returned to the original spokes of his drawing. The temple probably would give her more clues about this society and culture. Leah wondered if she could talk Hardy into taking her there. Thinking of venturing out again reminded her of the silver cuff that still rested nearby, in the center of the long table. She picked it up and looked at it more closely.

"Do you know what these markings mean?"

Hardy almost seemed embarrassed by the question.

"Do you mind explaining them to me?" She held the cuff out to him in the palm of her hand.

He didn't pick it up or touch it, but he pointed to details as he spoke.

"This text at the bottom says that you are property of the Tenth Clan."

She couldn't help but bristle at his words.

"This says you specifically are bound to Commander Keegan, with her rank, and this is her crest."

"A bird?"

"Yes."

Leah examined the engraved, ornate shape of a bird with outstretched wings. She'd have thought Keegan's crest might have been a bear, or a wolf, or something else equally stubborn and aggressive. But a bird? She could not have predicted that, and when Keegan had first placed the cuff on her arm she'd been unable to turn it in such a way to see these details.

"Will you help me put this back on?"

Now she was sure Hardy was blushing, but he agreed to assist anyway. Her fingers weren't strong enough to open the cuff or bend it back once it was around her arm. After replacing the cuff, Hardy respectfully backed away and resumed his protective stance near the door. Leah touched the silver band. It felt cool beneath her fingers as she rubbed them over the outline of the bird absently and studied the map on the table in front of her.

CHAPTER FOURTEEN

Hours passed, Leah wasn't sure how many. With no change in the sun's position, the passage of time continued to elude her and confound her. She was near the window when she saw Hardy come to attention in her peripheral vision. Footsteps echoed up the stone stairs, and she rightly assumed that Keegan was returning. Leah ran her fingers through her hair and swept it away from her face. She was partly hidden in shadow in the adjoining room when she saw Keegan, and the sight of her caused Leah's heart to pound more quickly, despite best efforts not to allow it.

Keegan was wearing long pants, over her boots, rather than tucked into the top as seemed to be her usual practice. This looked like some sort of dress uniform. Tan pants, pressed to a crease with a dark, fitted, long-sleeved shirt. The shirt was neatly tucked into the belted trousers. The pants fit snug and rode a little low on her narrow waist with a holster clipped to the belt over her right hip. Keegan's well-developed biceps and shoulders strained beneath the crisp shirt.

She hadn't noticed Leah yet. Keegan was speaking to Hardy quietly and Leah couldn't make out what was being said. She stepped from the shadows. Keegan glanced sideways and stopped talking, her mouth ajar as if she'd just been surprised by a ghost. But Leah knew this look. She'd seen this look before. This wasn't surprise or fear, this was appreciation; this was attraction. Her cheeks warmed under Keegan's penetrating appraisal, and she stepped closer.

Keegan cleared her throat and turned to Hardy. "Dismissed."

"Yes, Commander." He relaxed and slipped from the room. Leah heard his quick steps descend the stairs.

Leah had freshened up earlier and was wearing the blue dress that Esther had delivered. She was glad she'd decided to get Hardy to help restore the silver cuff. She noticed Keegan's gaze linger there before refocusing on Leah's face.

"I hope Esther informed you of the dinner tonight in the great hall." Keegan's stance was stiff; her hands were behind her back.

"She did." Leah clasped her hands in front, feeling like some shy teenager on a first date.

"Shall we go then?" Keegan extended her arm indicating that Leah should walk in front of her.

When they reached the landing at the bottom of the stairs, she felt Keegan's hand at her elbow, steering her toward a series of three double doors on the left side of the wide tiled corridor. Murmuring voices filled the large, open space. Leah thought the room felt like a cathedral, with stone columns at intervals around the oval shaped room, and decorative arches crossing the ceiling between each column.

"Keegan!" A young woman practically squealed and wrapped her arms around Keegan's neck the minute they entered the room.

Keegan returned the embrace, smiling.

"Kayla, this is Leah." Keegan turned to Leah. "Tonight's celebration is in honor of Kayla's eighteenth birthday."

Kayla didn't seem very excited to share Keegan's attention with anyone, but she smiled thinly before returning her full attention to Keegan.

"Dance with me later, please, please, please." She tugged at Keegan's arm.

"All right." Keegan patted her hand. "Okay, now, go greet your guests and come find me later."

Kayla trotted off and Keegan indicated that they should move away from the door. Leah was relieved to see Esther, a friendly face in a room full of strangers. Keegan left them and crossed the room to speak to an older man, seated at what appeared to be the favored seat at the head of a long, food-laden table.

"That is Chief Behn." Esther answered Leah's silent question.

"And that man?" Leah focused on a small cluster of people listening to a boisterous fellow wearing a dress uniform similar to Keegan's.

"That is Chief Behn's son, Tiago." Esther only glanced in his direction quickly and then looked away. "You should avoid him."

Leah should have followed Esther's example and looked away, but she was too slow. Tiago caught her eye from across the room. He handed his drink to someone and strode in their direction. Leah searched for Keegan; she had dropped to one knee and was listening intently to the chieftain, with her back to where Leah and Esther stood. As Tiago drew closer, Esther's stance stiffened. She averted her eyes and would not look at him. Leah on the other hand, could not seem to look away.

He was haughty, rolling his eyes from side to side as he crossed the room, so that his power over and simultaneous dismissal of others appeared in every movement of his body. He was average height, with a broad chest and a large head; his eyes were small, his beard was thin and well groomed. He had a flat nose and a swarthy complexion. He was not unattractive, but his energy was aggressive, even from a distance.

Tiago ended with one last, long stride, stopping just short of making physical contact. Esther shrank in the space, but Leah refused to give him room. He blatantly looked at her breasts and then at the cuff on her arm before he met her gaze.

"So, you are the prize stolen from the desert?" He seemed to ignore Esther, completely focused on undressing Leah with his eyes. He stepped closer, but still had not touched her.

"And who are you, sir?" Leah pretended she didn't already know.

"Keegan can keep you for now, but you will know me soon enough." He leaned close to her ear, whispering the last bit. Understanding the threat behind his words, Leah's skin crawled.

When he pulled back to face her, she refused to look away, defiantly meeting his direct gaze. Maybe the fact that she saw Keegan approaching out of the corner of her eye gave her courage. She stood firm but didn't respond to him. Leah did her best to keep her stance neutral but confident. Esther stood a half step behind her, looking at the floor. Everything about her posture said that she wanted to disappear.

Keegan reached in front of Tiago, putting her arm across Leah, essentially stepping between them. Tiago grinned at Keegan like some amorous frat boy caught attempting to steal her date. Keegan took Leah's arm and angled them away from Tiago toward empty seats at the table. Esther followed on their heels, but then took a seat nearer the chieftain.

Only after they were seated did Leah take a deep breath and release it. Everyone chose seats, and then the room grew quiet as the chieftain struggled to rise with the help of a steward. The young steward helped support his arm as he raised a cup in toast.

"We come together as family to celebrate with Kayla as she crosses the threshold to adulthood." He paused, glancing around the room at all the raised glasses. "To the Tenth Clan, I say, remain true…remain strong…" Men cheered. "To Kayla I say, choose well, live well, love well."

Cheers rang out, punctuated by clapping. Keegan and several others stood during the toast. The heavy wooden chairs scuffed loudly on the tile floor as everyone took seats again. Leah felt like an outsider at a reunion. She quietly sampled food as it was served over her shoulder onto her plate and tried to gather every detail she could from those in attendance.

Keegan reached for a thick slice of bread and noticed that Tiago was watching Leah from across the wide table. He thought nothing of challenging her or anyone else openly, and that pissed her off. She glared at him and struck the table with the side of her fist. The noise caught his attention. When he glanced her way, she pointed her dinner knife at him and he laughed. He had no fucking respect. Someone needed to put him in his place.

"I can ignore him." Leah spoke softly, so only Keegan could hear over the cacophony of random dinner conversation and banging dishes.

Keegan met Leah's gaze. "Don't ignore him. Be on your guard with him. Avoid being alone with him. And whatever you do, never challenge him."

Leah's eyes widened only the slightest bit at Keegan's advice. She wondered if this would be another instance where Leah would ignore her words of caution. Or if based on the brief encounter Leah just had with Tiago, she'd believe Keegan, for once.

As if in answer to her unasked question, Leah nodded and averted her eyes.

There was something different about Leah tonight. It could be that Keegan was seeing her in a different way because of the dress, which brought out both her figure and the pale perfection of her skin, but Keegan suspected that the difference had to do with something else. When she'd returned to her quarters, the sight of Leah had nearly taken her breath away. With effort, she'd tried not to show it, but every light touch between them caused blood to rush through Keegan's veins in a freefall. She'd noticed right away that Leah was wearing the silver cuff, so maybe something had changed, or was on the path toward change.

Keegan looked at Tiago again. He was distracted with one of the servers. Good. She didn't care for the way he looked at Leah. It made Keegan glad she'd stationed Hardy in her quarters. Although, if push came to shove, where Tiago was concerned, there wouldn't be much Hardy could do except run for help.

The food service was winding down. Dessert had been delivered and music echoed through the hall. Keegan was slouched in her chair watching Leah talk with Esther, who'd moved to an empty seat nearby. They seemed to like each other and that pleased Keegan. Slender arms wrapped around her neck from behind.

"Dance with me." She'd put Kayla off as long as possible, so she got to her feet and allowed Kayla to tug her toward a bit of open floor space cleared for dancing. Several other couples made room for them as they joined the fray.

"Are you enjoying your party?"

Kayla nodded and then waved to someone across the room. She was easily distracted. Oh, to be eighteen and optimistic again. Keegan had forgotten what that felt like.

"Is she here to stay?" She looked up at Keegan, Kayla's expression growing more serious.

"Who?"

"Leah." Kayla glanced in Leah's direction. "She seems... different."

Keegan had to agree, but not different in the way Kayla meant. Kayla probably meant foreign, and that assessment was equally accurate, but Keegan sensed a shift in Leah. She wasn't sure what to make of it. Leah was watching them dance from her seat next to Esther. The look Leah was giving Keegan stirred something deep, and she had the sudden impulse to go to her. As luck would have it, a young man asked to cut in and Keegan relinquished Kayla. She crossed the great room and weaved through the crowd with purpose, never taking her eyes off Leah.

"Dance with me." The request sounded more like a command than she'd meant for it to, but Leah nodded and accepted her outstretched hand.

Leah relaxed into Keegan's arms, following effortlessly as Keegan led her around the floor in small arcs. Their chemistry as partners was so smooth that it was if they'd always danced together. However, Leah would only hold her gaze for a moment and then look away, as if the couples around them were more interesting, or as if Keegan made her nervous.

They danced through several songs without a word passing between them.

"You dance well." Could she be more uninteresting? Keegan had been the king of one-liners tonight, none of them particularly interesting or inspired.

"You're leading. All I have to do is follow."

Was Leah making a joke? She'd been so serious all night that Keegan wasn't sure.

"Are you enjoying the party?" Keegan cleared her throat. "Maybe I should introduce you around a bit more. Esther is the only person you know."

"I'm fine, really. There's no need for further introductions."

Keegan wasn't sure what to make of that comment.

"We could leave if you like." Keegan tossed out the suggestion as a way to gage Leah's interest in being alone with her.

"Whenever you're ready, I'll follow your lead."

Leah's response hadn't revealed much. Keegan sighed.

But as they'd danced, the distance between their bodies shrank. At one point, Leah even rested her cheek against Keegan's shoulder. Was that affection or fatigue? Her heart fluttered in response.

She glanced around the room, her mood suddenly improved by Leah's small displays of affection. Her eyes settled on the chieftain, who looked tired. He motioned for Esther and she seemed to be struggling to help him up. Everyone else was too distracted with their own revelry to notice.

"Walk with me." Keegan dropped Leah's hand and strode toward the aging chieftain. For the first time, Leah followed without questioning. Possibly she'd anticipated where Keegan was headed.

"Thank you." Esther smiled gratefully as Keegan braced Chief Behn's other arm.

Leah watched with interest as Keegan gently supported him. She waited until he was stable on his feet before taking the first step. She fell in behind them as Esther and Keegan assisted Chief Behn to a door at the back of the grand hall. Leah was unsure if she should follow farther, but when she hesitated at the threshold, Keegan looked back and spoke to her.

"Close the door and follow us."

Their pace was slow, which gave Leah a chance to look around. She'd only been in Keegan's sparse quarters and seen a glimpse of the large kitchen downstairs but hadn't seen any other parts of the sprawling estate. The doorway they'd taken led to a short hallway, then another corridor to the right. That passage took them to a room darkened with heavy tapestries. A fire crackled on a stone hearth that faced two well-used, upholstered chairs. Each chair was more like a chair and a half, padded at the sides with additional cushions. Scrolls of what looked like a parchment sort of paper were strewn across a desk made of broad timbers. There were other places to sit, a small table, an ornate wardrobe, and leather journals of various sizes stacked along the base of the wall near the desk. The room was enormous. It seemed to be much more than just a bedroom. It was like bedroom and study combined and had a decided medieval feel, possibly because of the tapestries.

Leah watched Keegan help the chieftain with his shoes and then gently assist him as he reclined onto the bed. Esther brought him something to drink. Keegan started to turn, but Chief Behn caught her arm.

"Stay for a moment." His weathered hand gripped Keegan's forearm.

Leah was trying to remain a respectful distance from the bed, but she could still hear what he was saying.

"I'm here." Keegan leaned over him so that he could see her. He kept his fingers on her arm.

"You have honored me, more than most of my kin." His voice was raspy.

"I've given you an oath. And my word is stronger than blood." Keegan spoke quietly, but Leah heard her words clearly. Leah listened intently as they talked. Esther carried a blanket to the bed and spread it over him.

"This I know to be true." He paused, as if catching his breath. "If only you could take this charge from my shoulders. You would be wise and fair."

Was he saying he wanted to pass the title of chieftain to Keegan? Leah didn't know much of the social structure in this place, but that seemed like a big deal.

"You simply need rest." Keegan placed a hand on his shoulder. "Rest and I will come see you tomorrow."

"Time is my enemy now. It rushes toward me…with unsaid things…the regrets of an old man."

Keegan and Esther looked at each other as if they'd forgotten she was in the room, and Leah felt as if she were intruding on some private moment. She wanted nothing more than to recede into the hallway. But at the same time, something was at work here she felt she should bear witness to. A tectonic plate was shifting, changing the landscape. She sensed the tremors were coming and even as an outsider it scared her.

"You're a great man. You should have no regrets." Keegan clasped his hand and then settled it onto the bed at his side. "Rest."

He closed his eyes and said nothing more. Esther ushered them to the door.

"Thank you."

Leah followed Keegan back to the celebration. The excited chatter and music seemed a harsh contrast to the scene she'd just witnessed. Tiago was holding court with a group of men and women and hadn't seemed to notice his father's absence. Beside her, Keegan's mood had definitely changed. She scanned the crowd with a serious expression on her face, and Leah was dying to ask her what she was thinking. Tiago noticed them leaving the chieftain's quarters before she got a chance.

"Sucking up to the old man again." He practically spat the words at Keegan.

Leah fought the urge to face off with him in Keegan's defense. But Keegan stepped in front of her, offering a buffer against Tiago. She could see the set of Keegan's shoulders square off as she turned to face him.

"Go back to your entourage and leave me the fuck alone."

"You forget your place, Keegan."

"How could I when you're forever reminding me?"

"Soon I won't have to remind you." That sounded ominous. "And you..." He leaned past Keegan's shoulder to look at Leah. "I'd very much like a taste of—"

"Keegan, come dance again!" Kayla bounded up, oblivious to what she'd just interrupted.

"Can't you see I'm talking?" He bore down on Kayla, his tone as sharp as shards of glass.

"I'm sorry, I—"

"You're such a simple girl, only good for fucking or warming someone's bed."

Tears welled in Kayla's eyes.

"Enough, Tiago." Keegan drew Kayla in with a protective arm around her narrow shoulders. "You're drunk and you talk too much."

He leered at Leah again and sipped his drink. One of his friends tentatively approached and offered to refill his glass. That simple gesture seemed to derail the escalating tension between Tiago and Keegan. He shook his head and looked as if he might say something else, but he didn't. A slow smile spread across his face as he turned and walked back to the circle of men who'd stood several feet away watching the entire exchange.

"He's drunk. What he said isn't true." Keegan tried to sooth Kayla.

"I hate him." Kayla sniffed.

"Don't say that, and don't let him ruin your night." Keegan looked at him, but he was distracted again and seemed to be enjoying the sound of his own voice. "Just go back to your friends and avoid him."

Kayla nodded. She wiped at her wet cheeks with her hands and sniffed again. Leah admired her for trying to shake off his cruel words. Kayla left them and crossed the room to join a small group on the dance floor. Once she was gone, Keegan turned back in Tiago's direction. Tension oozed into the air around Keegan, and Leah was afraid she was considering confronting Tiago. She touched Keegan's arm, which seemed to snap her out of whatever trance she'd been in.

Keegan looked down at Leah's slender fingers against the fabric of her dark shirtsleeve. Leah's touch surprised her. She couldn't quite shake the feeling of foreboding that had followed her from the chieftain's chamber. Then Tiago had tried to bait her again into a fight. Leah's hand on her arm had brought her out of the fog of anger. This had been a strange evening, and it was definitely time to leave. She was no longer in the mood for a crowd.

"Let's go."

Leah nodded, but Keegan could see the questions in her eyes.

The celebration showed no signs of winding down as Keegan lightly held Leah's arm and headed toward the stairs up to her quarters. When they reached the narrow staircase, she motioned for Leah to walk ahead of her.

CHAPTER FIFTEEN

O nce inside, Keegan dropped the crossbar to lock the door. She wasn't sure where things were leading tonight, but regardless, she didn't want to be disturbed. The sound of the crossbar sliding in place caused Leah to turn and give her a curious look.

"I just wanted a little privacy. You don't mind, do you?"

Leah shook her head, but her expression didn't match her casual stance in the center of the room. Her eyes followed Keegan as she shuttered the windows and lit lanterns along the wall. Candlelight vastly improved the ambiance of the room. A hint of music could still be heard through the floor from downstairs. Leah hadn't moved when Keegan returned to the cupboard near the fireplace and opened a bottle of whiskey. She poured two small glasses, sipped one, and handed the other to Leah.

"Taste it. You'll like it." Keegan motioned for Leah to take the glass from her.

"What is it?" Leah sniffed before sampling as if she didn't trust the contents.

"Whiskey."

Leah sipped the amber liquid as she watched Keegan toss hers back and refill the glass. Keegan held up the bottle offering Leah a refill, but she declined. She wasn't much of a drinker and having eaten a light dinner, she knew this alcohol would go straight to her head. Keegan's edgy behavior was making her think she needed her wits about her.

She was alone with Keegan in the candlelit room and the door was barred. Her heart pounded in her chest. She took another sip and tried to relax. Just the night before she'd offered herself to Keegan. Maybe that had been an epic miscalculation. Maybe tonight was the night Keegan planned to call her bluff.

"Kayla seems sweet." Leah tried to sound casual.

Keegan nodded. She refilled her small glass a fourth time and then walked around the table to where Leah had been anchored to the floor. Reflexively, Leah took a step back, but Keegan advanced. Intensity vibrated in the air around Keegan, and Leah found that she had to fight to catch her breath. Keegan unfastened the top two buttons of her shirt. The collar fell open just enough to reveal the sensual dip at the base of her neck, between pronounced collarbones. Leah swore she could almost see the pulse of Keegan's heart in the hollow space. Her gaze was so focused there that she flinched involuntarily when Keegan touched her.

"You look beautiful tonight." Keegan leaned into her personal space, her lips inches from Leah's.

Leah stepped backward and Keegan followed her. She realized she was now in the bedroom. Keegan stepped around her, closed the shutters, and lit a lantern, lowering the amount of light in the room. It took a moment for her eyes to adjust.

She returned to stand in front of Leah. Keegan finished her drink, running the tip of her tongue across her lips.

Leah backed away, not really realizing her position in the room until she felt the back of her legs bump up against the bed. Keegan took Leah's drink and set it on the bedside table along with her empty glass. Leah dropped to the edge of the bed as Keegan slowly unbuttoned her dark uniform shirt, and then removed her undershirt, tossing them both to the floor.

Keegan never looked away, her gaze as sharp as a blade. It pierced Leah's chest, leaving a heat signature at its point of entry. Despite her bravado the previous night, Leah was afraid of what was about to happen. In some ways, their coupling seemed inevitable. Keegan was like a dense star with gravity so strong it could bend light, Leah's orbit was collapsing, Keegan was pulling her in.

Leah had had sex before, but this felt different. There seemed to be more at stake. This was probably not going to be like the polite, vanilla sex she'd experienced back on Earth. The energy that pulsed off Keegan as she shed her clothing was primal, uncontrolled, pure heat.

Keegan had removed her shirt to reveal small breasts, almost swallowed up by the muscles in her chest. With the body of an Amazon warrior, Keegan presented herself to Leah. Even in the dim light, Leah could see that Keegan's body had endured conflicts. Scars across her chest and ribs marked a history of combat, but still she was androgynously beautiful. Keegan's physique was an intoxicating mixture of symmetry, muscle mass, and female power.

Leah was like captive prey, mesmerized, frozen and still fully clothed. Keegan filled her fingers with Leah's hair and pulled Leah against her firm torso. Instinctively, Leah turned so that her cheek was pressed against Keegan's rippled abs. Keegan's fingers moved in her hair at the base of her neck, and then down, following the sensitive ridge of her spine inside the back of her dress. She tried to pull away, but Keegan held her.

She pushed against Keegan, both hands at Keegan's waist, until finally Keegan let go of her. Leah slid backward onto the bed, much the same way she'd done the previous night, but the power dynamic had clearly shifted. Her offensive display the night before had now become defensive.

Keegan followed Leah, crawling slowly after her. Keegan caught her by the hips and pulled her down onto the bed so that Keegan hovered over her, partially pinning Leah with her thigh. Keegan slowly unlaced the bodice that held the gown tightly around her waist. Once the bodice was gone, the fabric draped loosely in front. Keegan traced the edge of the neckline with her fingertip, pushing the fabric ever so slightly aside as she let her finger follow the contour of Leah's breast until her nipple was exposed at the edge of the fabric.

"Last night, when you undressed in front of me, is this what you had in mind?"

Leah inhaled sharply as Keegan brushed her nipple with her fingers.

"I don't know what I thought." Leah swallowed. "I was angry and…I was trying to make a point."

"You were right. This is how things work here. Some offer sex for protection." Keegan continued to distractingly tease Leah's erect nipple with her fingers. "Some have sex because they enjoy it." Keegan opened the gown farther, exposing more of Leah's midsection. She felt Keegan's warm breath on her skin as she looked down to sample the view.

Keegan stretched out casually beside Leah, propped on her elbow as if this happened every day, as if they'd been lovers for years. Her hand slipped inside the front of the gown and across Leah's stomach. Leah closed her legs, not giving Keegan easy access to slide her hand farther down. This seemed to annoy Keegan. She rolled on top of Leah and insinuated her thigh between Leah's legs, forcing them apart. She had so easily overpowered Leah.

Keegan pressed into her, kissed her deeply, searching with her tongue. Leah broke the kiss, her breath rapid, her cheeks hot. Keegan braced above her on arms she'd thought of touching. She'd imagined gliding her palms over the contours of Keegan's etched biceps. She'd secretly recently imagined the embrace of those arms.

There had been very little conversation so far. There had been no questions. Was this too much? How did Leah choose to be taken? Keegan asked nothing. Leah sensed Keegan would take what she wanted. Whatever happened now was possibly out of her control. She had a hard time relinquishing control and willed herself to be open, not to shut down.

"Keegan."

"Hmm?" Keegan's lips were against Leah's neck, moving southward.

"Keegan, what are we…"

Her words trailed off as Keegan's mouth reached her breast. Keegan took most of Leah's breast in her mouth, working her nipple roughly with her tongue. She ran her fingers over the soft stubble at the back of Keegan's head, unable to formulate clear thoughts at the moment.

Keegan kissed her way back up to Leah's lips.

"Your skin is so soft." Keegan kissed her neck again and let her hand drift over Leah's ribs to her ass. She pulled Leah against her.

Keegan was kissing her again now, swallowing up any words she'd planned to utter, until she sensed Keegan's hand moving between her legs. Keegan's fingers were so close. Leah gripped Keegan's forearm to stop her and broke the kiss.

"I'm not...I don't know if I want this." Leah's voice broke. Did she subconsciously want it? She'd let things go pretty far if she didn't. What was she afraid of? The truth was she didn't know what any of this meant. She didn't even know if Keegan had other lovers. She suspected that she did. It wasn't even that she required some declaration of love prior to sex, but she at least wanted to know where she stood, and in Keegan's case, she had no idea. Plus, the power dynamic between them made her want to resist on principle.

"I think you do want this."

Leah knew her body was conspiring against her. She was incredibly aroused. Her sex throbbed against Keegan's thigh. But was her head ready to deal with the fallout from this? She wasn't so sure. She needed a minute to catch up. Everything was happening too fast. And she was worried that Keegan was working out something else. That this was a symptom of the emotional encounter she'd just witnessed in the chieftain's chamber. In any case, Leah wanted to slow things down.

Keegan moved her arm and rested her palm on the lowest part of Leah's stomach, but when she opened the gown farther, Leah closed the fabric with her hand.

"Let me touch you." Keegan's breath was hot against the side of her neck just before she pressed her lips to the sensitive skin beneath Leah's ear, sending shivers down her arm.

"No." But Leah's response sounded almost more like a moan than a word.

"I've wanted to make love with you since the first moment I held you." Keegan's lips moved slowly down her neck toward her breast.

Leah sensed Keegan's hand moving across her stomach, almost touching her sex. She tried again to squeeze her legs together, but Keegan countered the move with her thigh.

"Stop." Leah pushed against Keegan's chest with her hands.

"What do you mean stop?" Keegan continued to kiss her neck and her chest. She captured Leah's hands, pressing her wrists against the bed above her head. With both hands now occupied, Keegan moved on top of Leah, stroking Leah's sex with her thigh.

"Don't. I said stop."

"What? Are you serious?" Keegan stopped kissing her and met her gaze.

"Yes, I'm serious…This doesn't…it doesn't feel…right." That sounded vague and unsatisfying. She wasn't sure what she was trying to say.

"What part of this doesn't feel right?" Keegan's voice was edged with frustration, she seemed genuinely confused. Leah imagined that *no* was a word Keegan wasn't used to hearing.

"You, pushing me to sleep with you…when I think you're upset about what the chieftain said to you." Leah struggled beneath Keegan but couldn't free herself.

"Don't pretend to understand whatever you think you heard." Keegan was getting angry.

"And I don't even really know you."

"You don't know me? I'm the one who saved you from certain death. I'm the one who's clothed and fed you these past days."

"So, I owe you?"

"Yes…I mean, no…fuck this." Keegan rolled off Leah and sat at the edge of the bed. She rubbed her face briskly with her hands then reached for her shirt and tugged it on.

Leah pulled the gown tightly around her chest and sat up. Keegan looked over her shoulder at Leah, her expression dark. For an instant, she thought Keegan might reach for her, but she didn't. She started buttoning her shirt as she stood up, no longer looking at Leah.

"You're leaving?"

Keegan scowled at her as she fastened the last two buttons.

"Can't we talk about this?"

"I'm not in the mood to talk." Keegan reached for Leah's drink and finished it with one swallow.

Keegan left the room and Leah heard the bolt slide from the door and then footsteps echoing down the stone stairway. She sank back against the pillows. Shaken, aroused, and angry. Was she angrier at herself or Keegan? She wasn't sure.

❖

The party was still going as Keegan passed by the Great Hall. She kept to the shadowed side of the corridor. She was not in a party mood. She was wrought up, angry. She clenched her fists as she stormed out into the street. It was late. Pedestrian traffic was light as most people had sequestered themselves in darkened rooms for sleep. Keegan was anything but sleepy. She thought of heading to Brooke's place, but sex for the sake of it wasn't what she wanted either.

She wanted Leah. She wanted Leah to want her. Now she was just pissed off, and only one thing would ease the adrenaline charging through her system.

A twenty-minute walk took her past the stages near the arena, and beyond that were darker places, underground rooms set up for cage fights for money. Keegan had frequented this place when she was younger and full of anger. It had been a while since she'd needed either the money or the physical release of a bare fisted fight. Tonight, she did.

Cheering and smoke traveled up the tunnel as she headed down beneath street level, down away from the sun, away from Leah and her life above ground. She shouldered her way through men and a few women gathered around a match in progress. The victor landed three successive blows to his opponent, dropping him near the far edge of the cage. The loser moaned, blood oozing from his mouth and nose, and he didn't get up. The troll-like referee held the victor's hand up to the cheering crowd. Bets were paid and drinks were sloshed about in the heat of the reverie.

"Who's next?" the referee called to the crowd as the nearly unconscious man was hoisted from the ring. "Who will challenge tonight's champion?"

"Here!" Keegan grabbed the bars and hoisted herself up from the floor. "I will fight him."

"We have a challenger!"

The crowd cheered, and then a few booed when she entered the ring. She'd sort of forgotten that she was still wearing the dress uniform. Some in the underground didn't care for the Tenth. Well, fuck them. Their dislike only fueled her aggression. She charged the cage wall, rattled it loudly, and yelled. Not really words, more like a battle cry, punctuated with clenched fists against the heavy gauge wire. The crowd surged forward, matching her cry with their own shouts, urging her on, cheering her predatory display. This was what they'd come for.

Someone shoved Keegan. She turned, ready to take a swing, but it was the referee signaling for her to take a corner. It was nearly impossible to hear any directions from him over the frothed and frenzied voices of the spectators. Keegan circled, facing her opponent, until her back hit the corner. The man she'd challenged had fought at least one fight already. She'd witnessed the finish of it. He had blood at his temple and bruising on his cheek. He wasn't entirely winded, but she was completely fresh and angry, so this hardly seemed like a fair match. Although, he probably outweighed her by sixty or seventy pounds, so she'd have that to contend with. He was thick and muscled, probably the result of heavy labor of some kind. He probably had stamina to match. He titled his head from side to side, adjusting some kink in his neck and then raised his fists in her direction signaling he was ready.

The referee stepped between them with outstretched arms meant to halt their advance.

"Everything is fair," he yelled above the noise of the crowd. "The fight ends when one of you doesn't get up."

She'd had four or five shots of whiskey and even she could follow those easy rules. The ref stepped away and Keegan's opponent lunged, aggressively taking the first swing. She dodged easily, stepped out of his way, and shoved him with her foot as he traveled past. The crowd laughed and cheered. This was too easy. Keegan turned to the mob waving her arms for the noise level to rise. She turned back just as a fist connected with her jaw. Her head snapped back painfully and she almost fell.

Fuck, that hurt.

He circled her, continuing to advance, but she regained her footing quickly, shook off the blow to her face and her ego, and shuffled backward a few steps ahead of his approach. When he lunged with a strong right, she ducked and landed a sharp elbow to his midsection. As he fought to catch his breath she came down on the side of his face with a solid left. He dropped to one knee. Keegan thought he was dazed, but she didn't move away fast enough. He grabbed for her foot and jerked. She hit the floor hard, flat on her back. His beefy fist was aimed right for her face when she rolled left and away from him. Still on his knees, he punched the floor. She rotated on her back and kicked him in the ribs with both feet sending him flying into the side of the cage.

She got to her feet just as he did and they circled each other. The noise of the crowd surged, she was sweating now under the dark shirt, her jaw ached, and she was winded. This felt right, but she was just getting started. Keegan taunted him to come for her again.

CHAPTER SIXTEEN

Hunger woke Leah. She sat up, rubbed her eyes, and tried to focus. Beside her, in the darkened room, Keegan didn't stir. She'd obviously slept in her clothes. Leah had fallen asleep, but she'd sensed Keegan's return at some point much later. She'd been lying on her side, facing the wall and pretended to be asleep. Keegan had fallen into bed without a word. Leah assumed Keegan was still mad so she made no attempt to talk to her. She planned to just let Keegan sleep it off.

As usual, Leah had no idea what time it was, but surely they'd slept for several hours after Keegan returned. She slipped from the bed and went to the cook area in search of food.

The lanterns from the previous night had long since burned out. When she opened the shutters, the room was bathed in light. Leah paused to look at the cloudless sky and wondered for a moment if it ever rained here.

Anna had delivered a fresh bowl of fruit the previous afternoon and there was bread. The coals in the fire glowed red when she stirred them so she added some small sticks for a fire. She placed two slices of bread in a pan to warm and sliced an apple along with some other fruit that looked like a small melon.

She'd searched the cabinets the previous day, but found no sign of coffee. What fresh hell was this? A planet with no coffee? That thought made her laugh. There were coffee rations on her ship, and if for no other purpose, that was reason enough to get back. A canister of loose tea leaves resided near the hearth. She set them in hot water over the coals to steep.

By the time she returned to the bedroom with a tray she was able to make a pretty decent breakfast presentation, a peace offering of sorts. She set the tray on the bedside table, and for the first time since she'd gotten out of bed, really looked at Keegan. The side of her face and the pillow was darkened with something. Was that blood?

Leah opened the shutters to allow partial light to filter into the room. With better light she could clearly see that the dark smear was blood. Keegan was asleep on her back. One hand rested on her stomach and the other at her side; both had bloody knuckles. Her shirt was torn and her trousers smeared with more blood and dirt. Keegan had taken time to remove her boots but nothing else. What the hell had happened?

Leah retrieved a basin from the kitchen area, filled it with water, grabbed a clean cloth, and returned to the bedside. Gently, she pressed the damp cloth to the blood on Keegan's cheek. There was a small gash over her eye and puffiness around it. As she dabbed the cloth across Keegan's cheek, her eyes fluttered. She seemed surprised to see Leah, possibly not remembering where she was, and then she swatted Leah's hand away.

"Stop it. You're hurt." Leah caught Keegan's hand and held it. She pressed the cool cloth to Keegan's scraped knuckles.

"What are you doing?" Keegan's voice was raspy with sleep.

"I'm trying to help you. What happened to you?"

Keegan blinked several times and then gingerly touched the gash at her temple with her fingers.

"You have a cut over your eye." Leah pulled Keegan's fingers away and applied pressure with the cloth.

Keegan relaxed and allowed Leah to tend to her.

"Why do you care if I'm hurt?" Keegan's question surprised Leah.

"What sort of question is that?"

"Last night you wanted nothing to do with me and now—"

"That isn't true." Leah dropped the cloth to her lap and sat back. "I might not have wanted to have sex with you last night, but I certainly don't want to see you hurt."

Keegan looked away. Leah's rebuff had hurt Keegan more than she'd thought possible; it was written all over her bruised face.

"Keegan, how did this happen?" Leah softened her tone. She turned Keegan's face so that she was forced to look at her.

"I got in a fight."

"Because of me?"

Keegan didn't respond, but her scowl told Leah everything.

"Did you win?"

"How can you ask me that?" Keegan leaned up on her elbows. "Of course I won."

"Then I definitely don't want to see the other guy." Leah tried not to smile.

"He's fine. I bought him a drink after he came to." Keegan slid back, propped against the pillow.

Leah held Keegan's hand in hers, dipped the cloth in water, and lightly wiped at the dried blood across her knuckles.

"Better?" Leah looked up and Keegan nodded.

An awkward silence settled between them as Leah continued to tenderly clean and inspect Keegan's injuries. She couldn't see what might be under Keegan's torn shirt, but she anticipated bruised ribs at the least. Given what had transpired between them the night before, she was reluctant to ask Keegan to remove her shirt. She cleared her throat and tried to redirect her thoughts.

"Are you hungry? I woke up needing food." Leah reached for a plate from the tray and offered it to Keegan along with a cup of tea.

Keegan sipped the hot tea and took a slice of the apple. "What time is it?"

"I have no idea. I don't know how anyone ever knows what time it is here."

Keegan rummaged in her pocket. Leah had to stabilize the plate balanced on Keegan's lap to keep it from toppling. "With this." Keegan held a small square device in her palm. "It's a solar clock. I got it from an antique dealer in the city market. We can find one for you if you like." Only then did Keegan register the time on the device. "Oh, shit. I'm late."

Keegan handed the plate to Leah and made tracks for the bathroom. Disappointment settled in the pit of her stomach along with her breakfast. She'd hoped they would have some time this morning to really talk. A lot had happened in the last two days, and in order to process it all Leah needed to talk it through. She'd hoped to do that with Keegan. Leah waited and listened to the sound of running water in the bathroom.

"I'm sorry I have to leave." Keegan's voice was muffled as she pulled a shirt on over her head and fished in the nearby chest of drawers for clean pants. Leah got a glimpse of what looked like painful bruises across Keegan's ribs.

"I was hoping we'd have some time to talk." But Keegan was in a hurry.

"Later." Keegan leaned over as if she was about to kiss Leah on the cheek, but she stopped midair, possibly rethinking the impulse. "I will see you later." At the door, she turned around and looked back with such intensity that Leah's stomach flipped over on itself.

Without another word, Keegan was out the door, again. Leah sighed and dropped back against the pillows. She sipped her tea thoughtfully. Something was changing between them and she couldn't quite sort it out.

Keegan was still shaking off tiredness after leaving her place. But she felt giddy, light-headed, distracted…and sore. She rotated her shoulder as she walked. The man she'd fought with the night before had put up a good defense, and she was fairly sure she'd be feeling it for days.

Already late, she quickened her steps toward the garrison. Morning roster was at nine, and the squadrons had already dispersed by the time she arrived at twenty after. Maddox gave her a curious look as she blew into the office. She was sure it was written all over her face, in addition to the bruises. *She likes me, I knew it.* Leah had brushed her off, but her kindness this morning had given her away. She *did* like Keegan, so why the cold shoulder? Maybe she'd have to adjust her usual seduction tactics where Leah was concerned. It didn't matter; she had time to figure that out. What mattered was that Leah obviously cared about her. This discovery was bound to be the best news of the day.

Maddox looked at her again, but he wouldn't ask how she'd gotten the cut over her eye and she didn't offer it up. He was old school, a gentleman who kept his exploits to himself and never pried about the exploits of others. She knew enough about Maddox to know he had a woman with whom he'd raised two children and she suspected a mistress or two on the side. He had an easy confidence and a strong but gentle manner. He gave the impression of a man who did well with women.

"Sorry I'm late." Keegan cleared her throat and poured herself a cup of hot tea from the pot warming on the small wood fired stove. "Something came up."

She took a seat and made a big show of shuffling items around on her desk. Maddox gave her one brief sideways glance but otherwise ignored her.

The door banged before Hardy could catch it. He grimaced and then came to attention in front of Keegan's desk. "Reporting for duty, sir, ma'am...sir."

"At ease, Private." Keegan fought the urge to laugh. "Aren't you supposed to be stationed at the Great House already?"

"Uh, yes, I mean...am I?"

"You're on security detail every day until I tell you otherwise. Got it?" She stood and swung her arm toward the door. "Now get going, you're already late."

"Yes, sir." Hardy let the door slam again as he left.

"That boy has a hard road ahead." Maddox shook his head.

"He's green, but he's motivated. He'll learn."

"He's lucky you've taken him under your wing, that's all I'm saying."

Keegan wasn't sure why, but she'd taken a liking to Hardy right off the bat. He'd joined up the minute he turned eighteen.

He'd weighed barely over a hundred pounds soaking wet. But this kid from the street had heart and determination. Keegan sought to reward that.

"The squad is running through exercises on the field out back. I'm going to go check their status." Maddox stood and slid his firearm into a holster on his belt. "Maybe rattle a few cages."

"Have fun." She looked up as he left.

Keegan was only granted a few moments of silence before Yates joined her.

"You're not running drills?" Keegan leaned back in her chair.

"Do I look like I need to run drills?" Yates poured herself a cup of tea and leaned against the front of Maddox's desk.

"You seem different this morning, what..." Yates's voice trailed off as a slow smile spread across her face. "Who'd you cross last night? Your face is telling a story this morning."

"You only think you see." Keegan was never able to slip anything by Yates, and that annoyed her no end.

"So, I guess she is still worth all the headaches she's caused you so far?"

"Every single one." Keegan couldn't help smiling.

She could tell Yates wanted to ask more, but she held back. Keegan, on the other hand, was feeling uncharacteristically like talking. She sensed Yates watching her from her perch on Maddox's desk.

"Do you ever wonder how you ended up where you are?" Keegan asked.

"What are you asking?"

"I mean, all the small decisions that you made to bring you to this place at this exact time. Do you ever stop to think about that?" Keegan let her eyes lose focus as she stared at nothing.

Before Yates could answer, an explosion echoed through the garrison.

"What the hell?" Keegan rushed for the door and Yates followed.

Debris fluttered in the air near the main entrance of the garrison. Keegan and Yates were the first to arrive because the rest of the squadron was still on the training field. An explosive device had been set off practically at the front door. Scrawled across the wall with white chalk was one word, Solas.

Keegan rotated to glance at the gathering crowd.

"Back up." Yates shouted at onlookers to move away, but they were slow to heed her request.

Keegan removed her firearm and sounded a shot skyward. That did it. The crowd immediately moved back forming an open arc around the bomb site. By the time she'd holstered the gun, Maddox and several soldiers had joined them. Maddox started issuing orders.

"Rope this area off. No one comes in here until we've combed for the detonator." He turned to Keegan. "Did you see anything?"

"No, Yates and I were in the office when we heard the blast."

She'd been the only senior officer nearby when the device was detonated, right on the front doorstep of the Tenth's command center. That seemed too bold for an outsider. The image of the raider she'd shot in the desert who carried the insignia of the Tenth rose from her memory. Was it possible that the Fain had infiltrated the Tenth? Was this detonation perpetrated by one of their own? That thought roiled her insides, but she had to consider it as a possibility.

Someone caught her eye unexpectedly, and she pivoted. There'd been a familiar face in the dispersing crowd, a man she thought she recognized as one of Tiago's men. Before she could get a clear view of him, he was swallowed up by citizens in the main thoroughfare. She bolted after him, weaving around carts and pedestrians.

CHAPTER SEVENTEEN

W hat was that?" Leah came to an abrupt stop, and Hardy, who was only a couple of steps behind, bumped into her. "I'm not sure. It sounded like it came from the garrison."

"Should you go investigate?" She secretly hoped he'd say yes and take her along with him. Leah was dying to see more of the inner workings of the city.

"No, ma'am. I'm to stay with you. Commander's orders." His expression was so serious that it was hard not to laugh.

Leah had convinced Hardy to take her to the city market area. She was anxious to see if one of the antique dealers might have other items that would give her some clues about when this city had been settled. The digital watch was something she couldn't quite accept without further exploration.

Hardy's hand on her arm stopped her just as she was about to step into the path of a slow-moving transport. She'd been distracted for an instant by strange markings over a door. Markings on buildings seemed to be equal parts words she recognized and glyphs.

The shadow of the building at her back fell across the transport as it passed. As it moved from shade to sunlight, Leah saw the woman she'd shared the cell with. The woman saw her in the same moment and recognition registered on her face. The cargo area of the large transport was a cage, covered with a weathered tarp, and it carried passengers, captives. Leah held the woman's gaze until they traveled so far down the avenue that the high walls along the narrow street hid her from view.

"Where are those people being taken?"

"A labor camp to the south."

"A labor camp?"

"That is where the farming is done."

"Why do they look like captives?" There'd been women, children, and a few men in the group inside the cage.

"Because they've done something to end up in a cage...broken the law...been picked up for stealing."

Leah remembered how easily she'd been plucked from the street. The memory made her shudder. She tabled additional questions for a quieter venue. The street was noisy, dusty, and weaving single file through pedestrians and vendors made it hard to have a serious conversation.

She visualized Hardy's hand drawn map in her head as they wound through the streets. If she was remembering correctly, they should be nearing the central hub of the city. After one more cross street, she saw a massive white stone structure up ahead. It looked like some ancient Roman temple, with wide stone steps and sculpted columns across the front.

"Hardy, is that the temple at the center of your map?"

"Yes, the Temple of the Nine."

"Would it be okay if I went in?"

He hesitated, but then relented. "You go in and I'll wait out front."

The door of the temple was enormous. A tall rectangular opening at least thirty feet high. The walls were thick, insulating the darkened interior from the light and warmth of the outside air. Leah hugged herself against the chilly space. In the middle of the huge open cathedral was a single skylight at the highpoint of a central dome, supported by nine columns. The light shone down onto a pattern in the tiled floor. Leah studied it for a moment, not sure if her eyes were playing tricks on her. She walked around the outside of the pattern in the floor to examine it from a different direction. The inlayed shape looked like a large V, the Roman numeral for five. A chill traveled up the tiny hairs along her arms.

She looked away from the central part of the temple toward the walls. It took a moment for her eyes to adjust to the dim, candlelit spaces that appeared at even intervals around the outside walls of the sanctuary. Little alcoves, curved spaces in the wall, framed on each side by smaller columns, each with a pedestal in the center. Leah had to lean very close to read the engraved plaque mounted on the pedestal. She covered her mouth. Her breathing became more rapid, and her heart began to beat so hard it threatened to break through her ribcage.

This couldn't be.

There had to be some other explanation.

She moved to the next alcove and then the next, only to discover the same type of plaque. Leah turned her back to the pedestal, sank to the floor, and began to sob. All the pieces were falling into place. The hypothesis she'd been afraid to utter aloud was true.

Keegan moved fast through the crowded streets, but so far hadn't seen the man again. Possibly he'd ducked into a doorway to wait for her to pass. The glimpse she'd gotten was so fleeting, maybe she'd been mistaken. She slowed her pace as she neared the city's center. She was surprised and then annoyed to see Hardy standing near the entrance to the Temple of the Nine.

Hardy shifted and straightened as she bounded up the steps two at a time.

"Commander."

"Hardy, I thought I told you to remain with Leah."

"You did, sir...and I am, I mean, she's here...in the temple."

Keegan squinted into the dark entryway but could see nothing. "Wait here." She frowned at Hardy and stepped inside.

It took a minute for her eyes to adjust to the dark interior. No one seemed to be about, and for a second she thought perhaps Leah had figured out another exit and left Hardy dumbly standing at the front entrance. A muffled noise was coming from the other side of the large, open chamber. Slowly, Keegan circled until she saw Leah sitting on the floor, head down, crying.

"Leah?"

Leah looked up from her crumpled position. Keegan extended her hand to help Leah stand. Leah wiped at tears with the palm of her hand, sniffed loudly, and jutted out her jaw. She glanced sideways at Keegan and then stepped away.

"What's wrong?"

"The Temple of the Nine." Leah hugged herself and walked back toward the lit area beneath the skylight. "Why do you call it the Temple of the Nine?"

"Because of the nine clans, the nine Great Houses." Keegan followed Leah.

"What is this?" Leah pointed to the large V shape on the floor.

"That's to honor the missing clan, the Fifth Clan, forever lost."

Leah covered her face.

"What's going on? Why are you so upset?" Keegan reached for Leah, but she pulled away.

"I'm from the missing clan."

"What? What are you talking about?"

"These plaques? These are the steel mission plates from each of the colony ships. They were mounted on the fuselage of the command modules of each ship." Leah pointed to one of the engraved metal plaques mounted on the nearest pedestal.

Keegan blinked rapidly, trying to get her brain to synthesize what Leah was saying. This didn't make any sense.

"How is that possible?"

"I am Dr. Leah Warren, a geologist from *Proxima Five*, the fifth of ten colony ships that departed from Earth for Proxima B." Leah took a deep breath. "The reason there is no fifth plaque is because my ship only just arrived. *Proxima Five* landed in the desert two days before you found me."

"This can't be—"

"True?" Leah shook her head. "But it is."

Then Keegan remembered something she'd heard in passing and dismissed. One of Maddox's squadrons had reported what they described as a weather anomaly, a cloud trail across the sky over the desert two or three days ago. Could that be what Leah was referring to?

Silence stood between them. Keegan considered the possibly that Leah was crazy, delusional, but then without prompting and without walking around the temple to read each plaque, Leah calmly recited the name of each Great House, without ever breaking eye contact with Keegan.

"The first ship, led by Hua Hsu, was charged with infrastructure and habitats, the second ship brought mechanical support, communications. Under the command of Frank Armus they were to establish the power grid." Leah listed the rest of the great houses. "Maclin, Sanneh, Yang, Rife, Chagall, Pan, and the tenth ship, led by Franz Behn, was responsible for military protocols."

"How can you know all that? How is this possible?"

"When you mentioned Chief Behn his name sounded so familiar, but I was still recovering from extended hibernation. Prolonged stasis has clearly affected my memory, and my ability to reason in some way..." Leah paced back and forth, talking with her hands.

"What happened to the fifth ship?"

"I don't know. Possibly a solar storm during transit affected navigation. I didn't have a chance to find out. I was only just bringing the ship's systems back to full power when...when those men found me." Leah looked at Keegan. Her eyes glistened with tears. "Our group represented the earth sciences team—physics, chemistry, biology, and geology."

"If you came here aboard a ship, where are the others?"

"Dead...they're all dead."

"How can you know those names?" Now it was Keegan's turn to pace.

"They are the last names of each ship's captain. I trained with all of them for this mission. We trained for months. I know... knew...I knew them."

Leah swayed on her feet and Keegan quickly moved to catch her before she lost her balance completely.

"How long?" Leah's voice trembled.

"What?"

"How long ago was this city established?"

"This place was seeded twelve generations ago." Keegan tightened her embrace to better support Leah's weight.

"Twelve generations." Leah looked up at Keegan, her eyes wide. "How long is that? I'm trying to do the math...wait, that's three hundred years...three hundred years." She repeated the words as if to herself. "We had the power to create a new world, and this is what we made." Leah began to tremble.

"You're not well. Let me take you home." Keegan tried to support her as she ushered Leah toward the door.

"Home." Leah's knees buckled. "I have no home."

Keegan scooped her up, cradling Leah's cheek against her shoulder.

"I'll take you home," Keegan whispered to Leah as she carried her toward the exit. She couldn't quite wrap her head around all that Leah had just said. There was no way it could be true, could it? She had described Leah as otherworldly, foreign, but this...this was far beyond that.

Keegan stepped through the door into the glaring sun. She didn't stop to explain anything to Hardy, but she knew he'd fall in behind her as she headed back to her quarters with Leah in her arms.

❖

Disorientation and nausea washed over Leah in successive waves as Keegan gently settled her on the bed. Leah rolled onto her side, facing the wall, and hugged her knees to her chest. Leah wanted to shrink away from this reality; she wanted to wake up and discover everything that had happened since her ship had landed was nothing more than a horrible, toxic dream. A delusional side effect of extended cryogenic hibernation and nothing more. But Keegan's hand on her arm was very real. This was no dream from which she could escape by falling blissfully back to sleep.

"Leah, what do you need?"

Keegan's question sounded surreal. What did she need? She needed to rewind three hundred years. She needed to sleep again and never wake up. She needed air, and space to breathe.

"I just need to be alone." Her voice sounded small inside her head.

Keegan's hand lingered on her arm, but then the warmth of her touch slipped away. She heard mumbled words as Keegan said something to Hardy, then footsteps, and she was gone. Leah had been granted her wish. She was alone. There was no fear, only numbness, oblivion. Leah was some other thing now, not in her own body, floating above a sun-fed summer field of grass, thinking of a past life she would never return to.

CHAPTER EIGHTEEN

L eah's revelation in the temple rattled Keegan, but she couldn't deal with that right now. She needed to find Tiago and report the explosion. The only question was how much of her suspicions should she reveal to him. Did she trust him? In all honesty, no. And if the man she'd seen was actually a member of his squadron he'd surely deny it to protect his own reputation. Tiago's men, the city squadron, had carved out more and more autonomy from the rest of the Tenth. And he'd been allowed to lead them as he saw fit. The chieftain either didn't know of Tiago's cruelties to citizens, or he was too tired to fight it. She wondered for a moment if she should press the chieftain to let her handle it, to take the burden from his shoulders and rein Tiago in. That was probably too much to hope for. After all, Tiago was his only son. Good or bad, blood was binding.

"Keegan." Esther approached from the other end of the corridor.

"What's wrong?" Even in the shadows of the hallway, she could tell Esther was upset.

"The chieftain needs to speak with you...he is not well."

Keegan followed Esther toward Chief Behn's residence on the first floor at the back of the Great Hall. Could this day get any worse? When she entered the chieftain's chamber she knew the answer was yes. Today would not be the day to talk with him about the growing threats to the city, by Tiago or anyone else. He was propped up, ashy and hollow cheeked against the pillows. His breathing was labored and shallow. Fuck, he looked like winded death. His feeble shaking hand reached for hers as she came to his bedside.

"No time now." He wheezed as he struggled for breath like a drowning man.

"Just rest, Chief."

"No, you...listen..." His words were swallowed by a coughing spasm that shook his frail body.

She glanced up at Esther. He squeezed her hand to get her attention, then whispered something she couldn't hear. She leaned closer.

"You...You must take my place."

"What?"

His eyes were wide and desperate.

"No..."

He shook his head. "It must be you."

Keegan turned to Esther, standing at the foot of the bed. Had she heard what the chieftain had said? Esther's expression told Keegan that she hadn't. Chief Behn squeezed her hand again, and she turned back. She leaned even closer so she could hear his whispered words.

"You...you must do this thing for me." He took a shaky breath. "Give me your word."

Before she could respond, a coughing fit overtook him. He coughed even more as he fought to take a breath. Keegan stepped away as Esther came to his side.

Keegan was tense, a little shell-shocked. He was in distress and seemed on the edge of panic. What had happened? Where was Tiago in his father's last hours? It was true that legally, the chieftain could name a successor other than a family member, but it had rarely been done and surely Tiago would challenge the decision, which the ailing chieftain was in no condition to combat. Who else knew of the chieftain's wishes? It would not be safe to carry this news alone.

He lapsed into sleep and Keegan stepped away. Esther came to her side. Esther put her hands on Keegan's arms, forcing her to make eye contact.

"He's been asking for you all morning. I sent a steward to the garrison for you, but he couldn't find you."

"I was…there was an explosion, and then…I didn't come directly here."

Keegan ran her hand across the stubble at the back of her head. Drawing strength from the mark in her scalp that she could not see, the physical sign of the oath she'd made to the Tenth Clan. The oath had given her a place, a home, and had given her life direction. She did owe the chieftain, and she did not carry that debt lightly.

"Where is Tiago?" Keegan searched Esther's face.

"He was here earlier."

"When?"

"He talked with Tiago this morning. Something happened yesterday. I don't know what it was, but Chief Behn became frantic, and first thing this morning after he spoke with Tiago again he asked to see you."

"What did Tiago say to him?"

"I don't know." Esther shook her head.

"What was Tiago's mood when he left this morning?"

Esther didn't answer. Her frightened expression told Keegan everything she needed to know.

There were proper channels for this sort of thing. The General Court needed to be involved to ratify a decision of this magnitude. Keegan had heard the chieftain's words, but she didn't really believe them. How could she rule in his place?

When she felt overwhelmed, Keegan tried to focus on whatever task was at hand. Action cleared her head, centered her. The explosion was the most pressing task at hand. In the short-term, she'd put her energies there.

"I have to go."

"Keegan, be careful."

Esther never told her to be careful. She looked back, feeling as if the words were some bad omen. She tried to shake off the dark cloud of unease as she left the room.

Yates met her on the steps as she was leaving the building heading back toward the garrison in search of Tiago.

"What is it?" Keegan stopped, standing a step higher than Yates.

"I brought your weapon." Yates handed her a rifle. "We got a tip that the bomber and his crew were just east of the city. Maddox wants us to check it out."

Keegan had been lost in thought, and then totally focused on Yates. For the first time, she noticed two crawlers parked nearby. Gage was driving the first vehicle, along with three soldiers from the Tenth. Yates and Keegan climbed into the second vehicle with two other soldiers. Yates was driving. The crawler lurched as they tailed the first vehicle. She thought of Leah, but there was no time. Too much was happening too fast. She could only focus on one thing at a time, and this was it.

The passage out of the city seemed to drag. Too many obstacles in the street, too many people, too much noise, and dust. All of it raised Keegan's anxiety. Something didn't feel right. Unease had settled around her like fog, and it was a distraction that she didn't need. Distraction could get you killed.

It wasn't until the tendrils of the city thinned that Keegan thought they were even on the right trail. She'd seen no signs of damage and wondered if they'd been sent on some wild chase for a phantom bomber. But as the buildings became sparser, they saw smoke on the horizon. As they drew close, she saw a scene she'd seen repeated numerous times. A smoldering structure, a kneeling woman cradling the head of a wounded man, and a half-starved child looking on.

One of the soldiers peeled out of the crawler with instructions from Keegan to take statements and see to the wounded while the rest of the squad followed the culprit's tracks east.

They were a half mile from the desert rim boundary when they spotted a small group ahead. Were these the culprits? Their rover must have run down, otherwise, why would they stop in the wide open? They were easy targets. The two crawlers were barely within range when a rifle shot pinged off the steel roll bar just above Keegan's head. That answered Keegan's internal question. Gage and Yates swiftly turned the vehicles to form a barrier as the armed squad spilled out, returning fire.

The soldier to Keegan's left took a hit to the shoulder. He sank to the ground as Keegan dispatched the shooter. From this distance, the shooters were nothing more than dark shapes against the blistering, undulating backdrop of the desert horizon. But it was only moments before the raiders, or whoever they were, were outgunned and only one remained. Keegan wanted to take one of them alive in hopes of gathering intel. Before they could reach him, the remaining renegade offloaded a two-wheeled rover. He fishtailed in the soft sand, but quickly righted the rover and sped off to the north. They were close enough now to know for sure this was a Fain raiding party.

"Yates, take one of the crawlers and follow him." They were halfway to the stalled vehicle when Keegan stopped to watch the dust trail recede north.

Yates and Gage looked back and forth at each other.

"Follow him and find out where these Fain raiders are hiding and then report back to us. It can't be more than thirty miles from here to the narrows. I'm guessing that's the cut through he's aiming for." Keegan let the idea sink in for a few seconds. "And then you come back, report to us, and we take multiple squads into the nest and clean it out."

Enough was enough.

"What about you and the rest of the squad?" asked Yates.

"We'll wait for the raider's cruiser to recharge and then we'll take that and the other crawler back to the city."

As she voiced the plan she wondered why they'd never done this before. It seemed so simple, so logical. Probably because she wasn't the senior military official who had the authority to launch such an initiative. That person was the chieftain. Why hadn't he done this before? Probably because Tiago had advised him not to. Because the lingering, guerilla conflict benefitted Tiago in some way. Without conflict, what was his role?

Yates started toward the military crawler, but turned back when Keegan spoke.

"Do not proceed into the Hollow Hills alone. Do you hear me?" Yates nodded. "You are only doing reconnaissance. Then you follow the dark lands boundary south, to the city. You report back to me and only me." Keegan paused, stepped closer, and lowered her voice so that only Yates could hear. "And you come to my quarters, not to the garrison...you got it?"

Keegan still didn't know if there was a Fain infiltrator within their own ranks, so she wasn't taking any chances.

Yates gave her a questioning look but agreed.

"We'll clean up here and head back to the city. Unless something unforeseen detains us, we should get back before you return." Gage followed Keegan toward the stalled cruiser.

They checked the bodies as they passed. Some lay face up, a few faced down, arms at odd angles. Dead. One man remained alive. He was badly wounded and sat with his back against the vehicle. He had a bleeding gash on his cheek, a shot to the leg, and a wound in his chest. His breathing was labored and his leg bled profusely. One of the soldiers applied a tourniquet to slow his blood loss, while Gage relieved him of his weapon.

Keegan knelt in front of him. He wasn't much more than a boy, probably no more than seventeen. Some of the others on the ground didn't look much older. A stone settled in Keegan's stomach. There was no honor in killing teenagers. Is this what the Fain had resorted to? Recruiting children? She remembered what she'd been like at his age—angry and ambitious, with nowhere to direct her energies until Chief Behn had pulled her from cage fighting and given her a place to serve the clan. If not for fate, she could easily be sitting in this young man's spot.

"Get him some water." Keegan spoke to the soldier who'd attended to his leg.

Keegan stood and checked the back of the crawler while the young man sputtered through a few sips from the canteen. There were random bits of clothing, a blanket, and some food stores. Not much of a haul if this group had come from the city's center. Something didn't add up.

"What's your name?" Keegan knelt again.

He blinked, as if he were struggling to focus, but didn't answer.

"Tell me your name. We'll help you, but I need some information from you first." She glanced up at Gage; his beefy shadow seemed even more ominous backlit by the sun.

The boy looked up at Gage, his expression shifting from fury to uncertainty to fear. Fear of death perhaps?

"Davis. My name is Davis." His voice was weak.

"Tell me, Davis, what do you know about explosives."

"Nothing."

"What about your friends here. Do any of them know anything about explosives?"

He shook his head. The motion made him cough and blood spattered near his lip.

"What are you doing here?"

He looked up at Gage and then scanned the soldiers loosely gathered around them. The reality of his situation seemed to be sinking in.

"We were looking for ammunition. We didn't mean to hurt anyone. That guy went for Allen, and that's when Rafe shot him… we weren't gonna hurt anybody…when we didn't find ammo were just gonna take the food and some blankets and leave." Once he started talking the details just kept spilling out.

This kid didn't strike Keegan as some insurgent mastermind or an explosives expert. As she listened to him she decided she believed him. Davis was telling the truth.

"Do you know who Solas is?" She might as well see what other intel the boy had while he could still talk.

"No, no one knows."

"What do you mean no one knows? Don't the Fain follow a leader named Solas? I see his name painted on the walls all around Haydn City."

"No one has seen Solas…so that Solas can stay safe. We don't need to see him to receive his message."

"And what is that message?"

The boy rallied for a moment, his eyes brightened. "That a free society run by an elite minority is not free."

He rattled off the words as if he'd memorized them, Keegan wondered if he even understood what he was saying.

"Those are big ideas…idealistic ideas."

"Think whatever you want. We're no longer going to sacrifice ourselves for selfish men, we—"

"Who is we?"

"The Fain..." He coughed, his breathing more shallow. He was fading. "We...we are the rising tide of change."

"You sound like a recruitment poster for discontented youth."

He scowled at her.

"You'll see. Solas will change everything...Solas will make things better...we just have to stay strong...He is coming..." His words trailed off as his drooped.

Keegan checked the pulse point at his neck.

"He's gone." He'd lost far too much blood, most of it from the leg wound.

She paced in front of his lifeless body, occasionally glancing down at him.

"I think he's telling the truth." Gage cradled his rifle to his chest in a relaxed stance.

"I agree." Keegan looked back at Davis. "The question is, who really set off those explosives. And who blamed these raiders."

"Yeah, something doesn't fit." Gage shifted. "They're all basically kids. This whole thing is fucked up."

Keegan nodded.

"We keep chasing our tails, putting out brush fires while we allow the embers to spread in front of the wind." Keegan paused. "I'm sick of this bullshit."

"You and me both." Gage's expression was serious.

"Where did Yates go?" one of the soldiers asked. He was looking north as if he expected to see Yates return.

"She's running an errand for your mother." He gave her a curious look. "None of your damn business, that's where she's going." Keegan made a circular motion with her hand, a signal for him to get moving. "Get these bodies loaded onto this vehicle. Two of you stay with it until the solar battery has recharged, then bring the bodies back to the garrison. On the way, you can stop and return what's left of the stolen goods to that family. The rest of you come with me. We're heading back."

Yates was a gifted tracker. She'd have no trouble following the runaway raider. Keegan would return to her place and wait for Yates to bring news of the Fain's location.

They were walking back toward the military crawler when Keegan noticed something approaching. A dust cloud signaled the approach of a large vehicle. As it got closer she could see it was a military transport. That seemed odd. Had more than one squad been issued the order to pursue the raiders? That seemed like a bad use of manpower.

The canvas covered carrier pulled to a stop in a swirling dust storm, just before reaching Keegan's parked crawler. It wasn't until the dust had subsided a little that she saw Tiago step from the truck. Her heart rate spiked and a tingling, warning sensation traveled up her spine. No one knew what had transpired in the chieftain's quarters, except possibly Tiago. The fact that he'd left the city to follow her squad raised alarms inside her head. Gage must have sensed her change in mood. Beside her, he stiffened. He didn't aim his rifle, but he repositioned it for ease of motion if he was required to. He'd never liked Tiago, for reasons of his own. Not many did like Tiago. They tolerated him because of his position, which he only retained based on his relation to the chieftain.

Her gut instincts told her something wasn't right. As the squadron of soldiers walked toward them, they raised their weapons. One of them discharged a round and the soldier to her left fell from a direct hit to the chest. Before Gage could fire, he was down also. Keegan shifted quickly and ducked. She reached beneath Gage's shoulders and dragged him to the cover of the crawler twenty feet in front of them.

She glanced up just as the two soldiers who'd stayed back with the fallen raiders were taken down as they ran forward to help defend Keegan's position. The one soldier who remained from her squad had dropped back to help his wounded comrades and was shot before he reached them.

What the fuck was going on? Was it possible that Tiago's men had mistaken her squad for the raiders? That seemed unlikely.

Keegan peeked over the hood of the crawler. Tiago and his men were striding toward her at an unhurried pace. She'd made it to cover, dragging Gage, without being hit. It was almost as if Tiago's men were shooting at everyone but her. Because she'd been an easy target as she'd dragged Gage to cover. She knelt beside him. He was breathing but unconscious. Strategies sped through her brain, possible scenarios considered for a split second and dismissed. She was outgunned, outnumbered, isolated, and there seemed no good options for surviving this. Firing on an entire squadron would serve no purpose. She raised her open palms to show that she had no weapon and stood slowly. Anger pulsed through her veins with every pump of her heart as she waited for Tiago to explain himself. The smug expression on his face as he approached made her blood boil. He signaled for one of his men to relieve Keegan of her weapon.

"Questions…questions." Tiago stood a few feet in front of her. "You have so many questions right now, don't you?"

She didn't respond. She balled her fingers into a fist, but he was beyond her reach. Keegan clenched her jaw and waited.

A few soldiers appeared behind Tiago carrying a cage, similar to the one the Fain raiders had used for Leah. They dropped it to the sand with a thud.

"You just shot soldiers of the Tenth Clan in cold blood." She said it loud enough for everyone to hear.

"No, we stopped a coup to overthrow the rightful heir to the chieftain's seat."

"What—"

"You are unmasked. There's no need to deny your true identity any longer…Solas."

"I am not Solas. And I want everyone present here to know the truth. I am loyal to the chieftain, I am loyal to the Tenth Clan, and my loyalty has never wavered."

Tiago stepped so close that only Keegan could hear him. "Except for today, I'm guessing."

"Maddox won't let this go. He'll find out the truth."

"Maddox is gone." He waved for the men to bring the cage. "It's done, Keegan."

Hands grabbed for her and she swung wildly at Tiago, but her arm was stopped before the blow found its mark. As two of his men held her, Tiago turned and punched her in the stomach. She doubled over, but then twisted sharply, breaking free and lunging at Tiago.

Three men were on her now, pressing her face down into the sand. She tried to rise despite a knee in her back only to have a boot strike her ribs, forcing her to drop. She tasted blood. "Don't worry, I'm going to leave you alive long enough to think of where you went wrong." Tiago knelt beside her. "And the prize you brought back from the desert? I'll take care of her for you. Think of all that I can offer her that you cannot."

Keegan struggled but couldn't break free.

"Fuck you."

"Oh, she'll fuck me…whether she wants to or not." He grinned and then got to his feet.

Keegan used the last of her strength to surge upward. She managed to topple one of the men who'd been holding her, but her maneuver met with the sharp strike from the butt of a rifle. Her head snapped back, her eyes fluttered. A second blow brought dizziness, and for a moment, everything went dim.

Her head lolled. It ached. Where was she? The cage was small. Once inside, she couldn't stretch her legs fully. As her senses returned she grabbed the bars and shook with force, but the gate was locked and wouldn't give way. Metal clanged as chains were fastened to the cage and then to the back of her crawler. One of Tiago's men drove forward, pulling the chain taut. The angle of the floor tilted, forcing Keegan off balance. She struggled to right herself.

"We'll follow in the transport." Tiago was talking to his men. He motioned for them to return to the vehicle. After they were out of earshot, he knelt beside the cage. "You were always more brawn than brains. I think that's why my father liked you. You were simple, uncomplicated, trusting, oblivious."

"You're Solas, aren't you?" It hadn't occurred to her until that moment, but she knew she was right. Her suspicions about an infiltrator, an inside job, were correct. She just didn't figure out who the traitor was, until now. "You're the one who's been supplying the Fain with guns."

"Maybe not as dumb as I thought." Tiago stood, looking down at her. "But in any case, too late to change the outcome."

"If you hurt Leah you will suffer for it."

"You're really in no position to threaten me, but I admire you for having the balls to try...while locked in a cage." He laughed. "We had some good times, Keegan. I can't say I won't miss you. But both of us can't sit in the same chair. And you are far too popular and fair-minded for my tastes."

"Chieftain is your position to claim." Keegan gripped the bars. "I don't want the chief's chair. You can have it." Her mind raced for some advantage, some way to reason with him. But the small space was beginning to close in, making it hard to think. Her heart thumped loudly in her ears, she struggled for air.

"Oh, yeah, you don't like cages, do you?" He bent down so he could see her face.

"Don't do this." She tried by force of will to slow her breathing, but she couldn't redirect her thoughts. Old wounds were pulling her under. She was drowning.

"Like I said, Keegan, it's finished. You are my last loose end."

He made a circular motion with his hand, a signal for his man to drive. The crawler lurched, jerking the cage along the sand. Keegan used her shirt to try to cover her mouth from the dust as she was dragged deeper into the desert. Tiago stood watching. He grew smaller and smaller until nothing was all that she could see.

She'd failed everyone. She failed Gage, left behind, bleeding out. She'd failed Chief Behn. She'd failed to save Esther. And Leah, she'd assured Leah that she could protect her. She'd failed Leah most of all.

CHAPTER NINETEEN

Leah went to the bathroom and splashed water on her face. She glanced up at her reflection. Her eyes were pink and puffy from crying. She'd basically lain in bed all afternoon, rolling everything over in her head, solving nothing. The facts remained that she was on Proxima B, exactly where she was supposed to be. Only she'd missed her target arrival date by three hundred years. Four light years from Earth, three hundred years too late. Time had become an enemy from which she could not escape.

She walked to the adjoining room, holding a damp towel against her eyes to soothe them. She was surprised to see Esther. Something was wrong. Esther had been crying also.

"What's happened?" Leah's stomach lurched, and she thought of Keegan.

"The chieftain is dead."

Leah noticed for the first time that bells were ringing in the distance. They sounded like bells from her church, from her childhood.

"When?"

"Less than an hour ago. I was hoping that Keegan was here."

"I haven't seen her since early today." Leah looked at Hardy for confirmation.

"She hasn't been back since we returned from the temple." He looked sheepish. Leah wondered if he'd gotten in trouble for allowing her to go there in the first place.

The Temple of the Nine. What a joke. A monument to mortal men and women, travelers, pilgrims from a faraway place, nothing more.

"Is there anything I can do?" Leah touched Esther's arm. She seemed so upset. It would be nice to focus on someone besides herself for a little while.

Esther shook her head. "Arrangements are being made. But I'm worried about Keegan…"

Esther didn't finish the thought.

"Why, what else has happened?" Leah had been wallowing in self-pity all day while a real threat had obviously been building. She'd been clueless and Keegan had said nothing to her. Leah hadn't asked why Keegan was at the temple. Did this have anything to do with the explosion she'd heard earlier?

Footsteps pounding up the stairs pulled Leah's attention away from Esther. Yates strode into the room and poured herself a glass of water without speaking to anyone. She looked dusty, road weary. Her lithe limbs glistened with perspiration. She finished the glass off and refilled it.

"Where's Keegan?"

That seemed to be the question of the hour.

"She hasn't been here all day." If Yates also had no idea where Keegan was, then Leah was definitely concerned.

"What do you mean she hasn't been here all day?" She took more gulps of water. "She should have been back more than two hours ago. They weren't that far outside the city when I left them." Yates glanced at the window with a puzzled expression on her face. "Why are the bells ringing?"

"Chief Behn is dead," Esther answered.

Yates looked as if she'd seen his ghost, her hand holding the glass stopped midair. She put the glass down and moved toward the door. Leah stepped in front of her, blocking her path.

"Where are you going?"

"I'm going to find Keegan. We were supposed to rendezvous here, and if she's not here then something stopped her from being here. I'm about to go find out what."

"I'm coming with you." This was the first thing Leah felt sure about in days.

"The commander asked that you stay here." Hardy spoke timidly from his post near the door.

"Well, the commander isn't here. Don't you want to find out why?" Leah watched his expression shift from doubt to resolve. He nodded.

"I'm going too." Esther filled a flask with water. "Keegan might be hurt. She might need this." Esther looked up. Everyone was watching her.

"Where are we going exactly?" asked Leah.

"East of the city. We followed a group of Fain raiders to the desert rim. We thought they might be responsible for the explosion earlier today at the garrison, but I don't think they were." Yates shifted impatiently, readjusting the strap of her rifle across her chest.

"The explosion was at the garrison?" Leah hadn't even asked Keegan about it when she'd last seen her. She'd been completely overwhelmed by her discovery at the Temple. But wait, east toward the desert meant they'd be headed in the direction of her ship. Leah went to the bedroom to get her gear bag. If Keegan was hurt they might need the medical supplies from her ship, and she'd need the locator to find it. "Okay, I'm ready."

"Wait, this is going to seem suspicious if we all leave at the same time." Yates held her arm in front of Leah to stop her. "I'll retrieve a crawler and meet you and Esther out front. Wait for a few minutes and then look for me on the street. I'll park away from the main entrance. Look for me."

Leah nodded, adrenaline rushing through her system.

"Hardy, you come with me." Yates motioned for him to follow her and the two of them left the room.

Leah turned back to Esther. "Are you sure you should leave?"

"I do not wish to be here without the protection of Chief Behn."

Leah was reminded of something Esther had said when they first met about having to serve Tiago after the chieftain's death. A chill ran up her spine. If the chieftain's death had Esther, a longstanding member of the Great House, this frightened, what did that signal for her? Probably nothing good.

They waited anxious moments. Every sound that echoed up the stone stairway was reason for alarm. Leah went to the window. People were crowded in the courtyard. Mourners? Possibly. Did she actually feel tension in the air or was it simply her own? It was hard to be sure.

After they'd waited as long as they could stand, Leah followed Esther down the stairway. They slowed their pace, walked calmly, eyes cast down to the stone tiles.

"Esther?" A woman's voice came from the kitchen as they passed.

They'd almost gotten beyond the three doors that opened into the large room where the birthday celebration had been hosted the previous night. Leah couldn't see the woman who'd spoken.

"Don't stop." Esther motioned for Leah to keep walking.

"I'll wait."

"No, go."

"We won't leave without you."

Esther nodded and turned back toward the kitchen. Leah continued down the corridor, but before she got to the front she saw Hardy walking swiftly in her direction.

"Where's Esther?" he asked.

"Someone stopped her. She didn't want me to wait." Leah was happy to see Hardy. She was feeling uneasy about leaving the main house. "I thought you were going to wait outside."

"The streets are jammed with people. Everyone is gathering around the main entrances. I was afraid you wouldn't find us." He took her arm and cleared a path for them as they left the shadows of the stone structure for the sun and dust of the street.

Hardy shouldered people aside, and she followed close behind in his wake until they reached the four-seated crawler.

"Where's Esther?" Yates rotated from the driver's seat.

"There." Leah spotted Esther several yards away weaving through people. Hardy walked back to meet her.

They were barely seated when Yates pulled away, snaking the crawler through the stream of mourners milling toward the Great House. They were moving against the tide in a sea of people. Leah felt closed in by the press of the crowd, sure someone would stop them, but the farther they got from the forum the more the gathering thinned. By the time they reached the city's boundary there was almost no one about, and the only reminder that something tragic had happened was the faint sounding of the bells in the distance.

They drove farther. Trees and other green thinned as they neared the desert rim. A tendril of smoke appeared on the horizon. After a few minutes, they were within fifty feet of the smoking structure, but nothing about the place stirred. Yates killed the engine and climbed out. Hardy shadowed her as she approached the dwelling. There were dark shapes on the ground, but Leah couldn't make out what the shapes were. Were they bodies? Yates stopped, stood for a few seconds, and then she and Hardy ran back to the vehicle. She seemed genuinely spooked.

"What is it? What's wrong?" Leah leaned between the front seats as Yates put the crawler in gear and hit the accelerator.

"We stopped at this outpost earlier. Keegan left a soldier here to take statements and help the wounded. He's dead now." Yates white-knuckled the steering wheel as the all-terrain vehicle lunged over a small rise.

"Who's dead?" Leah wanted specifics.

"The wounded civilian, the soldier, the children, all of them."

Leah dropped back to her seat. Whatever Yates thought this meant, it wasn't good. The stoic warrior was obviously shaken by what she'd just seen. They pushed on for another twenty minutes or so when more dark shapes appeared on the horizon. The desert landscape lay just ahead and Leah was having a terrible case of déjà vu. Her stomach sank as they drew close enough to see that these dark shapes were also bodies.

This time they all disembarked. Yates took the lead, and she and Hardy checked each body. There were heavy tire tracks in the sand. It looked as if more than one vehicle had passed over the area.

"Gage." Yates knelt beside one of the wounded men. He looked dead, but then his lips moved. Yates put her ear nearer his mouth. "Where?" He whispered something and then raised his fingers barely off the ground, pointing into the desert.

Esther knelt on the other side of Gage and attempted to give him something to drink. He sputtered. He'd lost a lot of blood from multiple wounds. A dark brown stain sunk into the soft sand and spread beneath him.

"We're going to get you to a doctor." Yates moved his arm and he grimaced.

His lips moved, but no sound came out. He blinked once and then his eyes remained open, but lost their focus. Yates sank back onto her heels.

"He's dead." Esther gently closed his eyes.

"Did he say something? What did he say?" Leah looked at the bodies around Gage. All of these people looked like soldiers. They wore the same clothing that Keegan did. And they'd all been shot multiple times.

"I can't be sure, but I think he said Keegan is out there."

"Out where?" Leah followed Yates's gaze toward the open desert.

"Look at this." Hardy pointed to a trail of some kind, a pattern in the sand, that led farther out into the desert. It wasn't a tire track. "It looks like something was dragged behind another vehicle." Troughs possibly made by wide, heavy tires bookended the pattern in the sand.

"Come on." Yates strode back to the crawler.

"We can't just leave them." Hardy wrung his hands helplessly.

"This is a triage situation. They're all gone…we might still have a chance to save Keegan if she's alive." Yates shook him. "Pull it together. I need you."

He nodded and they all hurriedly climbed back into the vehicle, but Yates's words echoed inside Leah's head. *If she's still alive.* Leah was suddenly overwhelmed by a sensation of loss she hadn't expected to feel about someone she hardly knew. But there was something between them, and she wasn't ready to lose the chance to find out what that was. Keegan had saved her life, and if it was at all within her power, she would do the same for Keegan.

They drove past other bodies. Two more soldiers. Hardy climbed out to check, but they were also dead. Then more bodies clustered in a loose circle on the sunbaked sand. They were young boys. They looked like teenagers. Leah's stomach tightened. This was a bloodbath. Someone went on a killing spree and had obviously no fear of recrimination for their acts of violence.

"These were the raiders who fired on us." Yates swerved around the carnage as they picked up the trail again.

Nothing. There was nothing for miles except sun, sand, and heat. Leah took some water from the canteen. It was hard to swallow around the lump of dread in her throat. Yates braked and stepped out of the vehicle, leaving it running.

"Do you see something?" Leah was scared. So many people dead and Keegan was not among them. What did that mean?

"These tracks double back and head south." Yates shielded her eyes with her hand.

Leah stepped out on the other side of the crawler. The other part of the trail, the part that looked as if someone had dragged a sled across the sand, extended ahead of them. A flat object of some kind had obviously been hauled into the desert. But what? And why?

"Get in."

Leah did as Yates directed and they continued east until something up ahead broke the monotony of the landscape. A dark spot, an unmoving shape sat, barely visible atop the razor thin horizon. Leah's heart sank as they got nearer. She had a terrible feeling. Yates stopped within a few feet of the cage and Leah rushed from the crawler. Keegan wasn't moving, and Leah's heart sank into her stomach. Her heart raced as she knelt and reached for Keegan.

"Keegan!" Esther joined Leah, kneeling in the sand.

"What the fuck?" Yates shook the cage door but it didn't give.

"Keegan, can you hear me?" Leah reached through the bars and touched her face. Her skin was dry and hot, possibly a sign of heat stroke. She was breathing but unconscious. Dirt covered her face and mixed with coagulated blood at her temple.

Yates returned with a crow bar, and she and Hardy took turns applying pressure to the lock. It finally gave way. Yates slid Keegan's feet out first. The cage was so small Keegan's knees were bent. It took all four of them to move her to the ground, into the shade of the crawler. Leah began to examine Keegan. She moved her hands slowly, methodically over Keegan's arms and legs. Then across her ribs. Nothing seemed broken, but she had a nasty oozing gash on her cheek and at her temple.

"We need to get her out of this heat." Leah left Keegan for a moment and rummaged in her bag for the location device.

"Let's load her into the crawler. We can lay her across the back seat. Hardy can ride in the cargo area." Yates gave directions. She looked up at Leah. "What are you doing?"

"I have a place nearby with a medical lab and supplies. It's much closer than the city." Leah held the device in front of her and waited until the blue dot appeared. "There." She pointed southeast. "We're very close."

"What do you mean you have a place nearby? That doesn't make any sense." Yates stood, her voice edged with frustration. "She's weak and she needs medical care."

"Look." Leah showed Yates the screen. "This measurement shows our distance. We are a little over eight hundred meters away from medical care."

Yates looked at the screen and then up at Leah.

"Trust me, Yates. I want to help Keegan as much as you do, maybe more." Leah was sure of it now. Her heart hurt at the sight of Keegan's motionless body in that cage. Leah would do whatever she could to bring her back.

Yates relented and they hoisted Keegan onto the seat. Leah held Keegan's head in her lap as they turned southeast. Blood from her head wound seeped into the front of Leah's dress. The crawler whined and lurched over the dunes and soft sand, but eventually they crested a rise and Leah caught the reflection of the sun bouncing off the sleek metal surface of the ship. Sand had blown against one side of the huge craft, but the cargo entrance was still clear enough to open. Leah eased Keegan's head to the seat and climbed out. She hurried to the ship and entered the code on a keypad to open the hatch. The huge door hissed as it released, and a blast of cool air swept past Leah. She motioned for Yates to drive up the ramp.

Once the crawler was inside the cargo bay, Leah punched the switch to close the door. Lights blinked on inside the darkened, cool compartment.

"What the hell is this place?" Yates sounded angry, but Leah considered that maybe her anger was the manifestation of fear instead.

"This is a colony ship, my ship, *Proxima Five*." Leah scanned their stunned faces. "I am from the lost clan." She'd been to the temple so she knew they would understand if she explained in those terms. "I promise I'll explain everything to you, but right now we need to get Keegan to the infirmary." Leah's head was clear. She was back in her ship. She was regaining some small amount of control, and it felt good. "Hardy, come with me. We'll get a gurney to more easily transport her."

They used a backboard to move Keegan to the gurney, and then Leah led them as they wheeled their way to the med lab. One more lift and slide and they transferred Keegan to a proper bed. Keegan was dead weight, unmoving, still unconscious.

"How long do you think she was in that heat?" Leah glanced briefly at Yates while she waited for the medical interface to come to life on the computer terminal.

"I don't know for sure. I left them eight, maybe nine hours ago."

Leah checked the digital clock overhead. It was twenty-three hundred hours; meanwhile the intensity of the sun and heat outside was equal to the level of midday. She looked up at the clock again. It was almost midnight. No wonder she was tired. The screen lit up and she started typing her search.

"Are you a doctor?" Yates hovered at her elbow.

"Yes, but not a medical doctor." Leah didn't look up from the screen as she scrolled the responses to her query. "But everyone on the team had basic medical training in case of accident or injury. I'm double-checking now to make sure I'm remembering correctly what to do."

Unasked questions hung in the air, but all of that would have to wait. Right now, Keegan needed Leah's full attention. This was science. With a clear course of action required, she was in her element. First, she confirmed Keegan's body temperature.

"She's too warm." Leah opened several cabinets until she found a cooling blanket.

"If she's too warm why are you getting a blanket?" This was the first time Hardy had spoken since they'd entered the ship.

"This is a cooling blanket. It will help lower her body temperature." She didn't have time to explain everything, but she tried not to sound impatient.

Esther helped Leah tuck the blanket into every crevice—under Keegan's arms, between her legs, and beneath her neck. It only took a minute after being plugged into a power source for the blanket to feel cool to the touch. After several moments, Keegan began to shiver.

"What's happening?" Esther was holding Keegan's hand and placed another hand on Keegan's shoulder.

"I need to give her benzodiazepine, it's a muscle relaxant." Leah prepped a syringe. "The shivering will increase her body temperature, making the cooling treatment less effective."

Leah administered the drug, and after another few seconds, Keegan stilled. She checked her temperature again, placing the device inside Keegan's ear and waiting for the beep.

"Good, it's going down." The overall tension in the room seemed to lessen.

Leah removed the blanket so as not to lower her temperature further. Once her temperature had leveled out, the next step in the protocol was hydration. She put a binding around Keegan's arm and looked for a vein to start a saline IV drip. After setting the IV, Leah looked up to see everyone watching her, wide-eyed. Yates was defiant, her fists at her sides. She looked like she was about to take a swing at Leah.

"These are fluids. This IV will help hydrate Keegan's body." Leah stepped away from the bedside, tossing the packaging for the IV needle in the trash.

Now came the waiting.

Hopefully, Leah had done the right things in the right order. She would know soon enough. Adrenaline ebbed in her system. Her head swam, and she leaned against the counter. She looked around the room. They were all tired and strung out. Esther looked lost, forlorn, and Leah was reminded of Chief Behn's death. Everything was probably about to change, but from Leah's perspective, all of that had been overshadowed by Keegan.

"There's nothing we can do at the moment." Leah touched Esther's arm. "Let me show you to the galley where you can get something to eat and drink. We've all been out in the heat too long."

Leah led the way as they shuffled out of the infirmary and down the long, sleek corridor to the kitchen.

CHAPTER TWENTY

Leah's mind wandered, replaying the events of the past few days, so that she wasn't sure how much time had passed when Keegan finally began to stir. She'd convinced the others to get something to eat in the galley. She'd needed food as well, as her energy waned. She'd left them in the kitchen and returned to check Keegan's status. The lights were dim, and she'd relaxed against the edge of the counter when Keegan's eyes fluttered.

"Hey." Leah tenderly rested her palm on Keegan's forehead. Esther had done her best to clean and bandage the wound at her temple. The dressing would need to be changed soon, as blood had seeped through the gauze.

Keegan blinked a few times and swallowed. "Water." The word came out like a raspy whisper.

Leah tilted Keegan's head up and brought a small plastic cup to her lips. The tiniest sip caused her to cough. She drank a little more, then swallowed a few times, and closed her eyes. After a few seconds, she opened them again. She looked at Leah and then her eyes widened.

"You're bleeding...are you hurt?" Keegan struggled to sit up, but Leah pressed her shoulder to the bed.

"No, I'm not hurt." She glanced down. She hadn't even thought to change out of the bloody clothing. "I'm afraid this is your blood, not mine. You took quite a blow to your head."

Keegan touched the bandage tentatively. "Oh." She relaxed and Leah stroked her forehead lightly.

"Gage? Is he..."

Leah shook her head. She didn't know Gage, but she'd been at Yates's side when they found him, and it was obvious that he was a close friend.

"I'm so sorry."

Keegan squeezed her eyes shut. The muscle along her jaw flexed.

"We were so worried about you." She stroked Keegan's forehead tenderly until she opened her eyes again.

"We?"

"Yates is here...and Esther and Hardy."

"What is this place?"

"We're on board *Proxima Five*, the colony ship."

"Your ship." Keegan spoke softly, as if to herself. She rotated, fixing her eyes on Leah. "You really are from the lost clan."

"Yes, I am." Leah squeezed Keegan's hand. Her knuckles were still scuffed from the fight she'd been in the night before. "How do you feel?"

"Like I was dragged through the desert." Keegan closed her eyes and let out a long sigh. "Considering that, I feel pretty good. My head hurts."

Leah stepped to the other side of the table and removed the IV. She placed a small bandage over the needle's entry and then helped Keegan sit up.

"Don't move too fast. Just sit for a moment."

Keegan nodded. Her hands were braced on the edge of the bed causing the muscles of her arms to flex. Leah couldn't help herself; she let her hand drift down Keegan's arm, over the contours of her bicep. Leah chided herself for thinking about Keegan's sculpted arms. She tried to redirect her thoughts. But what was wrong with acknowledging her attraction? She was just so happy that Keegan was alive and relatively uninjured. This whole situation could have gone much worse.

"If you feel up to it, you should let everyone see that you're up. Then I can show you where you can shower and we can both get some clean clothes." Keegan's shirt and pants were torn and smeared with dirt and dried blood.

Slowly, Keegan walked toward the galley, assisted by Leah. Conversation stopped the minute Keegan appeared at the door. Yates was the first to reach her, placing her hands on Keegan's shoulders as if to confirm she was real.

"You gave us a good scare." Yates didn't hug Keegan, but Leah was sure she wanted to.

"I gave myself a good scare." Keegan tried for levity.

Hardy didn't say anything. He just smiled and gave Keegan a little space. Esther didn't hold back. She embraced Keegan, pressing her cheek to Keegan's shoulder. Keegan returned the embrace. A tear slipped from Esther's lashes and slid down her cheek.

"It's okay. Everything is going to be okay." Keegan tried to offer words of comfort.

"Is it?" Esther pulled away and looked up to meet Keegan's gaze. "Chief Behn is dead."

"Well, then everything that happened today makes more sense." Keegan sank to a nearby chair. She leaned forward with her elbows on her knees and rested her face in her hands. "Fuck."

"You can't think about all of this right now. You need to eat something and rest. There's nothing any of us can do right now." Leah stood beside Keegan and rested her hand on Keegan's shoulder. Keegan nodded. "I'll get some food for you."

Keegan followed Leah down the corridor from the galley to the crew quarters. After eating, she felt better, but still fatigued, a deep-down-to-the-bone-marrow sort of weary. Leah had left Keegan in the kitchen alone while she got the others settled into sleeping compartments. It was nice to have a few moments alone with her thoughts, although, thinking of Tiago only made her furious. And she was too tired to deal with her anger just now. Satisfying her rage would have to wait.

They stepped through a narrow passage into a small space with three doors.

"This is the bathroom, with a shower. I'll show you how to use it." Leah opened the center door first, then the doors on each side of the bathroom. "These are both sleeping compartments…crew quarters." Leah's voice broke when she said crew.

She looked back at Keegan and smiled thinly.

Keegan stood by as Leah reached for soap and towels and then showed her how to turn the shower spray off and on. The square shower stall had a door to separate it from the toilet and sink area.

"I'll find some clothes for you, and I'll leave them on the sink while you shower." Leah backed out of the small space. "I think Eric was about your size. I'll get some things for you from his trunk." Leah looked at the floor as she talked.

This was Leah's world, or what was left of it. Keegan was seeing Leah in a different way. The dynamic between them had shifted, and Keegan wasn't sure exactly what that meant.

"Would you like to take a shower first?"

Leah looked down at her soiled clothing.

"No, it's okay." She met Keegan's gaze.

Keegan had the strongest desire to draw Leah into a protective hug.

"I want you to be able to rest. I can take a shower after." Leah slid past her and closed the door.

Keegan piled her discarded clothing in the corner and stepped into the hot spray. Reddish water pooled around her feet as the dried blood and dirt washed away. She tried her best to clean her face with a small hand towel without getting the dressing soaked. She wasn't sure she succeeded. The exterior door opened briefly and then closed. A shadowy figure was all she could see through the frosted glass that separated the shower compartment from the rest of the space.

She toweled off and slipped into a pullover short-sleeved shirt and boxers. Then she pulled on a pair of lightweight cargo pants.

Everything fit pretty well. The pants were a bit loose, but they felt good. And the shirt was softly broken in. When she stepped from the bathroom, Leah was seated on the bed in the room to the left. Leah looked up and smiled.

"You can sleep here. Everything is all ready for you." Leah moved away from the bed to make room for Keegan in the small compartment.

"Thank you." Keegan took Leah's hand. "For everything."

Leah nodded, seeming suddenly shy. She left, with clothing folded under her arm, to take her turn in the shower. The lights were dim, and the minute Keegan stretched out on the bed she knew she'd be asleep in seconds. Her limbs weighed a hundred pounds and her head was foggy. She was so tired that once she fully reclined, her senses warbled and she felt almost as if she was floating on water. Maybe she had a fever because that's what it felt like. Warm and exhausted, sleep came quickly. She dropped off to the sound of falling water from the shower.

CHAPTER TWENTY-ONE

Yates was leaning in the doorway of Keegan's room when Leah opened the bathroom door. She'd put on a clean shirt and shorts and was squeezing damp lengths of her hair in a towel. Showered and wearing her own clothes, she felt almost normal.

"I wanted to check on Keegan." Yates shifted her stance, crossing her arms.

It was as if she cared about Keegan but didn't want Leah to know. As if it weren't obvious to Leah already. Keegan was the hero of everyone's story, that was becoming clearer to her.

"Is she asleep?" Leah kept her voice low and leaned through the doorway to check on her patient. Keegan didn't stir. "After a good night's sleep, she'll feel much better. Thank God we reached her in time."

"Leah...thank you." Yates looked at her as if she were seeing her for the first time. She extended her hand and Leah accepted it. "Keegan is lucky to have you in her life."

Leah's cheeks warmed and she nodded but didn't know what else to say.

"You should get some rest too." Yates started to walk away, but then turned back. "And tomorrow you can explain all of...this...to me." She made an arc with her arm toward the outer corridor.

"Yes, tomorrow. Tomorrow I'll answer all your questions."

Yates nodded. "Good night."

"Good night."

Alone in the compartment, Leah considered her options. She was extremely tired, but also unsettled. She stood looking down at Keegan sleeping, and after a few moments decided she did not want to sleep alone. Leah hung the damp towel over a small metal chair in the corner. She carefully crawled over Keegan and snuggled into the open space between Keegan and the wall. She rolled onto her side, resting her cheek against the outside curve of Keegan's shoulder.

Keegan felt solid and real. The warmth of her body soothed Leah's frayed senses. She draped her arm over Keegan's midsection and took several slow breaths. They were safe. Keegan was safe. And they were together. It wasn't long before Keegan's deep, slow breathing lulled her to sleep.

❖

A sound woke Leah. At first, she thought someone was talking to her. The room was dark, and she fought through the cobweb of sleep that clung to her brain. She blinked a few times until her eyes came into focus. Beside her, Keegan jerked, making small movements with her arms at her side as if she were tied down and fighting it. Keegan mumbled something. That was the voice she'd heard. Leah sat up. Keegan jerked again, and the muted noise she made became more urgent, more like a wordless cry for help.

"Keegan, wake up." Leah gently shook her. "It's just a dream. Wake up."

Keegan thrashed about and swung her arm at Leah, causing her to bump the back of her head against the wall in the tiny sleeping compartment.

"Keegan, wake up." Leah reached across Keegan in an attempt to settle her, but Keegan was lost in some dark place. She lurched upward, and in one forceful move, tossed Leah on her back. She was straddling Leah's waist. One of Keegan's hands was at her throat, the other recoiled in a fist.

"Keegan! Keegan, stop!" Leah tugged at Keegan's fingers digging into her neck.

Breathing rapidly, Keegan opened her eyes. It took a moment for her to calm down. Once she realized it had only been a dream, she looked down at Leah and swiftly released her. She rotated her position so that she was sitting next to Leah rather than on top of her. Leah coughed. She sat up, matching Keegan's position.

"It's all right...it was a dream." She made slow circles on Keegan's back with her hand. "It was just a dream." Keegan slumped back onto the bed.

"I'm sorry." Keegan covered her face with her hands. "I almost choked you...I was out of my head..."

"Look at me." Leah pulled Keegan's hands away. She leaned over Keegan, braced with an arm on each side. "Hey, you didn't hurt me. You have nothing to feel bad about." The truth was, she'd been scared, but she didn't want to make Keegan feel worse.

"I dreamed I was in the cage." Keegan's voice broke. "I was trapped."

"Your experience today would give anyone nightmares."

"The cage was intentional."

"What do you mean?"

"When I was a kid, I got picked up in a sweep and thrown into a small cage for transport to Haydn City. Only, somehow, they forgot I was there. It was three days before someone found me."

"Keegan, that's horrible."

"Tiago knows that story. He specifically chose to put me in a cage...knowing it would bring everything back. He didn't simply want to kill me, he wanted to degrade me. He wanted to put me in my place. He wanted me helpless and suffering."

"Well, you're not dead." Leah touched her face again. "Hey, look at me. You're not dead and your place is wherever you decide it should be. He doesn't control you or me or Esther." Leah couldn't help getting angry.

Keegan met her gaze.

"You are very much alive, and you're going to stay that way." She rested her palm in the center of Keegan's chest. Something was different between them. Leah was no longer the captive. Keegan was no longer in a position of control. Keegan was allowing Leah to see a different view of the person she was, strong, yet vulnerable. She was beginning to open up to Leah; she could see it in Keegan's eyes.

Keegan's fingers were at the base of her neck. She tugged Leah down until their lips met. Keegan's tongue teased hers, and she felt the press of Keegan's hand against the small of her back. Leah held Keegan's face in her hands as the kiss pulled her under, the weight of her emotion, Keegan's strong arms around her, the heaviness of the day, all of it flowed through the kiss and away. Tenderly, softly, with eyes closed, Leah kissed Keegan's forehead and then her cheek and her neck before returning to her lips, warmed by the friction of desire.

"Thank you," Keegan whispered.

"For what?"

"Thank you for saving me."

"You saved me first."

CHAPTER TWENTY-TWO

I'm going back for Gage and the others." Yates didn't leave much room for discussion.

"Then I'm going with you." Keegan stood.

"No, you're not." Leah was leaning against the console in the galley. The others were loosely scattered at the table nearby, except for Yates who'd hardly sat down long enough to eat. And now Keegan was standing too. Leah could tell by the look on Keegan's face that she wasn't used to being told what she could and couldn't do.

"That's for me to decide." And clearly, she didn't like it.

"I'm sorry. I only meant that I don't believe you're in any condition to go back out into the desert." Leah kept her voice neutral. Keegan visibly relaxed but didn't sit down.

"Leah is right." Yates filled a canteen from the water station. "Hardy and I will go. I think it's better if Tiago thinks his plan succeeded. If you show up in Haydn City…well, I think it's best if you don't."

Leah watched Keegan's expression change. She was working things out. She must see that Yates was right. Keegan needed to rest and regain her strength for whatever happened next. And Leah really had no idea what that would be.

"I'd like to go also." Esther had been very quiet all morning. No doubt she was mourning the chief and in all likelihood, loss of the life she'd known.

Everyone was suffering and Leah didn't know what to do to help.

"I should be with you." Keegan's words undulated with emotion.

"I know." Yates put her hand on Keegan's shoulder. "This is a thing we must do without you. Gage would understand."

Keegan nodded and sank back to her chair.

"What will you do with..." Leah didn't finish her question. To refer to Gage as a *body* seemed callous and unfeeling.

"I'm going to take the crawler and a trailer I saw in the cargo compartment to retrieve our guys. Then I was thinking I'd take them to Chagall's precinct." Yates paused to wait for a reaction from Keegan, but she didn't challenge the plan. "Chagall's precinct is slow to get news from the city. I'll leave Gage and the others with the garrison there and see what I can find out about you."

Keegan nodded.

"But be careful." Keegan looked concerned. "I don't trust Chagall. He's always been clinging to Tiago's bootstraps. I'm sure he is not a friend to any of us now that the chieftain is gone."

Leah stepped closer to Esther. Leah was worried about her. She seemed unmoored and quieter than usual.

"Are you sure you want to go with them?" Leah reached over to help her fill a second canteen with water.

"I need to feel useful in some way." Esther smiled thinly. "Besides, I'm not a soldier so in this instance I might be able to run interference for them if necessary."

Maybe Esther was right. They had each showered and put back on their regular clothing. Leah had offered them things from the crew trunks, but that would only make them stand out.

Leah and Keegan followed them to the cargo bay. Leah gave Yates a location device and showed her how to read it so that they could find the ship on their return trip. She and Keegan stood in the gaping entrance of the cargo hold watching them drive away. Heat pulsed around Leah. The air was so hot and dry that it felt as if oxygen was literally sucked from her lungs. She couldn't imagine how Keegan must have felt trapped in the small cage, with no way to escape the unrelenting sun. Leah wondered what Keegan was thinking now, as she watched her friends drive toward the horizon.

After a few moments, Keegan looked at her, turned, and walked back into the ship. Leah followed, closing the bay door from the panel just inside. It would take a few moments for the air to cool even after the door was closed.

Keegan followed Leah back to the galley and reclaimed her seat. Leah served two cups of coffee from the console and took the seat across from Keegan. Coffee. This was her second cup. Across from her, Keegan took a sip.

"What is this?" She scowled at the cup of dark roast.

"Coffee." Leah smiled.

"It tastes awful." But she took a second sip just to be sure. "Terrible."

"Some, including myself, might refer to it as the nectar of the gods."

"Gods with horrible taste."

Leah laughed. "Let me make you some tea."

"Thank you."

When Leah returned to the table, Keegan's elbows were on the table and her face was in her hands. Leah touched her shoulder lightly as she set the tea in front of her.

"What can I do to make you feel better?" Leah wanted to break through the walls Keegan had been putting up all morning.

Keegan was receding into some dark place, and Leah desperately wanted to hold her back or follow her there. Keegan looked up and smiled weakly.

"Tell me something about yourself." Keegan sipped her tea thoughtfully. "When we were in the temple you said you were a doctor. And I'm fairly sure I'm here now because of your emergency medical skills."

"I have my doctorate in science, in geology. I study rock formations to be exact. Where I'm from they call you doctor, but it's not the same thing as a medical degree."

"So...I was saved by a rock doctor."

Leah laughed. A genuine laugh. She couldn't remember the last time she'd laughed for real. It felt good, and laughter lightened the air in the room. Even Keegan couldn't help smiling.

"Talk to me about where you came from." Keegan leaned forward. He undivided attention focused on Leah.

"Earth?"

"Yes."

"It's ultimately where you come from too."

"Yeah, I guess I hadn't thought of it that way."

"The Earth I left was in the last stages of debility. We abused the planet and…either because of us, or perhaps it was part of an inevitable cycle due to overpopulation and species decline, climate on Earth changed. Sea levels and water temps rose, weather patterns shifted permanently, causing droughts in some places and floods in others." Leah stared down into her coffee. "One of the most striking effects of climate change was its power to unsettle our basic expectations of the modern world. Humans no longer had a predictable future. Our planet changed into a strange and unstable environment, and it was a process outside technological control."

"How did that happen? There must have been warning signs."

"Oh, yes, there were warning signs…those warning signs were symptoms. The response was endless debates about what the cause of the symptoms were."

"What do you think was the cause?"

"I think the long-term overuse of fossil fuels disturbed the basic biogeochemical processes that made the Earth habitable. By the time the first Proxima ships left, the planet was at the threshold of a new geological epoch."

"What do you mean by fossil fuels?"

"Oh, right…we chose this planet for its endless sun. An eternal engine for solar power. You would never need oil or gas." Leah looked up and smiled. She'd forgotten that Keegan's world was a very different place from hers. "Fossil fuels are basically hydrocarbon deposits, such as petroleum, coal, or natural gas. They are derived from the accumulated remains of ancient plants and animals and burned as fuel."

"They're underground then."

"Yes. And carbon dioxide and other greenhouse gases generated by burning one of these types of fuel were considered to be one of the principal causes of global warming. The planet warmed and the weather changed."

"That explains the world you came from…but I was more interested in your world." Keegan was looking at her with that intensity that had become so familiar over the past few days.

"Oh." Leah sipped her coffee and averted her eyes. She took a deep breath. "My world was all about preparing for this journey. It seems odd to say that now."

"You planned to come here."

"Yes. I trained with my team for the voyage and landing." Leah rested her chin in her palm. "We were supposed to arrive right after the first four ships, early enough to help establish the initial colony settlement."

Keegan was quiet, absorbing what Leah had said. Once she'd started talking, words just tumbled out. She could finally reveal to Keegan who she was, what was at stake, and what had been lost. An unwanted tear slid down her cheek, and she wiped it away. Honesty was such a relief.

"Is this world what you imagined when you left Earth?"

Leah shook her head and more tears came. Keegan sat quietly and let her cry. She sniffed loudly and retrieved a paper napkin from the dispenser in the center of the long sleek table.

"I'm sorry. I don't know why I'm crying." Leah pressed the tissue to her eyes and held it there. "I'm not the only one who's lost something."

"You're sad and I'm angry." Keegan shifted in her chair. She reached across the space and touched Leah's arm. "We're perfect for each other."

She smiled and Leah laughed.

"How long do you think the others will be gone?" Leah dabbed at her eyes and then wadded the napkin up in the palm of her hand.

"Hard to guess. Twelve hours…maybe longer. If they feel safe enough in Chagall's precinct they might overnight. Yates has close friends there, people she trusts. She might go to them if things take too long." Keegan finished her tea. "It's hard to say."

Leah realized she was alone with Keegan for the first time, really alone. And now it seemed they might have up to twenty-four hours of time on their hands. Her stomach fluttered at the possibilities. But it was hard to read Keegan's mood. No doubt anger was simmering just below the surface given what she'd just been through. Maybe a distraction would help.

"Since we have some time, would you like to see the rest of the ship?"

"Sure." Keegan seemed distracted by her own thoughts, but agreed.

Keegan followed Leah from the galley into the passageway, which was a combination of smooth metal and an intricate array of piping overhead. She looked up as they walked trying to guess each one's purpose. She gave up trying to figure it out and trailed her fingertips along the cool surface of the passage. They came to a doorway and Leah turned left again. Dizziness passed over Keegan like a shadow. She shut her eyes and braced her outstretched arm, palm flat, against the wall.

"Are you all right?" There was concern in Leah's voice. She walked back to check on Keegan.

"I'm fine." But she was far from fine. This was like some nightmare, an out-of-body experience. For all she knew this was a dream, or the afterlife. Following the woman she'd wanted so badly through endless gleaming tunnels to nowhere. Wouldn't that just be her luck? But if this were a dream, or if she were dead, would her shoulder ache so badly from bouncing around in the cage?

"Are you sure? Maybe you should sit down. I can show you around later." Leah rested her hands at Keegan's waist and searched her face.

"I'm okay, really." She could tell from the look on Leah's face that she didn't believe her, but she nodded anyway.

Leah placed her hand over a sensor near a doorway at the end of the corridor, and the hatch, made of mostly glass, swished open. The oblong door was rectangular with rounded corners. It receded into the wall like a pocket door, and Keegan followed Leah inside. This seemed like a workspace of some kind. There was a long metal table with equipment at equal intervals along one wall. Above the table were cabinets. The room was very organized and sterile. It looked as if, whatever its purpose might have been, it had never been used. The floor gleamed from lack of foot traffic.

"This is my rock lab." Leah leaned against the edge of the long table and faced Keegan. "I had many plans for this lab. I guess that's all over."

Keegan was reminded that she wasn't the only one whose life had been completely shattered by recent events.

"What sort of things would you do, did you plan to do?" Keegan crossed her arms and slowly walked along the table, looking at the strange devices and metal trays.

"Well, initially I'd have taken soil samples to get a breakdown of the mineral makeup of the planet surface." Leah opened a cabinet door as if she were looking for something, but then closed it without removing anything. "On a larger scale, I'd have assisted in identifying hazards for the settlement...earthquake threats or landslide risks."

"I'm sorry."

"For what?"

"That things didn't happen for you the way they were supposed to."

"I'm coming to terms with it." Leah moved away from the table. Her mood shifted, and Keegan suspected that simply being in the lab was painful for her. "Do you feel up to seeing the rest of the ship?"

Keegan nodded and followed Leah out of the room.

Leah walked Keegan through the various cargo bays. There were additional food rations, crates of them, and machinery and other supplies. Keegan couldn't help thinking how valuable these things would be. How much the residents of the city would benefit from having this much food in storage. She knew that there were many residents that barely scraped by.

They passed by some of the crew cabins, and Leah shared random details about the people who'd traveled with her. Leah stopped at the door of the cryo bay, but they did not go inside. The entire chamber was dark and Keegan didn't press Leah about what lay on the other side of the door.

The cockpit, the control center of the ship, held the most interest for Keegan. There were six high-backed chairs facing a bank of controls and a huge display screen. The room was dimly lit so that small lights flickering on and off from the intricate dashboard caught her attention.

"Does this ship fly?" Keegan leaned over one of the chairs to look at the console more closely. She had no idea what she was looking at but was intrigued nonetheless.

"Yes, it will fly."

"Can you fly it?"

"I think so." Leah didn't sound overly confident. "We were all trained in simulators, and I flew on several test flights before we left Earth." She paused and looked at Keegan. "So, yes, in theory I can fly the ship."

Keegan couldn't help thinking that an airship might be a formidable asset. She just wasn't sure exactly how.

Leah led Keegan through a labyrinth of small passageways, the last one opened out into the cargo hold. Keegan stood next to the enormous hatch. She rested her forearm on the window and leaned her forehead against her arm. The desert seemed to extend forever. She studied the horizon for any hint of Yates's return, but it was too soon for that. She sensed Leah watching her. She lowered her arm and rotated away from the window. The ship's interior seemed barely lit now, compared to the glare through the glass of the endless desert.

They stood a few feet apart. The air around them swam with charged particles, but neither of them moved closer. An ache throbbed deep inside. Keegan considered reaching for Leah to soothe the ache, but something held her back. The rules of their engagement had shifted, and she was struggling to find her balance again. Her intense scrutiny must have made Leah uncomfortable because she looked away.

"Thanks for the tour." Keegan smiled thinly and brushed past Leah.

She wound her way to the small crew compartment she'd slept in the previous night. It was practically dark. A dim light along the floor flickered on when she entered the space. Keegan dropped to the side of the bed, rested her elbows on her knees, and buried her face in her hands.

CHAPTER TWENTY-THREE

Leah stood motionless, intensely aware of the emptiness of the room. Keegan left so abruptly. Should she follow? She pivoted in the space and tried to sort through her own feelings. Keegan had looked so tormented just now. Leah wanted to reach for her, but something had stopped her.

Leah hesitated, but after a few more moments of indecision, she walked back toward the galley to look for Keegan. She found Keegan sitting on the side of the bed they'd shared the previous night. Did Keegan need to be alone? It was impossible to read her.

She felt a strong pull to connect with Keegan, to know that she was okay. Quietly, slowly, she approached. When Keegan didn't look up or register her presence, Leah touched Keegan. She gently stroked Keegan's head, the soft stubble of her nearly shaved hair tickled her sensitive palm.

Keegan lowered her hands and looked up at Leah. Her eyes glistened, catching the reflection of the ambient light from the corridor. Leah leaned down, held Keegan's face in her hands, and she lightly brushed her lips against Keegan's.

Keegan's hands were on her hips now, drawing her close, so that she was standing between Keegan's legs. Keegan sank into her, resting her face against Leah's breasts. She cradled Keegan's head to her chest, careful of the bandage at her temple. After a moment, Keegan pulled back and with slow, confident movements, pulled her shirt up and off. Leah rested her hands on Keegan's broad, bare shoulders. The skin on skin contact warmed her entire body. She felt

Keegan's fingers at the hem of her shirt. Taking that as direction, Leah removed her shirt as well and then her bra.

Keegan's hands were on her back, hot and strong, drawing Leah closer so that Keegan could kiss her breasts. Leah felt her knees weaken as Keegan sucked and teased her nipples, one and then the other. And then Keegan cupped her breast with one hand, squeezed, and took most of her breast into her mouth. Leah was instantly wet. With one hand at the back of Keegan's head and the other braced against Keegan's shoulder, Leah did her best to remain standing.

Keegan's fingers were dipping under the waist of her pants now, easing them down over her hips. Once they were gone, Keegan pressed her closer, and unhurriedly swept her hands up and down over the curve of her ass as if she were waiting for Leah to offer up some sign of resistance. She felt almost weightless when Keegan lifted and swung her around and onto the bed. Almost instantly, Keegan's hand was sliding up the inside of her thigh.

She looked up, trying to read Keegan's expression. Leah needed to know what this meant to Keegan. Possibly, Leah was only a distraction to soothe Keegan's hurt. And even if that was the case she'd already let it go too far to stop it. She was hurting too, and Keegan's weight partially on top of her felt comforting, grounding.

Keegan's fingers lightly brushed over her sex, fleeting contact, but now there was no way to hide her arousal. She closed her eyes and swallowed, trying not to come undone.

"Look at me." Keegan's voice was low and husky.

Leah opened her eyes. Keegan smiled and kissed her. She was propped on one elbow. She stopped touching Leah, unfastened her trousers, and pushed them down until she could kick them off. Then she rolled on top of Leah, bracing above her.

"Open your legs for me."

Leah shifted until she felt Keegan's firm thigh between hers.

"That's it." Keegan adjusted, sliding her thigh across Leah's sex until an involuntary soft moan escaped.

"What are you thinking?" Leah's question was barely audible.

Keegan slid her hand over Leah's breast. Intently focused on every detail of its shape, she pressed her palm to the erect tip, and then moved her hand down to the place that throbbed to be touched.

"I was thinking that I've wanted to do this since the first moment I saw you." Keegan teased at her opening, stroked as she spoke, and then slid inside. Leah exhaled sharply and opened her legs farther. Keegan kissed her deeply as she thrust slowly but firmly, in and out, in and out, each thrust deeper than the last. "You are so wet..." Leah wrapped her arms around Keegan's neck and held on as Keegan moved on top of her and inside her. She pressed her open mouth against Keegan's neck. Was she still breathing? She rocked against Keegan's hand, then swept her fingers over Keegan's forearm, letting her fingertips follow the muscles flexed in Keegan's arm as she fucked her. Keegan owned her now, completely. Her entire body tautly vibrated as her orgasm built to a crescendo and then cascaded, dropping her over the edge into darkness. Keegan kissed her neck as she held her trembling body. Gradually, she withdrew her fingers and pressed her thigh against Leah's throbbing clit.

She caressed Keegan's face and then let her hands drift down Keegan's neck, across her shoulders and down her arms. She held Keegan's face in her hands for a moment before pulling her down into a kiss.

"I've wanted you like this too," she whispered. *I want you and it scares me. Because everything else about this place is so wrong. How could this one thing be right?*

Leah's limbs sank into the bed, her bones softened and limp. She closed her eyes but opened them when Keegan moved. It was clear that Keegan wasn't finished with her.

Keegan's sheer strength overpowered Leah. She positioned Leah where she wanted her; she rolled her over in one strong move and took her from behind. Leah felt Keegan's arousal against her ass, but could not reach her. Instead, she gripped the blanket with her fists and held on.

Keegan pressed against her. Keegan's body stiffened as she arched into Leah, who sensed it the moment Keegan climaxed. She thrust deep and held Leah tightly, scraping her teeth across Leah's shoulder. After the tremors passed, Keegan eased her fingers out of Leah and flopped over onto her back.

Their lovemaking had been intense, frenzied, and now that Keegan had released her, Leah was adrift. She rolled over. Keegan's eyes were closed and she was breathing as if she'd just run a race. Leah touched herself. Her sex was swollen and wet. Now that she'd allowed the barrier between them to be breached, she wanted more.

Leah slid her hand across Keegan's torso, then traced with her fingertips the outline of the muscles in Keegan's thighs. She explored the sensuous landscape of Keegan's reclined body, without touching the place between her legs. After a few moments of exploration, she realized that Keegan was watching her. What did Keegan want? What would she allow?

Tentatively, Leah rolled partially on top of Keegan and began to lightly kiss Keegan's stomach. She kept looking up at Keegan's face for permission to continue. When her lips reached the apex of Keegan's thighs, she felt Keegan's fingers in her hair. She hesitated, but Keegan made no move to stop her so she began to explore with her tongue. Beneath her, Keegan trembled and stiffened, and rose to meet her mouth. Leah held her hips, keeping contact as Keegan came. Leah held on, riding the wave as Keegan tumbled.

Leah slid up Keegan's body and kissed her, long and deep. Keegan's fingers drifted tenderly up over her hips to her shoulders and back again.

She rested her head on Keegan's chest and Keegan caressed her hair.

They'd made love barely speaking a word. Leah marveled at this. But why was she surprised? Keegan rarely talked and certainly not about feelings. Never in her experience had so much distance coexisted so comfortably with such intimacy.

Keegan lay on her back with her arm behind her head. Leah spooned at her side, snuggled against her shoulder, the sensual curve of her hip highlighted by soft light from the passageway. Relaxed, but still aroused, Keegan brushed her fingertips lightly over Leah's shoulder trying to figure out if Leah was awake.

"What does the bird mean?" Leah ran her finger over the silver cuff.

Leah had asked the question without looking up, so Keegan didn't know she was awake until she spoke. She was naked, except for the silver band around her arm, just above her elbow.

"What do you want to know about it?"

"The silver band has the engraving of a bird." Leah raised up on her elbow to look at Keegan. Her hair was adorably tousled. "Hardy said it was your crest...I think that's what he called it."

"Hardy talks too much." Keegan smiled. She wasn't really angry. In fact, she felt lightened in every way. Was that all Leah's doing? Or was this ethereal state a result of her escape from Tiago and the pressures of her post in Haydn City? It was hard to know. The chieftain's slow decline had been a weight she'd carried for weeks. And now that was gone too, although sadness had remained in its place. "Birds aren't tethered to the ground. Flight awards them the ultimate freedom. Freedom from gravity itself."

A bird could also be caged.

When she'd chosen this animal as her crest, she hadn't thought of it. Caging a creature capable of flight seemed unusually callous, regardless of the kindness of the captor.

Leah was quiet. She placed her hand in the center of Keegan's chest and then slid it down to her stomach. Leah's touch sent aftershocks through Keegan's system. She tried not to react to them because she sensed Leah had something else to say. It was almost as if Keegan could see the gears inside of her head churning.

"You don't have to wear it any longer."

"What?" Leah had a confused look.

"The cuff...I can remove it if you want." Keegan couldn't look at her, so she looked at the ceiling. "I have nothing to offer you now."

"Keegan, look at me." Leah's words were soft. "Now we are both untethered. I like this better."

"What do you mean?" Keegan studied her face in the low light.

"When you found me, those first days, you held all the power in our...arrangement." Leah paused. "I know that I was angry and I pushed you away...I was struggling to come to terms with everything, and I don't relinquish control easily. I'm a scientist. I feel most comfortable in a controlled environment, with parameters

I understand. This…everything that's happened…has been hard for me."

Keegan brushed Leah's cheek with the back of her curled fingers.

"So, you like it that I'm an outcast, with no home, no fortune, and no prospects?" Keegan smiled.

"Yes, actually, I do." Leah smiled back. "I like you, Keegan. Whatever your role in the Great House is…or was…it doesn't define you. You are the most amazing person I've ever met…strong and sensual and—"

Keegan cut her off with a searing kiss. She wanted Leah again. Leah opened her legs as Keegan rolled on top of her, kissing her deeply. She rocked against Leah, and Leah in turn wrapped her legs around Keegan, holding her tightly. Keegan pressed Leah's silky thigh against her ribcage so that she could grind against Leah's other leg and still touch her. She wanted to come with Leah this time. She used her thumb, sliding inside, and cupping Leah's ass with her fingers. The combination of thrusts and mutual friction brought them both rapidly to the edge. Leah was so wet and so was Keegan. Leah was about to climax. She tightened around Keegan's thumb.

Keegan rocked on top of her, increasing the friction and pressure between them so that just as Leah cried out against her shoulder, Keegan followed her. She groaned loudly and tumbled as successive waves of orgasm shuddered through her body. Then she was floating, weightless, a scattered starburst against the darkness of forever night.

She didn't pull out right away. Keegan wasn't ready to lose that most intimate contact. She cradled Leah and kissed her as she slowly withdrew her hand from between Leah's legs.

"Leah, I…" Her words were raspy, barely a whisper. What did she want to say? She'd almost told Leah that she was falling for her, that she loved her. What did that matter now? She'd meant what she said when she told Leah she had nothing to offer. It would be selfish to keep Leah, regardless of what Leah said. Leah was foreign to this world and had no idea how things really worked.

Chapter Twenty-four

Before Keegan's heart rate had slowed to normal, before she could finish her thought, an alarm sounded. It echoed through the passageway and bounced off the sleek metal walls of the sleeping compartment. She jerked up, ready to engage whatever enemy was upon them. Leah captured her arm just as she was about to bolt from the bed and reach for her clothing.

"It's a proximity alert." Leah sat up. Her cheeks were flushed with color. "I set it to sound an alarm if someone approached the ship."

"Yates."

"Probably. I didn't want anyone else to surprise us." Leah shimmied to the foot of the bed and started pulling on clothes. "We can turn off the alarm from the cargo compartment."

The alarm reverberated down the long, narrow passageway as they hustled toward the cargo bay. Leah stood in front of a console a few feet from the bay door. Several key strokes brought the monitor to life. Keegan looked over her shoulder at an image of the desert and a vehicle approaching. It was definitely Yates. Her long dark hair and the military crawler were unmistakable.

"That's her." Keegan braced her hands on her hips.

"Hit that red circle to open the bay door." Leah pointed toward a large button a few feet away.

The huge metal door opened, and a blast of hot air flooded the compartment. Tendrils of dust traveled with the heat as Yates pulled the crawler up the ramp and killed the engine.

Keegan had the urge to bear hug Yates as soon as she climbed out of the seat. What was happening to her? Her emotions were a bit out of her control at the moment. This was new territory. As it turned out, she didn't need to reach for Yates because Yates didn't hesitate to embrace her. It wasn't their usual distant *comrade* sort of hug either; this was a full body embrace. Yates fell into her and hung on. Keegan returned the embrace with equal intensity. Esther rounded the front of the crawler and was next in line. She wrapped her slender arms tightly around Keegan's neck and kissed her cheek. With one arm still around Esther's waist, Keegan reached for Hardy. She put her hand at the back of his shaved head and pulled him in for a one-armed squeeze. Esther released Keegan and hugged Leah.

Her friends were back. They were safe. Relief filled the crevices of Keegan's bruised heart. They were weary and dust covered and had returned to the ship sooner than expected. She wasn't sure if that was good news or bad.

"You can take showers if you like. I can prepare some food when you're ready to eat something." Leah looped her arm through Esther's and followed the others down the passage toward the galley.

"I will help you." Esther patted Leah's arm.

Keegan peeled off near their sleeping compartment. She wanted a shower too.

The spray had only just warmed when she saw the shadow of the door opening through the fogged glass. Leah opened the shower door and stepped into the tiny space. She faced Keegan as she reached for the soap dispenser mounted on the wall under the showerhead. She lathered the liquid between her hands and soaped Keegan's chest, shoulders, then her arms.

Keegan began to massage her soapy fingers through Leah's hair. The shower was only intended for one. Leah's body, slick with suds, made contact with Keegan's as she rotated to rinse her hair. Keegan wrapped her arms around Leah from behind. She caressed Leah's breasts and then let her hands drift down across the soft curve of Leah's stomach. She was so beautiful.

Leah rotated, draped her arms over Keegan's shoulders and kissed her.

"I hope you don't mind. I wanted to be close to you." Leah paused and kissed her again. "The way we had to jump out of bed didn't feel right."

"You're so beautiful." Keegan had thought it so many times, she wanted to say it out loud. She wanted Leah to hear it. She brushed wet hair off Leah's forehead and let her hand drift down, along the outside curve of her breast to her hip. "I like being close to you."

She wanted to be close to Leah, in fact, she wanted to tug Leah from the shower and take her to bed again. But she needed to get Yates's report. She'd be on edge and distracted until she heard what was going on back in Haydn City.

"We need to change this bandage." Leah touched her forehead. She kept forgetting about the injury. She looked down. There were bruises on her torso and on her right arm. She had other scrapes on her knuckles, and those were just the things she could see. Keegan figured she looked a little like the walking wounded.

They stepped out of the shower, and Leah began to towel Keegan off. What had happened? Why was Leah suddenly so sweet and attentive? It couldn't only be that they had had sex, could it? Keegan was puzzled.

"You seem so...different."

"Do I?" Leah cocked her head and quirked the side of her mouth up in a half smile, but offered no explanation.

Keegan finished drying off as Leah wrapped her hair in a towel and squeezed. This might have been a completely normal thing, a few moments of post-sex intimacy, if she weren't so acutely aware that she was standing aboard a spaceship, in the middle of the desert, having just barely survived attempted murder.

"Put on some clothes and I will dress that wound." Leah's voice pulled her out of her head.

Leah gave her a questioning look. Keegan smiled thinly and gingerly pulled a shirt on over the damp bandage at the side of her temple. It felt strange to wear someone else's clothing, but whoever this guy was, he'd been about Keegan's size. She tugged on a pair of clean trousers and followed Leah, barefoot, to the infirmary. The shiny metal floor was slick and cold under her feet. She rather liked the sensation and thought the chill underfoot might snap her out of whatever fog she kept getting lost in. Maybe she was in shock and just didn't realize it. She did feel a little outside herself, as if she was walking a half step behind, watching her own body move through the passageway with Leah.

"Sit here while I get supplies." Leah motioned toward the nearest bed.

Keegan hopped up and let her legs dangle. Leah rummaged in drawers across the room and then returned. She stood between Keegan's knees as she lifted the edge of the gauze. Keegan studied her face. Leah wasn't making eye contact. She was completely focused on her task.

Leah discarded the used bandage in a nearby bin. She used a soft tipped tool to apply some sort of goo to the cut.

"This is an antibacterial cream." Leah still wasn't making eye contact, but she must have sensed Keegan's unasked question.

"What's that for?"

"It will help the cut heal faster." Leah peeled the backing away from a square bandage and tenderly covered the injury. Only then did she look at Keegan.

Leah's gaze was so sharp that Keegan blinked reflexively, or perhaps defensively. Leah's palms rested on Keegan's thighs. Heat radiated from her hands, despite the lightness of her touch.

"How are you feeling?"

The question surprised Keegan. How was she feeling? She had no idea. "I'm fine." And even if she wasn't, she couldn't explain it. Not yet anyway. "Let's go find Yates. I'm anxious to hear from her."

Keegan was pretty sure her response to Leah's question had been unsatisfying, but Leah didn't press her for more. She nodded, stepped away, and followed Keegan out the door toward the galley.

CHAPTER TWENTY-FIVE

Leah focused on Keegan's shoulders as she trailed her toward the galley. Her shoulders seemed to carry weight, the heaviness of some object invisible to the naked eye. Leah had lost her world so she could relate in some ways to how Keegan might be feeling. But Leah's loss had been caused by some possible machine malfunction. Her demise orchestrated by neutral computer functions. Keegan had lost her world through betrayal. That was an entirely different thing altogether.

Yates, Esther, and Hardy were in the kitchen when they arrived. Hardy was struggling with a food console.

"Here, let me help you." The food synthesizers would be confusing for anyone not used to using computers. They weren't entirely intuitive even if you were.

"Thanks." He lifted the food from the tray as the small hatch opened, and then took a seat at the end of the table where Yates and Esther were seated.

Leah wasn't hungry, but she hit the button for a white coffee. Now that she was back aboard ship with easy access to coffee, she couldn't seem to get enough. She leaned against the edge of the console and sipped, letting the earthy, slightly bitter warm liquid sit on her tongue before swallowing.

"Talk." Keegan stood with arms crossed at the head of the table.

"I left Hardy and Esther in Chagall's province and went to Haydn City myself." Yates shifted so that she straddled the bench seat with one leg on each side. She leaned on one elbow. Her position was casual, but she was anything but at ease. Leah could see her jaw tighten from several feet away.

"You took too much of a risk going back." Keegan frowned at Yates.

"I needed to see for myself."

"And?"

"Haydn City is in mourning. People were clamoring at the doors of the forum, but no one would answer them. People are afraid. I could feel it. And without Maddox controlling the Tenth, chaos is inevitable."

"Tiago said that Maddox was gone…I wasn't sure what that meant." Keegan swept her hand across her face.

"Maddox is dead, and without him, and without the chieftain, the Tenth will be bound to answer to Tiago."

"What happened?"

"An explosion near his quarters." Yates paused. "It's my guess that the bomb that detonated at the entrance to the garrison was meant for Maddox. Except that he was on the training field and not in the command center where he was meant to be—"

"You and I were in the command center."

"Yes."

"And Tiago had other plans for me."

Yates hesitated before responding. "Yes." She took a deep breath. "I think the device was detonated in error and the graffiti from Solas was just a distraction. And…you should also know Tiago has posted bulletins naming you as Solas. He's claiming you were killed to stop a rebellion."

"Who is Solas?" Leah couldn't follow what Yates was saying.

"Solas is the shadow leader of the Fain." Keegan sounded so calm. She clearly wasn't surprised by what Yates had said.

"Are you Solas?" Leah asked. Keegan glared at her.

"No." Keegan's shoulders sank. She looked at the floor. "Tiago is Solas. He admitted that to me before he dragged me into the desert. He also said he was going to blame the actions of Solas on me."

"No one will believe him." Hardy had been intently listening.

"Yes, they will." Keegan was resigned to the situation. "I found out from one of the raiders we caught that no one knows who Solas is. No one has ever seen him. The people will easily believe that Solas could be me. I would benefit from overthrowing the leadership and taking the chieftain's position."

"Which is exactly what Chief Behn wanted, isn't it?" Esther's spoke softly, her words full of emotion.

"Yes, it was." Keegan looked at Esther. "Which gave Tiago even more reason to be rid of me. He must have known too. And I believe the escalating violence from the Fain is all Tiago's doing. One of the raiders who captured Leah had the insignia of the Tenth tattooed on his scalp, under his hair."

"You said nothing of this." Yates sounded hurt.

"The conversation with the chieftain happened right before you came to the Great House to get me. I didn't have a chance to say anything to you." Keegan paused. "And I felt telling you would only have put you in danger." Keegan shifted and looked at the floor. "And my suspicions about Tiago and the Fain infiltrators were confirmed just before Tiago dragged me into the desert."

"I don't follow." Hardy looked up from his half-eaten food.

"Think about it." Keegan's expression darkened. "The Fain have been around for decades, but the theft, the killing…that only started in the past few years. I'm convinced that's all related to Tiago and his men. He's been building his own takeover all along."

"It seems we were all in danger either way. But he was going to inherit the chieftain's seat anyway."

"Unless the chieftain passed it to me. Tiago must have known." Keegan crossed her arms. "He needed to pin his fake coup on me to win the people's approval as their new leader. If he convinced them that he took out Solas, he'd be above reproach. No one would challenge him."

Everyone was quiet for a moment.

"So, be Solas." Leah moved away from the console and put her empty cup on the table.

"What?" Keegan glared at her again, but this time with more surprise and less anger.

"This Solas figure is supposed to be the leader of the Fain. No one has seen Solas. Tiago thinks you're dead and no longer a threat." Leah paused, letting the idea partially sink in. "We could go to where the Fain are, and as Solas you could rally the Fain and retake Haydn City."

No one spoke. Did they all think she'd lost her mind?

"Leah is right." It was Esther who finally endorsed her proposed plan. "The Fain are made up of orphans and discontent youth. Before joining the underground they hovered at the edge of society, with no prospects of a better life. Keegan, you could easily have been one of them. You share a common origin with them. Leah is right. You should be Solas and lead a true rebellion." Esther stood and touched Keegan's arm for emphasis, forcing Keegan to look at her. "Your greatest strength may be as a symbol of a commoner, taken in and elevated in the military by Chief Behn. You are a true symbol of what is possible."

Silence again. The expression on Keegan's face told Leah she was considering it. And her stance had shifted, her shoulders squared, hands on her hips. She looked more like the warrior Leah first encountered in the desert. Yates was waiting for Keegan to speak, and Hardy simply leaned back with a shocked expression.

Esther continued. "You cannot leave the people in the hands of Tiago, a man who has no mercy, no empathy, no sense of fairness."

"There are only five of us and possibly a hundred Fain fighters." Keegan shook her head. "We'll be no match for the men Tiago will now command. He'll have Chagall's garrison, plus his own, plus the Tenth."

"I saw hundreds of Fain raiders, maybe thousands from the high cliffs of the narrows." Yates leaned forward with her elbows on her knees.

Keegan had forgotten the tracking mission she'd sent Yates on before everything had gone to hell. She looked at Yates now for confirmation.

"Thousands?" Keegan found that number hard to believe.

"Yes, possibly thousands. There was some sort of gathering at the entrance to the caves. Even from a distance I could see

that the crowd was huge. Many more than we've ever believed."
Yates looked down at her hands. She was puzzling something out.
When she looked up again her eyes were clear, focused. "I think
the Fain possibly have a social structure we don't know anything
about. There was clearly some sort of ceremony taking place, which
implies a culture of some kind."

What Yates said made sense. On some level Keegan knew it
must be true.

"I should have guessed it. There would have to be more than
petty thievery luring converts to the Fain all these years." Keegan
had been arrogant and insulated in her own world. She'd never
actually tried to figure out the motives of the raiders beyond the
simple act of lashing out and burning things down. But Yates was
right. Behind it all, underneath it all, there must be something more
meaningful.

"Solas is an Irish sun deity."

"You've heard this name before?" Keegan pivoted. What the
hell was Leah talking about?

"If you love rocks, which I do, then you must make a pilgrimage
to Ireland." Leah was pacing and talking with her hands. "On Earth,
where I come from, the Irish have a rich, ancient mythology. It's
coming back to me now…Solas was a deity associated with the
sun…with light." She looked up, her face brightened as she talked.
"It makes so much sense that a culture developing in darkness would
worship light."

Leah put her hand on Keegan's arm. There was a fierceness in
Leah's eyes that she hadn't seen since the day Leah had bloodied
her nose.

"I think you should be who Tiago says you are." Leah turned
to Yates. "I say we go to the Hollow Hills and see for ourselves.
Tiago has set you up to be Solas. I say we bring light to the dark
places." She looked at Keegan. "You, Solas, will bring the Sun to
the darkness and claim your Fain army."

A tingle of adrenaline spider webbed through Keegan's entire
nervous system. Could she do this? Was this her destiny? She'd
only ever wanted freedom, and now even that had been taken from

her. There was truth and valor in what Leah was saying. Even if they started a fight they couldn't win, she'd rather go down on a battlefield than fade away, hiding in the desert, losing her life to a brutal tyrant.

"So…exactly how will Keegan bring the Sun?" Hardy quietly asked.

"This ship has floodlights." Leah smiled broadly.

Keegan ran through possible scenarios in her head. Even for someone who loved risk and embraced violence, this seemed like a bold plan.

CHAPTER TWENTY-SIX

Everyone should get some rest." Keegan needed to be alone with her thoughts.

Yates nodded. She and Hardy left the galley for sleeping compartments.

"I'll go prep the ship." Leah stood to leave.

"Is there anything I can help with?" Keegan asked.

"Not yet." Leah touched her shoulder as she left the kitchen.

Only Esther remained. She sat across from Keegan quietly studying her.

"How are you feeling?"

Esther asked the same question Leah had asked, and Keegan still didn't know the answer.

"I don't know." She couldn't hide the truth from Esther. They'd known each other too long.

"I know that you don't see your greatness, but I do." Esther reached across the table and entwined her fingers with Keegan's. "And I think finding Leah was no accident."

"You believe all this is fate?"

"Fate, destiny, your true calling…" Esther trailed off. "You are a great soul, courageous, fearless, loyal. People feel it when they are near you."

It was hard to hear this from Esther. She felt exposed and had to look away. Esther squeezed her hand.

"You think too much of me." Keegan smiled thinly at Esther.

"I see you, Keegan, for who you really are."

A chill traveled up Keegan's arm. True greatness came at a price. Was she ready to pay that price? She wasn't sure. She'd never run from a fight before, but this one seemed unwinnable. If what she really desired was freedom, why not just take Leah and run away? Far away. She could find a place beyond Tiago's reach in the unsettled lands far to the south.

Almost as soon as she considered it, she abandoned the idea. That was not who she was. Esther was right on some level. Keegan would never be able to live with herself if she didn't see this through. Whether she survived or not. Her one concern would be keeping Leah and Esther safe. Yates and Hardy were soldiers. They knew the risks and could make the decision to join her or not, but she would not put Leah and Esther at risk.

"I will leave you alone to think and prepare." Esther kissed her forehead before leaving.

Keegan's mind was a jumble of thoughts and emotions. She needed to get clear. Emotional distractions would cloud her thinking. Distractions could get you killed. If she was really going to take on Tiago she needed to harness every skill she'd ever had. She knew enough about him to know that if challenged, this would not be a fair fight.

She filled a cup with water and sipped slowly, thoughtfully. The Fain had guns, but how many? And how many of them were willing to fight? There were many unknowns that would not be answered until they traveled to the dark side of the planet.

She'd been past the edge of sunset only twice, and even on those excursions not very far. The darkness was so absolute that it closed in on her. She felt vulnerable in it. Before she'd lost sight of the glowing pink halo of the horizon, she'd turned around, allowing the raider she'd been pursuing to disappear into the shadow lands.

As a child, she'd heard whispers about the Fain. That they came while you slept, that they tempted lost souls to the darkness, never to return. How much of those stories were folklore meant to control citizens who lacked hope? Now she had doubts that anything she'd ever believed was true.

She surveyed the sterile metal room with the gleaming tools of food delivery along one wall. Humanity had excelled at some point, that much was clear. They'd traversed vast space and time only to regress. Or so it seemed now.

Maybe Esther was right. There was a reason she'd found Leah. Maybe this was all part of her destiny. She'd saved Leah, Leah had saved her, and now together they were about to attempt to save the world.

❖

Leah rotated in the pilot's chair. She'd checked power levels and engine status and run through the various steps of preflight. They could take off whenever Keegan was ready. She'd need someone in the copilot's seat to assist with a few stages of liftoff, but she felt confident she could get the ship off the ground if Yates could direct them to the location of the Fain.

"So, this is your ship. This is where you came from." Yates leaned against the back of the chair next to hers.

"Yes, this is my colony ship." She smiled up at Yates. "Take a seat."

She'd lowered the opacity of the cockpit window so that it looked tinted and only allowed partial sunlight into the space. Otherwise, it would be far too bright to sit at the console while she prepped the ship.

"I don't even know where to start with questions." Yates sat down and scanned the intricate array of controls on the console.

"It is hard to know where to begin." Leah leaned back and looked out at the desert in front of them. "I'm still figuring it all out."

"I suppose I was never much of one for history. The Temple of the Nine was a relic to me, a place I never put much stock in." Yates ran her fingertip along the arm of her chair. "I lived intentionally, keeping my world small."

"That's not necessarily a bad thing."

"Keegan is different with you."

Leah looked over at Yates, but Yates was facing the horizon. "Different how?"

"She's always a little distant. Even though I know she'd do anything for me or anyone she cared about…she never asked things of anyone for herself. I think she's been afraid to truly need anyone." Yates turned to Leah, resting her head against the back of the chair. "She's allowing herself to need you."

Leah busied herself with the preflight checklist. She felt as if Yates wanted some response from her, but she wasn't sure what that would be. She sighed and dropped the portable tablet screen to her lap. "I think I need her too." That was the truth. She not only needed Keegan, she wanted her.

"You are good together. I can see it."

Leah smiled at Yates. "Thank you." An endorsement from Yates meant a lot.

"Well, I'll let you work." She touched Leah's shoulders as she stood to leave.

Leah returned her attention to the console. The hardest part of liftoff would be leaving her crewmates in the desert. The most sensible decision was to disengage the cryogenics bay and leave it behind. The most sensible but not the easiest. Over time, the huge cryogenic compartment would no doubt be swallowed up by the ever-shifting sands. A mass grave of sorts, with each member of her team forever encapsulated in failed stasis.

Leah needed to see them.

She left the cockpit and walked toward the stasis chamber. She walked through the darkened space, occasionally stopping for a moment to rest her fingers on the glass of various stasis tubes. Her friends. Her crew. Until she reached Kris's, then she came to a full stop. She stood at the end of the sealed sleeping unit and studied the peaceful expression on Kris's face.

A single shaft of light cut across the darkened room the way a small, high window allowed the sun to pierce a cathedral. But this was no cathedral. It was a tomb. Light from the small oval window that had roused her the first day on Proxima B sliced through the space, hitting the floor several yards away, near her open and empty cryo bed.

Leah was unsure how long she'd been standing there, looking at Kris, when she heard Keegan's voice behind her.

"I'm sorry, Leah." Keegan didn't reach for her. She was standing with hands in pockets a few feet away.

"This is Kris. I'm sorry that you won't get to meet her." She turned toward Keegan. "Or the rest of my crew. They were all great people. They'd have—"

A sob swallowed up her words. Keegan drew her into a hug. Keegan stroked her hair. She tucked her head under Keegan's chin and lost herself in Keegan's strong arms.

This was good-bye. She'd known this day would come. There'd been a time, only a few days ago when she'd feared she might never see her ship again. She was relieved to be back, even if for a short time, to say farewell to Kris and the rest of her friends.

She wiped at tears with her palm and cleared her throat.

"I'll undock this compartment before we take off." She paused. "I just wanted to see Kris one more time."

"Was she…were the two of you…" Keegan was struggling to phrase the question, but Leah knew what she was trying to ask.

"No, but we were close friends. She had an easy laugh and was a loyal friend."

"Loyalty is something I value also."

Leah smiled. She already knew that about Keegan.

"Something else you and I have in common." Leah took Keegan's hand and pressed her lips to Keegan's palm. And then she settled her cheek against the spot she'd just kissed.

"What other things do we have in common?" Keegan was standing so close now.

"A sense of fairness. A love of truth, and…"

Keegan kissed her.

"And yes, that." Leah smiled against Keegan's lips.

Keegan put her arm around Leah as they walked back toward the compartment door.

"Maybe you should get some rest too." Keegan stood aside as Leah sealed the door. "Who knows what waits for us in the Hollow Hills."

Leah held Keegan's hand as they made their way to the sleeping compartment they'd been sharing. On some level, she knew they were about to fly into the unknown, but somehow, the unknown seemed a lot less frightening with Keegan at her side. And besides, her intuition was telling her this was the right thing to do. When she was on the path, the right path, things always seemed to start falling into place. Every cell in her body told her that Keegan was her true north.

If her life were charted on a graph as a straight line, she was standing at the center of it. For whatever reason, her fate was entwined with Keegan's, and there seemed no other choice but to proceed. There was no such thing as going back; there was only going forward into the darkness. Into uncharted lands. Into the unknown.

Her future lay beyond the horizon, past sunset, in the land of eternal night.

CHAPTER TWENTY-SEVEN

The cargo hold contained gear and supplies for almost anything the architects of this voyage could anticipate. There'd been a proposal to explore the dark regions of the planet after the colony was established, assuming that there would be stores of frozen water waiting there to be unlocked.

Leah used the hydraulic arm of the robotic lift to lower containers full of winter wear. Subzero coats with hoods, face masks, gloves, boots, LCD head lamps, basically everything they would need to breach the deep cold and utter darkness of the sunless side of the planet. Once the necessary gear had been excavated, they all headed for the flight deck.

She felt chilled, possibly from nerves. Leah tugged on her crew jacket before she took her seat.

"What's that?" Keegan caught her arm as she passed.

"What?" Leah turned.

"That patch on the shoulder of your jacket."

"Oh, that's the *Proxima Five* mission patch. Every mission had one." Leah craned her neck to look at it. "The V is the Roman numeral for five and that's an—"

"Eagle." Keegan looked at her. "A bird."

"Yeah, a bird." And then she realized what Keegan meant.

"I just think that's worth noting." She looked pale.

It did seem eerily like fate that the mission patch was a bird, just like Keegan's crest. Leah shivered and tried to shake it off. She needed to focus.

"What are you guys doing back there?" Yates swiveled in the forward seat so that she could see them.

"I'm coming." Leah took the captain's chair and strapped in. She engaged the primary engines and gave them a few minutes to cycle up.

"That series of orange buttons on the console in front of you need to be green." Leah pointed, and Yates, seated in the copilot's chair, nodded. "Mimic what I do. As I press one, so do you, until all of these lights are green."

"Got it."

A simmering vibration could now be felt through the soles of her shoes. Leah slowly eased the throttle in the central console forward. Keegan, Hardy, and Esther were strapped into seats behind the two forward chairs. She realized this would be very strange for them since she was the only one of the group who'd actually flown before.

"How is everyone doing?" She glanced over her shoulder.

"We're good." Keegan nodded.

Keegan watched with interest as Leah toggled switches and used levers to control the engines. She wasn't used to relinquishing control to anyone, and she'd just put her life and the life of those closest to her, in Leah's hands. She'd expected to feel upended, but she didn't. Leah seemed confident and sure of herself. The change in her demeanor since they'd arrived at the ship had been remarkable. Or perhaps Leah had been this capable, confident woman all along and Keegan just couldn't see it. Leah's confidence and intellect only made her more attractive.

"Okay, I haven't done this in a while, so takeoff might get a little bumpy." Leah returned her focus to the console.

The ship dipped and rocked ten degrees or so in each direction until Leah was able to stabilize the craft. Keegan let her head rest against the seat. She clenched the arms of the chair as her body sank into the chair from the upward thrust. Through the forward windows she could see the horizon line tilt and disappear as the ship gained altitude. The seat belt held her fast as the ship banked and circled. Now there was green on the horizon, but they were much higher.

Her stomach seemed to fall away as they banked. It was an odd sensation to know the ground was so far below. She tried not to visualize the distance to the surface.

Yates was saying something to Leah and pointing, but Keegan couldn't hear what they were saying. She unclipped the belts across her chest and moved closer. She leaned against the back of Leah's seat, dipping down so that she could hear.

"See that dark line?" Yates was pointing northeast. "That's the Narrows. If we follow that, then I can get us close to where I saw the raiders gathered."

Keegan's skin tingled. They were actually going to do this. She needed to mentally prepare.

"This is amazing." Leah looked north and south as they crossed the green zone.

Keegan had to agree. Flight not only offered freedom, it offered perspective. The smallness of the world below struck her for the first time.

The Narrows was a thin dark ribbon, a charcoal mark on the ground from this altitude. The sun's reach marked the boundary of the green zone, and beyond that was darkness. Shadows swallowed the command center as the light receded. Interior lights blinked on automatically in response to the change. Leah toggled switches to her left and a display replaced the view of the sky. A grid of some sort.

"What's that?" Keegan studied the pattern but couldn't quite make it out.

"Since I can no longer depend on visual landmarks, I've switched to computer navigation. This grid shows us the topography of what is up ahead even though it's invisible in the darkness. See... that is a land mass of some kind, a rise, to the left." She angled the ship away at a safe distance.

"Incredible." Keegan was out of her depth and in awe of Leah's skills.

Esther's hand was on Keegan's arm. She and Hardy had also come forward for a better view. Although now all they could see was the computer rendered landscape, but still, it was like nothing she'd ever seen before.

"That open area resembles the place where I saw the crowd gathered." Yates pointed to a low place in the diagram ahead of them, surrounded on almost all sides by high cliffs. "I was following the drop-off there."

Leah pulled levers back, and Keegan had the sense that the speed of ship had slowed.

"Please take your seats while I try to land this beast." Leah swiveled in her seat. "I'm kicking on the flood lights. I'll disengage the computer navigation now."

The horizontal glass in front of them was once again a window. The lights of the ship followed the contours of canyon walls on either side of the craft. Leah lowered the ship until it hovered just above the ground. She turned the angle of the ship and started the landing sequence. Alarms sounded, and a hissing noise filled the compartment, and then a small jolt as the landing gear made contact.

"We're down." Leah looked at Yates. "Hit all those green buttons. Down from the top, until they're all orange again."

Light from the ship flooded the darkness, and slowly, the open space began to fill with people. They kept a safe distance from the craft at first, shielding their eyes from the intensity of the lights. So many upturned faces.

"I'm going to adjust the lights a bit." Leah toggled switches until the lighting shifted up and down. "I've rotated them at a thirty-degree angle so some are pointing at the ground and some at the sky." She rotated in the chair to look at Keegan. "Are you ready?"

They decided that Yates and Hardy would stay back aboard ship with Esther. Keegan had no idea what fate awaited them here. She wanted Leah to stay behind also, but Leah insisted on joining her.

"If something goes wrong, you're the only one who can fly the others out of here." Keegan's words were hushed but urgent. Leah was putting on a heavy coat with a padded hood. She wasn't sure Leah was listening. "Leah, did you hear what I said?" Keegan grabbed Leah's arm.

"I heard you." Leah stopped moving and looked at her. "If something goes wrong we're not leaving you."

Keegan knew it was pointless to argue with her.

"Stay close to me and do as I say."

Leah nodded.

Keegan looked back one last time at Yates, Hardy, and Esther. Leah opened the forward hatch so that they could exit down a ramp directly under the flight deck. Leah left the hatch open, and the two of them walked away from the ship. This was Keegan's first glimpse of the aircraft from outside. The wingspan was huge. The wings swept forward like an enormous bird in mid-flight. The body of the craft had multiple floors, which seemed obvious from the windows in neat rows along each level. She'd obviously only toured the main decks.

Leah fell in step behind Keegan. She was afraid, but she took comfort in Keegan's steady shoulders in front of her, and anyway, there was no way she was going to let Keegan face this alone. Especially since it had been mostly her idea.

As they walked, Keegan seemed as fascinated by the ship she'd arrived in as she was by the mystery of the place they'd landed. Keegan's pace was slow and steady as she continued to look in both directions, taking in all the details. Some of the lights angled up from the ship and disappeared into darkness. Others pointed down and illuminated much of the open area they were now entering. The space had slowly been filling with people since they'd arrived. Yates was right; the crowd was larger than a hundred. Leah guessed there were close to a thousand people emptying into this canyon ringed natural stage.

Keegan stopped. Leah stood a step behind her, scanning the crowd. She didn't feel a threat, only curiosity, possibly edged with fear. But it was hard to separate her own fear from what might be the unease of others.

"Who is in command here?" Keegan shouted. Her voice echoed off the canyon walls.

Leah could only imagine what Keegan looked like to these people. Six feet tall, wearing all white, heavy strange clothing, her head under the oversized padded, arctic hood, backlit by powerful floodlights. All those details combined to make Keegan an intimidating figure, larger than life, like some extraterrestrial being from another world.

Keegan hesitated. Leah wondered if she was having second thoughts. But then she spoke, and when she did, her strong voice was clear and confident.

"I am Solas."

The crowd rippled with sounds of awe or possibly disbelief.

"Solas is dead," someone shouted.

"I am not dead. Despite efforts by those in power to end my life." Keegan paused. "I stand before you, very much alive." She waited a moment for the crowd to settle. "I come to you as your champion."

Keegan seemed unsure of what to say next, and the crowd around them began to murmur amongst themselves.

"Say what I say." Leah stood just behind Keegan and whispered. Keegan glanced over her shoulder.

Keegan nodded. She whispered to Keegan and Keegan repeated each phrase to the crowd.

"I come to you as your champion." Keegan said it again, louder. "I come as your champion."

The crowd fell silent.

"I'm aware of your suffering. The continued indifference to the evil that created such conditions is worse than evil itself." Keegan paused.

Leah fed her more words. Words she'd carried in her head. Words full of her own hopes for the future, a world that might have been.

"In a free society, all are responsible for the common good. All should benefit from their own labors and share in the wealth of this planet. Together we will create a new order."

Keegan extended her arms. The last statements were her own.

"The time for revolution has come. I have brought the light!"

The crowd erupted in cheers and shouts. As the raised voices subsided, row by row, people began to kneel. Until Keegan and Leah alone were standing. Their silhouettes cast long shadows, like spears across the center of the crowd.

It was impossible to gauge age, race, or gender of the people in the crowd. Clothing layered against the cold made it impossible to discern details. The crowd shifted. Someone rose, stepped past those who were in front, and walked toward them. The person stopped several feet away and removed the cloth from their face. She could see now that he was a man. Every bit of skin had been covered except his eyes. He looked to be in his thirties. His face was lean, his expression intense.

"I will take you to speak with the Collective."

"What is your name, friend?" Keegan extended her hand.

"Janus." He looked up at her and accepted her hand.

"I am Solas and this is Leah."

Keegan looked back toward the ship and motioned for the others to join them. They waited for a moment as Yates, Hardy, and Ester descended from the ship. Leah closed the hatch remotely before Janus led them through the crowd. As Keegan passed, people began to stand and follow her passage with their eyes. The entire scene felt surreal, and Leah's skin tingled with excitement or nerves or both.

They entered the underground settlement through a central cave, although Leah noticed several smaller cave entrances on either side of the larger one. Once inside she realized the tunnel was a lava tube. The floor was clearly basaltic lava, mostly smooth, with a slightly ropy surface in places. The walls were marked with curbs from former lava flows at various levels. This was fascinating. These tubes must be prehistoric.

As they traveled deeper into the honeycombed passages, the air warmed. Fires were lit at intervals, vented through small earthen holes. Leah hoped the others were paying attention to the route they'd taken. She'd been focused on staying close to Keegan and wasn't sure she could find her way back to the ship if necessary.

Finally, Janus stopped outside a door. "You asked who was in command. We have a different structure here than Haydn City."

People had followed them inside, and a large cluster gathered around their small group. Some had removed the coverings from their faces to reveal every age and race. This community was certainly not homogenous and certainly not made up entirely of young men, as she'd been led to believe. There seemed to be families here, women and children. Leah tried to catalog specifics without staring. Although people seemed to feel no shyness about staring at her. She wondered if it was her clothing or something else that piqued their interest.

"Wait here." Janus leaned against the heavy door and disappeared inside.

Keegan turned to face the throng and smiled. A few people standing near enough to do so reached out and touched the sleeves of her coat, as if they were unsure she was a solid entity.

Janus opened the door. "The collective will see you." He looked only at Keegan.

"She must come with me." Keegan motioned for Leah to follow her. "Yates, the rest of you wait here.

Leah and Keegan entered the chamber, leaving Yates, Esther, and Hardy surrounded by the gathering of curious cave dwellers.

An elderly woman stood and walked toward them. She wore a white gown that nearly touched the floor. Her long gray hair was braided and hung down the center of her back. Her skin was light brown, and her pupils were lost inside dark irises. She stopped a few feet away from them and waited for an introduction.

"This is Solas. This is Leah." Janus motioned toward Keegan. "They have come in a ship from the sky."

"Leave us." The woman's voice was firm but kind.

Janus bowed slightly at the waist and left them.

"You have many questions. I see them in your eyes."

For the first time, Leah noticed the data drives. This room looked as if it had been carved from the earth like some prehistoric cave, and all along the edge of the walls sat computer data towers. They looked like the data drives aboard her ship. Past meeting future, or past meeting past. Leah stepped closer. She recognized this equipment. It came from a colony ship. Not hers, obviously, but definitely from one of the others. Or from all of them, she silently counted the drives, not realizing that the woman had been watching her until she turned around.

"I am Naomi, the Collective Elder." She turned to Leah. "You recognize those don't you?"

"These are data towers from the colony ships." Leah turned to face her fully.

"Yes, they are."

Naomi grasped Leah's hand between hers and held her gaze, smiling. A door opened at the other end of the large room, and four robed figures entered. Their robes were gray rather than white. Three men and one woman. Their ages varied.

There was a long rectangular table in the center of the adjoining room. Naomi motioned for them to take seats. She sat at the head of the table, her elbows casually at the edge, with two gray-robed individuals on each side. They must be what Janus referred to as the Collective. The whole scene was surreal. Leah had tumbled through the looking glass and the entire world seemed upside down.

"You are the leader of the Fain?" Keegan was seated at the opposite end of the table. "How can you lead? You are so…"

"Frail? Old?" Naomi seemed immune to any insult about her age. And Leah was sure that Keegan had meant none. She'd simply voiced the thought both of them had. How could a woman of her advanced age come to any position of power in this world?

"Do you know about the elephants of Earth?" Naomi looked at Leah. "I'm sure you do."

Leah nodded.

"Is it so surprising that I would be the Seanchai, the Story Keeper? In elephant families of old Earth, it was the ancient, long-barren females who held in memory the migration routes and watering holes—whose heads were full of what the extended clan needed to survive."

A young woman Leah hadn't even noticed moved from the shadows with a cup of water. Naomi thanked her and took a drink.

"Is anyone else thirsty?"

Keegan and Leah shook their heads. Leah leaned forward, anxiously waiting for Naomi to continue.

"Knowledge lost its value and place in Haydn City long before you were born. Perhaps, six generations ago now." She looked around the room. "When I was a young girl I aspired to more than the life of a companion to a person I might not choose for myself. It was easy for me to decide to follow the Fain. They promised another way. Their ideas appealed to my deepest yearnings for identity, faith, and self-actualization."

Leah opened her mouth to speak, but thought better of it. She was a stranger and she had no idea what was acceptable behavior in this place.

"You have a question?" Naomi smiled at Leah.

"Yes, but I don't want to seem too...forward."

"An honest inquiry is always welcome here."

"How did knowledge lose its value? How did things destabilize so quickly?" Leah wanted to know why the colonies had failed to achieve their stated goal, the mission to establish an egalitarian community. She'd seen enough in Haydn City to know the vision for Proxima B had not been realized.

"When terra forming a foreign, potentially hostile environment, you make certain choices to ensure that life will survive. There will always be those who take and those who stand by and watch as the weak are abandoned. Systems were put in place that favored the strongest of our species. But in so doing, important values were lost, seen as weakness."

Leah covered her face with her hands. Humanity had been doomed from the beginning because mankind would never rise above its basest impulses.

"We replaced one illusion with another, didn't we?" She looked at Naomi for confirmation of her hypothesis. "It is hard, after all, to accept that the Earth's problems might be insoluble; much easier to believe that the challenges can be surmounted just as soon as the status quo is torn down and a new Earth constructed in its place. The only problem is, we're still human, we're still who we are. We've repeated all of our original mistakes."

Naomi settled back in her chair, her brittle and delicate wrists dangling off the arms. "Like truth, understanding must be sought. Compassion must be fostered."

Naomi's four companions still had not spoken. They seemed to study Keegan and Leah, their expressions neutral.

"Twelve generations since the world was seeded and six generations since the reign of the Behn Clan, the Tenth Clan."

Keegan leaned forward, resting her arms on the table. "And citizens in the city and the provinces suffer under repression and poverty."

No one spoke.

"I need your help to change that." Keegan looked at Naomi. "Did you know that when a fire gets large enough it creates its own wind? The air thins and the flames rise, creating a firestorm. And when the flames reach the crown of the trees, the highest points, there are only two things left to do. Run away or pray for rain."

Leah wondered if Naomi always spoke in parables.

"Why are we talking about fire?" Keegan sounded impatient.

"Because a fire has been building, and Tiago has fanned the flame with fear and distrust and violence. And as his flame grows it will create its own wind. It will destroy everything good."

"That is why I'm here. I'm asking the Fain to rise up and help me stop him."

"You claim to be Solas, but we both know that Solas is a myth." Naomi paused. She wasn't angry. Her expression was as neutral as before. "A savior myth that originated around cook fires. A myth told and retold to bring hope to the neglected."

Keegan didn't respond.

Naomi continued. "Nonetheless, we held a funeral ceremony when we heard Solas had been killed."

That must have been the huge gathering that Yates had seen.

"So, if you are not Solas, who are you?" Naomi asked.

"I am Keegan, adopted by the Behn Clan, commander of the northern legion of the Tenth."

"And I'm guessing, a credible threat to the new chieftain."

"Yes." Keegan sat back, her voice softened. "Although, a threat I never intended."

"True strength frightens the weak."

Keegan was quiet. She seemed to be considering Naomi's words. Leah wanted more than anything to support Keegan, but now she was wondering if the whole idea had been folly. Humanity would never change. They could defeat Tiago, and who was to say that another like him wouldn't rise up in his place? Did she have so little faith? She felt defeated before the fight even began.

CHAPTER TWENTY-EIGHT

They decided to return to the ship for food and rest. Janus had given them a brief tour of two of the tunnels after their conversation with Naomi, but it was clear that the leadership of the Fain, the Collective, needed time to consider Keegan's request. They'd been dismissed without the other four members of the Collective saying a word.

It was obvious that the people residing in the Hollow Hills had used the naturally formed lava tubes as the primary arteries for their underground settlement. It was genius actually. The tubes were already there, had been there for a millennium, the perfect protection from a harsh surface environment. The challenge must have been fuel and food, but both problems had been solved. Steam venting from underground chambers, from somewhere deep in the center of the planet, warmed the tunnels, and harnessed steam provided power for small arrays of ultraviolet tubes for subterranean grow rooms.

Leah wondered if some of the earliest settlers to the planet, engineers perhaps, had split off to form this underground community. It was easy to imagine that after arriving on the planet ideologies might not have aligned. Once the military reached Proxima B, if they'd wanted control they could easily have taken it. And that seems to be what transpired.

The others had eaten in the galley, but Leah hadn't been hungry. She'd taken a cup of coffee and gone to the command console to think. She lounged in the large captain's chair, one leg thrown over the arm, her other foot propped on the edge of the console. She'd turned off all but two of the floodlights, leaving just enough illumination so that she could see the surrounding terrain. She'd also reengaged the proximity alarm. The Fain seemed welcoming, but she wasn't taking any chances.

The data logs came to life as she entered her password. She'd begun the data download the day she'd first come out of cryo but had never gotten a chance to study it. The logs would hopefully tell her what had gone so horribly wrong in transit from Earth. She scrolled through screen after screen of the ship's log. It was hard to decipher what she was seeing. She entered a search using *cascading collapse* as key words.

The screen filled with failure alerts. She checked the dates.

Jesus. She rubbed her eyes and looked at the screen again.

Ten years after departing Earth, a solar storm had knocked out navigation and damaged some key systems. The ship was off course for nearly one-hundred and fifty years while the automated piloting system rerouted fried circuits and attempted self-repair. She clicked the keypad, jumping ahead in the logs.

Radiation readings were off the charts. Luckily, over the course of three hundred years of deep space travel, the radiation had dissipated and returned to normal levels.

But why had the cryogenic tubes failed?

Leah sipped her coffee as she hit the down arrow, skimming lines of text for a clue. Then she saw it. A microburst of meteor debris. The data log recorded a hole the size of a baseball in the shielding of the cryogenic compartment of the ship. It could have been made by a meteoroid as small as a marble. Most small particles less than one centimeter posed no catastrophic threat, but they would cause surface abrasions and microscopic holes. This had obviously been something bigger.

The greatest challenge for deep space travel was medium size particles, objects with a diameter between one centimeter and ten, because they were not easily tracked and were large enough to cause catastrophic damage to a spacecraft fuselage.

Proxima Five was fitted with the heaviest shielding ever flown, but it had not been enough. The rock must have struck at just the right speed and just the right angle to pierce the shielding. Critical components were severed, and all but one tube failed.

Leah sank back into the chair and blinked at the screen.

Her crew had been dead a hundred years before they ever reached the planet. It had to be some sort of miracle that she'd survived. Or it truly was fate. At least now she knew. Her theory of what had happened had been confirmed by the ship's computer logs, and now she even had the timeline to go with it. Somehow, she'd expected conclusive data to make her feel better. It didn't.

"Would you prefer to be alone up here?" Keegan rested her forearm across the back of the copilot's chair.

"No, not really." Leah partially swiveled as Keegan sank into the second chair. She definitely wasn't in the mood to be alone.

"What are you reading?"

"I was trying to scroll through the ship's data logs to find out what went wrong."

"And did you find anything?"

"Yes...It was no one's fault." She never really thought it was, but she voiced the thought aloud anyway. "Unlucky. *Proxima Five* was unlucky."

"I'm sorry about your friends, but I'm glad you are here." Keegan reached over and took her hand, entwining her fingers with Leah's.

Leah squeezed Keegan's hand. "Thank you for saying that."

For a few minutes, neither of them spoke. Keegan seemed lost in thought.

"What do you think the Collective will decide?"

"I'm not sure." That was the truth. Leah didn't feel overly optimistic. "If they decide not to follow, not to help us, what will you do?"

"I'll face Tiago either way."

"What? No...that was not what I intended."

Keegan looked over at Leah. She had an expression of utter calm on her face.

"Don't be afraid for me." Keegan had decided the only thing she could control in this scenario was herself. She'd already made the decision to face Tiago, regardless. She would live or die, succeed or fail, and that would be the end of it. She wasn't going to hide from this and she wasn't going to run away from it, with or without the support of the Fain.

"Keegan..."

"Just promise me that if things don't end well, if I fail, that you will take the ship and leave."

"No, Keegan—"

"I'm serious, Leah. You take Esther, Yates, and Hardy, and you fly south...beyond the provinces. You make a new life. You have enough supplies on this ship to last you a lifetime." She turned away from Leah and looked out into the darkness. "And think of me fondly."

Leah climbed into Keegan's lap, capturing Keegan's face in her hands.

"Keegan, I'm in this with you, regardless of the outcome. I'm not leaving you." She kissed Keegan.

"I'd never have made it this far without you, Leah. You've done enough. If I fail you must promise to save yourself."

"I'm not making that promise, and I think you know me well enough by now to know you can't make me do something I don't want to do."

Keegan laughed.

"You laugh because you know I'm right." Leah lightly punched Keegan's shoulder.

"Hey, don't make me make you." Keegan scooped Leah in her arms and rotated her so that she had the advantage.

"Okay, okay." Leah slapped at her chest. She was practically hanging upside down off Keegan's lap.

Keegan drew Leah up and close; their lips were inches apart. Keegan tenderly brushed her thumb over Leah's cheek. "I'm starting to think you saved me from more than a cage in the desert."

Leah kissed her. A kiss to carry her through the darkest hours to come. A kiss filled with hope and passion.

"We saved each other." Leah whispered the words against Keegan's parted lips.

Leah settled across her lap, resting her head against Keegan's shoulder. They held each other, looking out at the darkness. And Keegan wondered again if she should just take Leah and run away. It was a fleeting thought, and then it passed.

CHAPTER TWENTY-NINE

Keegan tried to find sleep, but that was impossible. She'd lain down beside Leah, and after Leah drifted off she'd tossed and turned. She gave up and walked to the galley to look for a drink. She needed something stronger than water, something with alcohol content.

She was looking through cabinets and finding nothing.

"Lose something?"

Keegan peered over the open cabinet door to see Yates holding a small flask.

"I'm glad one of us packed the necessities." She accepted the small metal flask from Yates and took a long draw.

"I couldn't sleep either." Yates sat down.

"Is this a crazy idea?" Keegan didn't sit. She paced and took another sip from the flask before handing it back to Yates.

"Yes."

"Are you telling me not to do it?"

"No."

Keegan sat down. She exhaled and waited for Yates to offer more than a one-syllable comment.

"While you were talking to the Collective behind closed doors I listened to the crowd gathered outside."

"And?"

"They are ready for change. I think your call to action is well timed."

Keegan rubbed her face with her hands.

"What did you hear from the Collective?" Yates passed the flask across the table.

"Riddles." Keegan took a swig. "The Collective is led by an old woman who tells stories." A twinge of guilt for her dismissive comment shot through her gut. Maybe she was as bad as Tiago, only valuing a particular kind of strength.

"Were they good stories at least?"

Yates tried to lighten Keegan's mood. That was impossible.

"I suppose we'll know tomorrow." Keegan held the flask out to Yates. "The last sip is yours."

"Get some rest."

Keegan glanced at Yates. "You too."

She walked back toward the sleeping compartment, trailing her fingertips along the sleek metal of the passage as she went. The ship's interior was so foreign, and yet familiar, almost as if something she'd seen in a dream or had some genetic memory of.

When she stepped through the door she saw that Leah was awake.

"Is everything okay?" Leah sat up against the pillows.

"Just couldn't sleep. I'm sorry if I woke you."

"Come here." Leah crossed the bed on her knees.

When Keegan got within reach, Leah fisted the front of her shirt and tugged her closer. She teased with her fingers at the hem of Keegan's shirt then slid her hands across Keegan's ribs beneath the soft fabric.

"What are you doing?" Keegan was amused.

"I'm helping you relax."

"I'm not sure relaxed is what I'm feeling right now." Keegan held Leah's face in her hands and kissed her.

"Good. Lie down." Leah shoved Keegan onto the bed and straddled her waist. She pushed Keegan's wrists over her head onto the pillow. "Now, stay there."

Keegan couldn't help smiling. She reached for Leah.

"No." Leah pushed her hands back to the pillow. "I said stay."

Keegan watched with rapt attention as Leah seductively removed her shirt and her underwear and then began to tug Keegan's shorts down before resuming her position. Keegan groaned. Leah was so wet. Leah braced with outstretched arms against her stomach and began to move slowly on top of Keegan.

Once again, she reached for Leah. She wanted to put her hands on Leah's hips and grind into her sex. Leah captured Keegan's wrists, and this time when she forced them above her head Leah lingered long enough to kiss her.

"Leah, let me touch you."

Leah took Keegan's lower lip between her teeth and tugged. "No."

This was a side of Leah she'd never seen, and it was driving her crazy not to take control. But Leah wouldn't relent. Leah slowed the roll of her hips grinding on top of Keegan until an involuntary groan escaped. Leah was going to make her come.

Leah pushed Keegan's shirt up and began to trail kisses across her chest. Leah teased her highly sensitive nipple with her teeth before soothing it with her tongue. Keegan's entire system vibrated.

"Leah, please...let me touch you." She knew if she touched Leah she'd instantly tumble over the edge. She was so close, too close, painfully close.

Leah slid up Keegan's taut body, her lips skimmed the edge of Keegan's ear as she whispered, "Fuck me."

Keegan slid her hand between them. Leah raised up enough to give her room. Leah was so wet that Keegan's fingers easily slid inside. Above her, Leah closed her eyes and moaned softly as she rode Keegan's hand. Leah grabbed the crumpled front of Keegan's shirt and held on as Keegan thrust with her fingers. She placed her other hand at the base of Leah's neck, beneath her hair, across her slender shoulder, and applied pressure. Leah's breasts glistened with a light sheen of sweat as she pumped harder. Leah tossed her head back and gripped Keegan's arm. One last deep thrust and Leah arched against her hand.

"Oh God, oh God..." Leah stiffened and shuddered, then collapsed on top of Keegan. "Oh, baby, that was so good." Leah kissed her neck as she slid her wet center down over Keegan's thigh.

She rolled Leah over and kissed her deeply. She was on the verge of an orgasm, so aroused, but she hadn't come. She took Leah's hand and placed it between her legs. Leah looked up at her with the most soulful expression as she slipped her fingers inside.

"Am I hurting you?" Keegan whispered the question. She knew she was riding Leah hard; she was so fucking close.

"No." Leah's response was breathless.

She quickened the speed of their rhythm, riding Leah's fingers, and pressed into Leah's sex with her thigh as she rocked against Leah's. Every muscle was as taut as a bowstring about to snap. And then it did. She lost herself in Leah, holding tightly as she rode the crest of the wave. She sank into Leah and let the successive waves carry her off into oblivion.

Leah pressed her lips to Keegan's throat and then her jaw.

"I've got you." Leah whispered. Her arms tightened around Keegan. "And I'm not letting go."

CHAPTER THIRTY

Janus escorted Keegan and her small entourage back to the chamber where she'd first met the Collective. As had been the case the day before, a gathering of cave dwellers fell in behind them as they walked. By the time they reached the chamber quite a large group had formed. She wondered if the Collective held complete sway over the Fain or if, regardless of the ruling, a group of fighters might not follow her anyway. Having lived with soldiers, she knew enough to recognize the signs when a group was itching to fight. The atmosphere inside the caves fairly hummed with the expectancy that something was about to break loose or be set free.

Keegan stood facing the door to the chamber, quietly waiting, lost in her own thoughts. Leah brushed against her arm. She was close. Yates, Hardy, and Esther stood behind Leah.

A scuffle erupted. Leah jostled against her and almost fell. She rotated, catching Leah in her arms. Hardy had toppled into Leah as he struggled with someone, a man. Keegan tried to get past Leah to intervene. There was a flash as the knife blade caught the light. The crowd contracted as if all the bodies were one, recoiling from the scuffle. Keegan glimpsed Yates fighting to free herself from the tight cluster of arms and shoulders. But Hardy was on the ground already. She lost sight of Esther in the sea of faces.

The attacker stood frozen for an instant, the bloodied knife in his right hand, as if his own actions were a surprise. Keegan shoved Leah behind her and lunged for the assailant. She grabbed his right wrist and twisted in an attempt to disarm him. With her other hand, she grabbed the front of his shirt and shoved, putting her full weight in play to move him away from Hardy and Leah.

He was a large man, not easily toppled. He twisted out of her grasp. He swung wide with the knife, aiming for her midsection. Keegan bowed her stomach, narrowly avoiding contact with the blade. She circled him and he mirrored her movement. The crowd slunk back, creating a larger open space for them.

"Stay back." Yates was at her side, ready to engage. Keegan held up her hand to stop Yates.

Keegan was itching for a fight too, and this one was hers. Stupidly, she hadn't carried a weapon. That was sloppy, careless. Her carelessness had given this asshole the upper hand.

He was impatient, rattled, off balance. He lunged at her. She shifted, capturing his wrist again as he thrust past her. She forced his arm down in the same instant that she landed a powerful blow to his jaw with her elbow. He staggered. She punched him again, hard. A right hook that dropped him to one knee. She sprang on him, using her forearm against his throat to press him to the ground. He struggled beneath her in an attempt to sink the knifepoint into her shoulder. But she had the advantage. She raised up so that he missed his mark. Her hand was on his as he gripped the handle. He strained against her as if they were in a deadly arm wrestle, but she finally won, sinking the blade into his chest. He shuddered, gasped, and then stilled.

Keegan rocked back on her knees, straddling his body. Yates was on high alert, scanning the crowd for other attackers, but it seemed this man had acted alone. Behind her, Leah cradled Hardy in her arms. Blood pooled underneath his slender frame and soaked the front of his coat.

Keegan rushed to his side. She knelt and cradled the back of his head in her hand. She looked up at Leah. Leah's eyes glistened with tears. She shook her head. In Leah's arms, Hardy was trying to say something. Esther knelt next to Leah, resting her hand on his leg. Hardy blinked slowly, his lips moving.

"Protect...Leah..." He coughed and blood pulsed around his fingers. Leah covered his hand with hers over the wound, but the pressure would not stop the bleeding.

"You did. She's safe." Keegan kept her hand on his shoulder.

"Protect you…"

"I'm okay, Hardy. We're all safe, thanks to you." She squeezed his shoulder as he glanced up at her. For a moment, he seemed to regain focus. "You're a warrior of the Tenth, brave and true. You have brought honor to the oath…You did good."

He smiled weakly and blinked, keeping his eyes closed for a few seconds.

"Hardy?" Tears slid down Leah's cheeks.

He opened his eyes and looked at Leah but said nothing else. His body convulsed once, his leg jerked, and then he was still. Keegan closed his eyes with her fingertips. She stayed there for a moment, head bowed, eyes closed. Rage pulsed through her arms to her clenched fists. Leah quietly sobbed.

Keegan stood abruptly and went to the man's body. She rolled him onto his side and checked his scalp. Under his shaggy brown hair, she could see the tattoo. He was from the Tenth. Tiago's paid mercenaries had infiltrated the Fain. Like the man who'd captured Leah. What had he offered them to turn against their own and abandon their oath? She wondered how many more lurked in the caves. She dropped his lifeless head to the ground and turned to see Naomi and the other members of the Collective watching from the open door. How much had they witnessed of what had just taken place? She stood to face them. Leah still cradled Hardy at their feet.

"We will follow you to Haydn City." Naomi's voice sounded oddly calm given the carnage that surrounded her. "The Fain are yours to command."

Keegan had decided to start for Haydn City as soon as possible. Word had already arrived from a Fain scout that Tiago had killed the head of one of the Great Houses for refusing to fall in line. She'd guessed correctly that the only House to offer any resistance had been Armus, and he'd been killed for it and his estate claimed by Tiago. But it was only a matter of time before the other Great Houses fell. Keegan felt sure of it.

She stood next to Leah, watching from the observation deck as the Fain assembled near the ship, waiting to embark on their journey.

"I want to go with you." Leah turned to face her.

"We've been over this. I can't focus on what I need to do if I'm worried about you." Keegan angled her head and gave Leah her best pleading look. She held Leah's hands in hers and kissed them. "I need for you to stay here. Stay with Esther. Stay with the ship."

Keegan had decided to take one of the crawlers and travel with the Fain raiders back to the city rather than have Leah fly her there by airship. It was the only way to keep Leah at a safe distance from what she had to do. It would take eight hours to reach the arena on foot, which is where she planned to call Tiago out. She wanted Leah far away from whatever was about to happen. There were far too many unknowns. Keegan might have to switch tactics at a moment's notice.

The Fain had guns, thanks to Tiago's smuggling efforts, but she had no idea about their abilities in combat. For all she knew they were green and would turn and run at the first sign of a skirmish. Or worse, scatter in confusion and fire on one another. She had hopes that a clear show of force would tip the scales in her favor and that a full-scale military assault wouldn't be necessary. But where Tiago was concerned it was best to plan for every scenario.

"It's time." Keegan shouldered her rifle.

"I don't want you to leave."

Keegan laughed and swept her hand affectionately up Leah's arm.

"What's so funny?"

"I remember a time, not so many days ago, when you didn't want to be anywhere near me." Keegan cocked her head with her forefinger on her chin. "If memory serves, you punched me in the nose."

Leah playfully shoved her. And then she wrapped her arms around Keegan's waist and rested her cheek on Keegan's chest.

"Things are different now." Leah's words were muffled against Keegan's heavy coat.

"I know, sweetheart." Keegan held her close and kissed her hair.

"You called me sweetheart." Leah's voice was full of emotion.

"Don't let that get around...I have a reputation to protect."

"Too late." Yates leaned against the doorway, a smirk on her face.

"Don't make me hurt you." Keegan pointed at Yates and scowled, keeping one arm affectionately around Leah's shoulders.

"Your troops await, Commander. We can leave whenever you're ready." Yates adjusted the rifle strap across her chest.

"I'm ready."

Yates left them alone.

"Come back to me." Leah kissed her.

"I promise." Keegan hesitated. "But Leah, if—"

"Don't...don't even suggest it." Leah pressed her fingers to Keegan's lips.

"If I can't get back to you, promise me that you'll stay safe. Don't take any chances. Stay with Esther and take care of each other."

Leah nodded, but didn't respond as she started toward the door.

"Keegan?"

Keegan turned back. "Yes?"

"I love you."

Keegan swept Leah up, almost lifting her off the ground, and fiercely kissed her. Then she looked back one last time at Leah standing in front of the huge window of the observation deck. She felt things for Leah she'd never felt for anyone before, but she couldn't say them now. She would not say them now. Having not said them would stay with her through this long night. Those unsaid things would give her courage to fight, to live. She had so much more to fight for than ever before.

CHAPTER THIRTY-ONE

L eah stood at the window. She watched the throng of Fain fighters follow Keegan's crawler through the narrow canyon and away from the ship. It gave her some comfort that Yates was with Keegan and that such a force had committed to follow her into this battle. But nothing, no assurances, could completely soothe the knot in her stomach. The floodlights from the ship lit their path, until after a time, the soldiers were swallowed up by darkness. And still she lingered, reluctant to move from the spot where she'd last embraced Keegan.

"It's time." Esther touched her sleeve.

Leah nodded and followed Esther away from the window. They decided that she and Esther would see to Hardy's burial. As was the custom on this world, he would be cremated on a funeral pyre. Leah had never witnessed such a ceremony and was taking her lead from Esther.

The ship felt huge and forlorn as they covered the distance between the observation deck and the exit ramp near the forward compartment. Leah used a remote device to raise the ramp and close the hatch once they were on the ground. It was so strange to Leah that this place was forever in darkness. She kept expecting the sun to crest the cliffs, but it never did, and it never would.

The funeral site was far from the central entrance. It took several minutes to walk there. A group of women carried Hardy's body, wrapped in simple white cloth, on a wooden platform. Leah,

Esther, and a small group of people followed the bearers as they carried the body to the pyre. Naomi and the four other elders waited near the structure as the fire was lit. No one spoke, but reverence for the ceremonial bonfire was palpable. As if there could be no words to compensate for the loss of a life, and the dead could only be honored by silently witnessing their return to dust.

The blaze grew, challenging the darkness. Sparks rose, mingled with the stars, and disappeared. She thought of her crewmates, forever entombed in the desert. Leah slipped her arm around Esther's waist and leaned into her shoulder. She wiped at tears with her free hand. Was she crying for Hardy or for Keegan or for herself? She was unsure. Emotions churned in her chest. She and Esther held each other. No doubt bonded in their worry for Keegan and Yates. She drew strength from Esther, her first real friend on this strange new world.

❖

Six hours at a steady march brought the regiment of Fain fighters to the edge of the dark lands. Keegan decided they should make camp in the shadows behind a low ridge, before crossing into the light. Once this army crossed into the green zone, Tiago would no doubt be warned of their coming and have time to prepare a defense.

The soldiers organically broke into small groups. Dinner would be cold rations or food carried along from the caves. Cook fires would draw attention so Keegan ordered no fires. She walked through the ranks, making her presence known among the men and women who had joined her on this journey. Some of them looked so young, or maybe she was suddenly feeling older.

She'd led soldiers before. She'd never wavered in her command. But somehow this felt different. These were not well-compensated professional fighters. These were mostly young people who believed in a cause. Their only reward was the promise of change, the establishment of an ideal.

Eyes followed her in the near darkness as she walked among them, faces upturned, hopeful. She smiled back. She offered in her demeanor the only thing she could, conviction. Confidence that they would succeed. If only she knew with certainty that her confidence was not unfounded.

One young man stood as she approached. When she reached him, she put a hand on his shoulder.

"You should get some rest."

"I feel too restless." He reminded her of Hardy. Hopeful, eager. Esther and Leah had stayed behind to bear witness to his passing. Keegan felt a twinge of guilt that she hadn't been with them.

"A soldier must clear his mind so that he can give his body what it needs to succeed." She patted his shoulder. "Eat and rest."

She turned and took a few steps toward where Yates was camped near the crawler.

"You'll be with us tomorrow?"

She paused. "I will be with you. We're in this together."

"Are you afraid?" His voice grew quiet, as if he didn't want the others to hear.

She walked back and stood in front of him. "Only a fool has no fear." She placed both hands on his shoulders and gave him her full attention. "A strong person, a brave person, overcomes that fear for the sake of others…and for themselves."

He nodded.

"Get some rest now. Because tomorrow we change the world."

He grinned. She turned again and walked away.

Yates had unpacked their bedrolls from the crawler by the time Keegan made the rounds. She hadn't walked like the rest, but fatigue was pulling her under. She unzipped her coat, lounged against the side of the crawler, and took a long drink from her canteen. Yates tossed her one of the protein bars they'd brought with them from the ship. It tasted bland and chalky, and she had to keep drinking water with every bite to choke it down. She needed to eat and rest too and was in the mood to do neither. A shiver crept up her arm. Not from the temperature. They'd traveled beyond the deepest cold, the air was still cool, but that wasn't it. She wasn't chilled and yet, her skin tingled. Possibly from anticipation or nerves or adrenaline.

"You should get some sleep." Yates wrapped a blanket into a makeshift pillow and reclined against it.

"Yes, Mother."

"I'm serious." Yates kicked Keegan's boot playfully.

"I'll do my best, but I'm not sure I'll be able to."

"My eyes will remain open so you can close yours." Yates settled herself to take the first watch.

Keegan nodded. It took a minute to shuck off her boots and climb in the sleeping bag she'd been sitting on. She lay on her side, facing Yates. When she closed her eyes all she could see was Leah. The memory of Leah stirred her insides, tumbling the food she'd just ingested until her stomach felt as hard as a stone. What was Leah doing right now? What was she thinking?

CHAPTER THIRTY-TWO

A communal meal followed the funeral. Food was the last thing on Leah's mind, but refusing the invitation seemed impossible. Maybe being with people was best right now. If she were left to her own inclinations she'd have skulked back to her ship and curled up in bed to cry. Being here, among the Fain, kept her from withdrawing. Esther sat a few chairs away at the long table. They'd barely spoken. Mostly Leah responded to questions when asked, but wasn't in the mood for casual conversation. She did her best to be gracious when offered more food that she wouldn't be able to eat. She barely managed to swallow a few bites of potato and some fresh baked bread. Her stomach had revolted, and every other minute she felt the urge to bolt from the room in order to be sick.

Keegan was out there, somewhere, in the darkness.

Intellectually, Leah knew that Keegan wasn't alone, but emotionally that's how it felt. Or was she simply projecting her own sense of isolation? She wasn't sure. It was as if Keegan's absence was a physical presence. Leah was unable to direct her thoughts in any other direction.

She felt someone touch her thigh. A child, probably no more than three or four, leaned against her leg and looked up at her expectantly. When she finally made eye contact, a smile spread across the little girl's face. The light from nearby candles danced in her dark eyes. Leah opened her arms, and the little girl wriggled up and into her lap. The child leaned back against Leah's chest and kicked at the edge of the table.

"Katie, don't put your feet on the table." A woman, Leah assumed was the mother, claimed the empty chair next to hers. "Is she bothering you?"

"No, not at all." Katie gripped Leah's fingers with her tiny hand, balancing herself as she reached for leftover food on Leah's plate. "She's adorable."

"I'm afraid I spoil her. I'm Mary." Mary held the edge of the plate so that all the food didn't toppled onto Leah's lap and the floor.

"I'm Leah."

"My partner is with them too." Mary's expression grew more serious.

"Your partner?"

"Katie's father." Katie offered Mary a piece of bread. "No, thank you, sweetie."

Mary was the first person in this underground community that Leah had actually connected with other than casual brief comments, aside from Naomi, who seemed quite separated from the average Fain.

"I want her to see the sun." Mary was looking at Katie, then she shifted her gaze to Leah. "All children should have a chance to play in the sun."

Leah stepped outside of herself for a moment and looked around. Women and children and a couple of elderly men were gathered loosely in the communal space. Eating, drinking, talking in low voices. These people were not scary or threatening. They were just trying to make a life for themselves and their children. How they had all come to be here was a mystery to her, but regardless of the reasons, it didn't seem fair that they should have to hide underground in order to live the way they chose.

"How did you…why did you come to this place?" Leah held a cup of water for Katie to sip.

"My sister was taken as a companion. She died from cancer in service to a man she did not choose. I refused to suffer the same fate. Katie's father was part of a work detail in the southern province. We decided to run away together." She smiled. "That was six years ago."

"Do you miss it?"

"What? The sun?"

"Any of it…any part of your old life."

"Of course. To live freely I had to be willing to give up certain things. The trade-off was worth the risk."

Katie reached for her mother, and Leah helped her hop into Mary's lap.

"Sometimes risk is the only barter you have." Mary brushed crumbs from Katie's clothing as she squirmed. "Sorry, I should probably put her to bed. She missed her nap today, and I think we're only moments from witnessing a meltdown."

"Of course." Leah reached for Katie's hand. "It was nice to meet you, Katie. And your mother too."

Leah was ready for bed too. If not to sleep then at least to be alone with her thoughts. She looked for Esther, but somehow Esther had slipped past without Leah's notice. She found her standing outside the main entrance looking up at the stars. Esther hugged herself. Her breath puffed in white clouds into the night.

"There you are." Leah stopped and looked up. None of the constellations looked familiar to her. "I'm walking back to the ship if you're ready and would like to go with me."

"Yes, thank you."

The soft sound of voices echoed from the tunnel as they made their way toward the floodlights of the ship. They walked in silence almost all the way.

"Where do you think they are right now?" Leah used the remote to lower the ramp after opening the door.

"I think they would have stopped somewhere on this side of the green zone to rest. Certainly, Keegan will want the fighters to be as rested as possible to meet Tiago's forces."

Once inside, Leah sealed the hatch.

"What do you think will happen?"

"I don't know." Esther's expression telegraphed worry, despite her attempt to sound neutral.

"Should we have gone with them?"

"I don't know." Esther walked beside her toward the sleeping compartments.

"I'm having second thoughts." What had Mary said? That sometimes risk was all you had to barter. So far, she'd risked nothing and she'd watched as Keegan had marched off to face an unknown fate without her.

"I've never fought for my freedom and maybe I should have." Esther sounded wistful, possibly regretful. "I've sublimated my own desires in return for protection, safety, but now I wonder at what cost."

One life ends and another begins. Every choice came with some cost, didn't it? History bore witness to those choices, some made by humanity, some made for humanity by a select few. And through it all, mankind had driven the species forward, carried into the future by spear tip or spaceship in search of some undiscovered utopia. A perfect world that didn't exist because in order to create such a world people would have had to figure out a way to overcome the limitations of humanity—frailty, mortality, selfishness, and greed. Despite all of that, children were born having no control over how or where they came into the world, and yet, they arrived with joy, hope, and possibility.

Katie reminded her of everything that was possible. Maybe this place wasn't the world she'd imagined, but who was to say it couldn't be?

"Esther."

"Yes? What are you thinking?" Esther waited expectantly for an answer.

"Esther, have you ever fired a gun?"

CHAPTER THIRTY-THREE

The Fain soldiers crossed the threshold into daylight very early. Everyone was as restless as Keegan and anxious to reach Haydn City. Camp had broken quickly, and the throng of fighters entered the city with no resistance by late morning. If it was true that strength came with numbers, then Keegan felt empowered as they neared the arena. She planned to organize the Fein in squadrons and she'd designated more seasoned fighters to lead each group. Janus was one of them.

"The runners are away." Janus looked over his comrades standing quietly in tight groups.

They'd sent two messengers to the forum to call Tiago out.

Now for the waiting.

If a show of force had been her goal, she'd achieved it. At least five hundred Fain warriors stood, ready for the command to fight. How the tables had turned. Three weeks ago, even a week ago, she'd chased Fain raiders into a gunfight at the edge of the desert. Or so she thought. Now she realized the Fain had been set up and betrayed by Tiago just as she had. Today they were unified against a common enemy. Today she stood with them; she stood for them. And they stood with her. How could she have been so misguided? Why had she never bothered to try to see their side of the conflict? In truth, the Great Houses had perpetuated the conflict by shoring up the caste system in the settlements, and she'd been eager to help them enforce that system in trade for a place at the table. She'd sold out her own kind and hadn't even realized it. She'd bought into the entire fucked up system because it seemed too big to change, too entrenched.

The crowd of soldiers stirred and looked up, then she looked up. Leah's ship was just east of their position. It looked like she was going to set it down right on the field behind them. The soldiers scattered into two large groups, making room in the center of the field for the enormous aircraft.

Dust swirled around the landing gear, and the sun bounced off the reflective metal surface like small flashes of lightning, so that Keegan had to shield her eyes from the glare. What was Leah doing here?

A ramp lowered from the forward door. Leah and Esther calmly walked toward her, followed by Naomi.

What the hell?

Keegan strode toward them with Yates on her heels.

"Let me talk first." Leah held up her hand.

Leah was dressed in trousers and a simple V-neck shirt. A rifle strap cut across the shirt between her breasts. She stabilized it with one hand as Keegan grabbed her by the other arm and hauled her away from the group.

"Keegan, hear me out."

"I asked you to keep a safe distance. I asked you to take care of Esther." She didn't give Leah a chance to speak.

"We don't want to be at a safe distance." Leah was defiant. "I'm not letting you do this alone." She swung her arm in an arc toward the ship. "There's no better show of force than my ship. You know I'm right."

Keegan had to concede that the colony ship with its wingspan covering the width of the field like some enormous raptor, was intimidating.

"And since when do you carry a rifle?" Keegan pointed at the gun.

"I never said I didn't know how to shoot. I just prefer not to." A breeze wisped past, and Leah tucked her ruffled hair being her ear.

Keegan was about to say more when the sound of many boots on the ground pulled her attention to the approaching garrison across the open arena. Now it was her turn to be intimidated. She'd never faced her own troops before. And from the look of it, Tiago had brought every soldier of the Tenth that he could muster. They presented themselves in a formidable line across the entire field, ten soldiers deep.

"Formations!" Keegan signaled for the squadrons to reassemble in front of Leah's ship. She walked the front line, checking their spacing, and occasionally coaching one of the fighters on the proper defensive stance with their firearm.

Keegan faced her Fain army. Young men and women, some of them barely teenagers. She saw herself in them. Young, idealistic, and angry.

They looked to her and waited for the call to advance.

But something darkened her thoughts. She saw death on the field as well, and some of the wounded were too young to perish, the children of Proxima B, bloodied and strewn in the dust. She halted her review of the squads and really looked at them.

This was a conflict they hadn't asked for and shouldn't be required to wage.

This was *her* fight.

She looked back at Leah and held her for a moment with her eyes. This wasn't Leah's fight either.

Abruptly, she spun and walked toward the center of the field. Yates rushed to follow her, as did Leah. She saw Tiago break away, flanked by two of his men. They met near the center of the large open field, keeping a few yards between them. Yates gripped her rifle in front of her. Keegan was wearing a sidearm and kept her rifle slung over her shoulder.

Tiago didn't seem overly surprised to see her. Maybe he'd already received word somehow that she'd survived. His cocky arrogance made her want to close the space between them and pummel him with her fists. She took a breath and squared her shoulders.

"So I see someone sprang you from you cage, little bird."

"Disappointed?"

"Hardly." He leered at Leah, which pissed Keegan off. "I've defeated you once, I'm happy to do it again...with an audience."

"These are better odds."

"Yes, I see you brought your Fain army with you this time, Solas."

She bristled at the name but let it hang in the air uncontested.

"I challenge you, Tiago."

"What?" For the first time, the mask slipped away and she saw a glimmer of uncertainty in his eyes.

"I challenge you to a death match." She pointed at her chest and then his. "You and me. That's what this is really about. You and me."

He didn't respond. He shifted his stance and looked back at his men.

Keegan stepped away and shouted to Tiago's squadron and hers.

"You are my witnesses. I challenge Tiago to a death match. Here. Now."

Leah's heart began to beat wildly in her chest. What was Keegan doing? She didn't have to do this alone. That's why Leah and the others had come. She started toward Keegan, but Yates stopped her. Yates looked at her and shook her head.

"Do you accept my challenge?" Keegan shouted at Tiago.

He looked like a man who wanted to run away, but then his expression darkened and he handed his firearm to one of his men.

"I accept this challenge. This is a match long overdue."

His acceptance set things in motion. At his direction, several soldiers from the Tenth broke ranks and began to use levers in the center of the field to raise high walls of a cage. The walls of the cage had been flat on the ground, covered with dust so that she'd not even noticed them.

"Yates, what's happening?" Leah was afraid she already knew.

"Keegan and Tiago will fight."

"In that?" She motioned toward the cage taking shape in front of them.

"Yes. With no weapons until…"

"Until what?"

"Until one of them is dead."

Keegan walked toward them and began to unload her weapons onto the ground at Yates's feet. She didn't look at Leah. Her focus was laser sharp on what she was doing. Janus had joined them now. He shouldered Keegan's rifle, along with her sidearm. Everyone seemed to understand what was happening except Leah.

"Keegan, what are you doing? Don't do this."

"This is my fight, Leah." Keegan straightened and looked at her. "I'm not sacrificing any of these people for a conflict that isn't theirs."

"This is too much. I won't let you—"

"What prize do I get if I win this challenge?" Tiago stuck out his chest.

Keegan rotated to face him as he approached.

"If you win, you will have the chieftain's seat. But what will I have?" He looked at Leah. She felt his eyes pass over her leaving goose bumps on her arms.

"You get to keep your kingdom and your life." Keegan stepped in front of Leah, blocking his view.

"But I already have this kingdom. You must offer me something worthy of the challenge. I will accept your prize from the desert."

Keegan's reaction was instantaneous. "No."

"I offer myself." Leah spoke only to Keegan, but Tiago heard her.

"I accept." Tiago motioned for his men to take Leah.

"No. This is not part of the agreement."

"No prize, no challenge." Tiago glared at Keegan, daring her to back out of the fight.

One of the men relieved Leah of her rifle and then gruffly tugged her away from Keegan.

"Wait." Keegan raised her hand to stop him. "I need a minute."

"Take some time to say good-bye. I think that is wise." Tiago smirked. He tipped his head, signaling for his man to oblige Keegan's request.

Keegan rested her hands on Leah's arms. Leah wanted nothing more than to fall into her and disappear. To take Keegan by the hand and escape. She shivered despite the warmth of the air.

"Remember when I said I had to come back to Haydn City because all my things were there?" Leah looked up at Keegan. "I was wrong. Everything I need is right here." Keegan touched the center of her chest. "You have made me see things differently, Leah. For that I will always be grateful."

"Keegan, don't talk like this. You are going to defeat him. I know this, or I wouldn't have offered myself." Leah wanted Keegan to know that she had no doubts Tiago would be defeated.

"But if I don't—"

"You will win."

"Enough!" Tiago cut their conversation short.

Leah was tugged away from Keegan. Nearby, the cage was readied for the match.

Keegan watched as Leah was led away. Emotions fought for dominance—fear, anger, love…yes, love. Adrenaline began to build in her system. "What have I done?"

"You've done what you had to do." Yates rested her hand on Keegan's shoulder and squeezed, but Keegan couldn't look at her. "Whatever else happens today, you have saved many lives."

"Have I?" She rotated to look at the Fain fighters. "I should have anticipated this and come alone. I've put all of you at risk."

"Hey, clear your head." Yates stepped in front of Keegan, forcing Keegan to look at her. "Clear you head of everything but victory."

Keegan nodded and turned toward the cage. The time had come.

Tiago stood waiting inside the mesh walls. The crowd pressed closer as the door closed. Keegan looked for Leah one last time. Leah had wagered her life that Keegan would win. She turned to face Tiago. Yates was right. She needed to regain focus. Tiago's bid for Leah had unbalanced her, but it had also raised the stakes. Maybe that would be enough to push her over the top. She rolled her shoulders in an attempt to loosen up. She needed the reassurance of one more resurrection. Liberated from one cage, she'd willingly chosen another, but this would be the last. Win or lose, there would be no more cages.

Chapter Thirty-four

L eah struggled for a clear view. She needed to see Keegan. Tiago and Keegan circled each other. Tiago swung and Keegan easily dodged. Then Keegan advanced, but her swing did not find its target. They were testing each other, at least that's what it seemed to Leah. They must know each other well enough to anticipate certain tactics from one another. Surely, hopefully, Keegan would use this to her advantage.

Bare fisted and with no weapons, they continued to circle and lunge. Keegan was the first to make contact. Tiago recoiled from the blow, staggered, but immediately sprang forward with a right and then a left. Keegan took a hit to her gut and doubled over as she scuttled away from his next swing.

A flurry of blocked punches and then a loud smack as Keegan took a blow to her jaw. She swiped at blood near her mouth with the back of her hand.

Leah wanted to hide her face, and at the same time, she couldn't look away. Her fate was entwined with Keegan's now. She'd risked herself to give Keegan what she wanted, a one-on-one challenge match with Tiago.

The bodies of the soldiers pressed against her, carrying her closer to the cage. She searched for Yates but couldn't find her. Cheers erupted, and she returned to the match just as Keegan fell to one knee. It was hard to tell if the cheers were against her or to encourage her. Tiago kicked her in the stomach, and she tumbled sideways. Before he could get to her, she reached for the wire mesh and pulled herself up. She used the cage wall to springboard out of his reach. She shook her head a few times.

Blood ran in a thin stream from the gash that had only recently begun to heal. Leah ached to reach for her, to draw her close, and protect her. She grabbed for the mesh and bent her fingers around the thin gauge, only to be tugged back by her captors.

❖

Keegan blinked several times to clear her vision. Clumsy. She'd been clumsy. She'd let Tiago tag her solidly. Her vision blurred and then cleared. She scuttled in an arc away from him. She needed to buy some time to regroup. He was more fit than she remembered, or possibly she was less so. She'd barely recovered her strength and she'd hardly slept the night before. And it was a struggle not to think of Leah as his prize.

"You've gone soft." He taunted her. "I expected more from you."

She didn't respond.

"I'm surprised you'd choose another cage so soon. Did you enjoy the last one?"

"I think you're angry that I wasn't so easily dispatched. I'm like the rival you can't shake. The harder you try the more determined I become."

He scowled and lunged at her, but missed. She shoved him as he passed so that he stumbled into the cage.

"And the way you set up the Fain as the enemy. They were never our enemy. They only wanted to coexist."

"There can be only one way and that's the way of the Tenth."

"I am the Tenth. You have stolen the Tenth…you distort their mission for your own greed and ego." If she lost this match she wanted those gathered around them to hear the truth.

"Stop talking and fight." He lunged again and she dodged.

Breathe. Calm down. Anger will cause mistakes. Keegan coached herself silently and rocked back on her heels, forcing Tiago to go on the offensive again.

"I will have her in my bed tonight, and I have you to thank." He smiled, confident that he would triumph. Confident that threatening Leah was the key to unbalancing her.

She lurched as if to volley, and when he recoiled she changed direction. Her knuckles cracked against his jaw, erasing the smug expression from his face. Her tactic had surprised him, and before he could right himself, she struck him twice, once under his rib cage. He staggered backward and she raised her leg straight in front of him, sinking the heel of her boot into his abdomen. She knocked the wind out of him. He hit the dirt with a solid thump.

Keegan launched herself toward him with the intention of landing with an elbow against his ribcage, but he rolled and her elbow made hard contact with the ground. She swiveled, using her legs as a vise around his neck. He rotated and broke loose. Dust filled her vision and made her cough. Her view momentarily impaired, she didn't see the knife until it sliced through the sleeve of her shirt. She shifted at the last possible second so that the knife tip skimmed through her shirt. A thin red line seeped at the edge of the torn cloth.

Fuck.

A death match was supposed to be hand to hand, with no weapons. He'd decided to make his own rules, and it was too late to disarm him. The door wouldn't open until one of them was dead.

The crowd roared. It was impossible to make out individual voices or words. It was impossible to discern who they were rooting for. She tried to block out the noise.

Her arms felt heavy, sluggish. Fatigue and adrenaline warred in her system. Leah. This fight had begun as something much larger, but now all she focused on was Leah. Winning for Leah.

Keegan got to her feet just as Tiago stabbed for her midsection. She sidestepped and grabbed him from behind, her arm around his throat.

He sliced her forearm and tossed her over. She hit the ground hard. He was standing over her now. But just as he was about to fall on her with the blade, she rolled away. She swiveled and kicked his knee out from under him. He cried out and dropped on top of her.

"Enjoy your last moments of life." He grunted.

Keegan braced both arms against his as he tried to sink the blade into her chest.

"Fuck you." She jerked her head, making contact with his nose. For an instant, he lost focus. She swung up with her elbow, breaking his bloody nose. He rolled away and took her with him. The knife slipped neatly between his ribs as she pressed her weight on top of him.

He regarded her with wide eyes.

He'd never expected to lose.

His lips moved. Blood oozed at the corner of his mouth.

"You're finished, brother." She twisted the blade and drove it deeper.

Leah broke free and elbowed her way to the front. She could see Keegan's prone body through the haze of dust in the ring. She wasn't moving, but neither was Tiago. Her heart seized. Her throat closed and she couldn't breathe. She clung to the cage wire with her fingers. The crowd quieted.

Slowly, Keegan stood. She scanned the spectators until her eyes met Leah's. She walked toward the door and opened it. The sea of soldiers parted for her as she reached for Leah and drew her into her arms. Her shirt was bloodied and sweat-stained. Keegan was alive. Keegan was in her arms. It was over. They had won.

Yates pierced the crowd. She cupped the back of Keegan's head with her hand. Esther was there too. Leah felt Esther's embrace at her back, a group hug. Then Yates and Esther stepped away and hugged each other.

The soldiers of the Tenth mixed with the Fain surged forward with a deafening, roaring cheer. They grabbed Keegan and hoisted her up on their shoulders. Clearly, the crowd had been in her favor, the loyalty of the Tenth never wavering.

Keegan leapt from their shoulders to the hood of Tiago's crawler. She motioned for the cheering to subside, and once she could be heard she shouted to the gathered throng.

"Tiago is defeated!"

Deafening cheers again. With outstretched arms, she attempted to quiet them.

"This victory is not mine alone. This victory is for all of us. This victory is for our fallen chieftain. This victory is for the lost tribe."

The crowd murmured and restlessly shifted.

"There, amongst you…that woman is Leah Warren, the leader of the lost Fifth Clan." Keegan pointed in Leah's direction, and an open space spread around where she was standing. She walked toward Keegan. "I am your champion, but it is the Fifth Clan who should lead us. Leah is the one who carries the vision for a better world for all of us."

Keegan jumped down and stepped closer and knelt in front of her.

"What are you doing?" Leah wanted Keegan to stand.

"There are other ways to be strong." Keegan smiled up at her. "This is the first day of a new beginning. You are the one who carries the vision of what that new beginning can be."

"Keegan, I…"

"This world can be better. Change begins here…now…with me." Keegan raised the bloody knife to Leah, resting across the palm of her hand. "I am your champion, but it is you who should lead us."

Cheers erupted from those gathered. Leah took the blade from Keegan, leaned down, and tenderly kissed her.

"Your victory is for all of us. You *are* my champion…my life, my love." Leah touched Keegan's face.

The world was changing. The world had changed. Despite being tidally locked, Proxima B had just shifted on its axis for Leah. Those who dwelt in the darkness of the Hollow Hills had moved into the light. The Collective could hold court in the forum. A process of reconciliation between the Great Houses and citizens from all the provinces, including Haydn City, could begin. Her vision for a new world, a better world, now had a real chance. She dropped the knife. It sunk, blade first, into the ground at their feet.

Leah was bound to Keegan as Keegan was now bound to her.

Around them soldiers cheered and embraced. In the midst of the cacophony of celebration, all Leah could see was Keegan. It was as if everything else dropped away. Keegan filled her vision and her heart.

Keegan was standing now, cradling Leah in her arms.

"I still remember those first hours when I was something else."

"Something else?" Keegan looked puzzled.

"Angry, hopeless, clinging to the illusion of a world I thought I would never see."

"I was clinging to my own illusions." Keegan caressed her cheek. "What are you now?"

"Happy." As Leah said the word, she knew it was true.

"So am I." Keegan kissed her. "Leah..."

"Yes?"

"I love you." Keegan hugged her more tightly. "Let's build the world we want, together."

"I love you, Keegan." Leah rested her cheek on Keegan's shoulder and closed her eyes.

Keegan was safe and in her arms. Changing the world would have to wait because she just needed to hold Keegan a little longer, maybe forever. Yes, forever.

The end

About the Author

Missouri Vaun spent a large part of her childhood in southern Mississippi, before attending high school in North Carolina and college in Tennessee. Strong connections to her roots in the rural South have been a grounding force throughout her life. Vaun spent twelve years finding her voice working as a journalist in places as disparate as Chicago, Atlanta, and Jackson, Mississippi, all along filing away characters and their stories. Her novels are heartfelt, earthy, and speak of loyalty and our responsibility to others. She and her wife currently live in northern California.

Books Available from Bold Strokes Books

A Fighting Chance by T. L. Hayes. Will Lou be able to come to terms with her past to give love a fighting chance? (978-1-163555-257-7)

Chosen by Brey Willows. When the choice is adapt or die, can love save us all? (978-1-163555-110-5)

Death Checks In by David S. Pederson. Despite Heath's promises to Alan to not get involved, Heath can't resist investigating a shopkeeper's murder in Chicago, which dashes their plans for a romantic weekend getaway. (978-1-163555-329-1)

Gnarled Hollow by Charlotte Greene. After they are invited to study a secluded nineteenth-century estate, a former English professor and a group of historians discover that they will have to fight against the unknown if they have any hope of staying alive. (978-1-163555-235-5)

Jacob's Grace by C.P. Rowlands. Captain Tag Becket wants to keep her head down and her past behind her, but her feelings for AJ's second-in-command, Grace Fields, makes keeping secrets next to impossible. (978-1-163555-187-7)

On the Fly by PJ Trebelhorn. Hockey player Courtney Abbott is content with her solitary life until visiting concert violinist Lana Caruso makes her second-guess everything she always thought she wanted. (978-1-163555-255-3)

Passionate Rivals by Radclyffe. Professional rivalry and long-simmering passions create a combustible combination when Emmett McCabe and Sydney Stevens are forced to work together, especially when past attractions won't stay buried. (978-1-163555-231-7)

Proxima Five by Missouri Vaun. When geologist Leah Warren crash-lands on a preindustrial planet and is claimed by its tyrant, Tiago, will clan warrior Keegan's love for Leah give her the strength to defeat him? (978-1-163555-122-8)

Racing Hearts by Dena Blake. When you cross a hot-tempered race car mechanic with a reckless cop, the result can only be spontaneous combustion. (978-1-163555-251-5)

Shadowboxer by Jessica L. Webb. Jordan McAddie is prepared to keep her street kids safe from a dangerous underground protest group, but she isn't prepared for her first love to walk back into her life. (978-1-163555-267-6)

The Tattered Lands by Barbara Ann Wright. As Vandra and Lilani strive to make peace, they slowly fall in love. With mistrust and murder surrounding them, only their faith in each other can keep their plan to save the world from falling apart. (978-1-163555-108-2)

Captive by Donna K. Ford. To escape a human trafficking ring, Greyson Cooper and Olivia Danner become players in a game of deceit and violence. Will their love stand a chance? (978-1-63555-215-7)

Crossing the Line by CF Frizzell. The Mob discovers a nemesis within its ranks, and in the ultimate retaliation, draws Stick McLaughlin from anonymity by threatening everything she holds dear. (978-1-63555-161-7)

Love's Verdict by Carsen Taite. Attorneys Landon Holt and Carly Pachett want the exact same thing: the only open partnership spot at their prestigious criminal defense firm. But will they compromise their careers for love? (978-1-63555-042-9)

Precipice of Doubt by Mardi Alexander & Laurie Eichler. Can Cole Jameson resist her attraction to her boss, veterinarian Jodi Bowman, or will she risk a workplace romance and her heart? (978-1-63555-128-0)

Savage Horizons by CJ Birch. Captain Jordan Kellow's feelings for Lt. Ali Ash have her past and future colliding, setting in motion a series of events that strands her crew in an unknown galaxy thousands of light years from home. (978-1-63555-250-8)

Secrets of the Last Castle by A. Rose Mathieu. When Elizabeth Campbell represents a young man accused of murdering an elderly woman, her investigation leads to an abandoned plantation that reveals many dark Southern secrets. (978-1-63555-240-9)

Take Your Time by VK Powell. A neurotic parrot brings police officer Grace Booker and temporary veterinarian Dr. Dani Wingate together in the tiny town of Pine Cone, but their unexpected attraction keeps the sparks flying. (978-1-63555-130-3)

The Last Seduction by Ronica Black. When you allow true love to elude you once and you desperately regret it, are you brave enough to grab it when it comes around again? (978-1-63555-211-9)

The Shape of You by Georgia Beers. Rebecca McCall doesn't play it safe, but when sexy Spencer Thompson joins her workout class, their non-stop sparring forces her to face her ultimate challenge—a chance at love. (978-1-63555-217-1)

Exposed by MJ Williamz. The closet is no place to live if you want to find true love. (978-1-62639-989-1)

Force of Fire: Toujours a Vous by Ali Vali. Immortals Kendal and Piper welcome their new child and celebrate the defeat of an old enemy, but another ancient evil is about to awaken deep in the jungles of Costa Rica. (978-1-63555-047-4)

Holding Their Place by Kelly A. Wacker. Together Dr. Helen Connery and ambulance driver Julia March, discover that goodness, love, and passion can be found in the most unlikely and even dangerous places during WWI. (978-1-63555-338-3)

Landing Zone by Erin Dutton. Can a career veteran finally discover a love stronger than even her pride? (978-1-63555-199-0)

Love at Last Call by M. Ullrich. Is balancing business, friendship, and love more than any willing woman can handle? (978-1-63555-197-6)

Pleasure Cruise by Yolanda Wallace. Spencer Collins and Amy Donovan have few things in common, but a Caribbean cruise offers both women an unexpected chance to face one of their greatest fears: falling in love. (978-1-63555-219-5)

Running Off Radar by MB Austin. Maji's plans to win Rose back are interrupted when work intrudes and duty calls her to help a SEAL team stop a Russian mobster from harvesting gold from the bottom of Sitka Sound. (978-1-63555-152-5)

Shadow of the Phoenix by Rebecca Harwell. In the final battle for the fate of Storm's Quarry, even Nadya's and Shay's powers may not be enough. (978-1-63555-181-5)

Take a Chance by D. Jackson Leigh. There's hardly a woman within fifty miles of Pine Cone that veterinarian Trip Beaumont can't charm, except for the irritating new cop, Jamie Grant, who keeps leaving parking tickets on her truck. (978-1-63555-118-1)

The Outcasts by Alexa Black. Spacebus driver Sue Jones is running from her past. When she crash-lands on a faraway world, the Outcast Kara might be her chance for redemption. (978-1-63555-242-3)

Alias by Cari Hunter. A car crash leaves a woman with no memory and no identity. Together with Detective Bronwen Pryce, she fights to uncover a truth that might just kill them both. (978-1-63555-221-8)

Death in Time by Robyn Nyx. Working in the past is hell on your future. (978-1-63555-053-5)

Hers to Protect by Nicole Disney. High school sweethearts Kaia and Adrienne will have to see past their differences and survive the vengeance of a brutal gang if they want to be together. (978-1-63555-229-4)

Of Echoes Born by 'Nathan Burgoine. A collection of queer fantasy short stories set in Canada from Lambda Literary Award finalist 'Nathan Burgoine. (978-1-63555-096-2)

Perfect Little Worlds by Clifford Mae Henderson. Lucy can't hold the secret any longer. Twenty-six years ago, her sister did the unthinkable. (978-1-63555-164-8)

Room Service by Fiona Riley. Interior designer Olivia likes stability, but when work brings footloose Savannah into her world and into a new city every month, Olivia must decide if what makes her comfortable is what makes her happy. (978-1-63555-120-4)

Sparks Like Ours by Melissa Brayden. Professional surfers Gia Malone and Elle Britton can't deny their chemistry on and off the beach. But only one can win... (978-1-63555-016-0)

Take My Hand by Missouri Vaun. River Hemsworth arrives in Georgia intent on escaping quickly, but when she crashes her Mercedes into the Clip 'n Curl, sexy Clay Cahill ends up rescuing more than her car. (978-1-63555-104-4)

The Last Time I Saw Her by Kathleen Knowles. Lane Hudson only has twelve days to win back Alison's heart. That is if she can gather the courage to try. (978-1-63555-067-2)

Wayworn Lovers by Gun Brooke. Will agoraphobic composer Giselle Bonnaire and Tierney Edwards, a wandering soul who can't remain in one place for long, trust in the passionate love destiny hands them? (978-1-62639-995-2)

Breakthrough by Kris Bryant. Falling for a sexy ranger is one thing, but is the possibility of love worth giving up the career Kennedy Wells has always dreamed of? (978-1-63555-179-2)

Certain Requirements by Elinor Zimmerman. Phoenix has always kept her love of kinky submission strictly behind the bedroom door and inside the bounds of romantic relationships, until she meets Kris Andersen. (978-1-63555-195-2)

Dark Euphoria by Ronica Black. When a high-profile case drops in Detective Maria Diaz's lap, she forges ahead only to discover this case, and her main suspect, aren't like any other. (978-1-63555-141-9)

Fore Play by Julie Cannon. Executive Leigh Marshall falls hard for Peyton Broader, her golf pro…and an ex-con. Will she risk sabotaging her career for love? (978-1-63555-102-0)

Love Came Calling by CA Popovich. Can a romantic looking for a long-term, committed relationship and a jaded cynic too busy for love conquer life's struggles and find their way to what matters most? (978-1-63555-205-8)

Outside the Law by Carsen Taite. Former sweethearts Tanner Cohen and Sydney Braswell must work together on a federal task force to see justice served, but will they choose to embrace their second chance at love? (978-1-63555-039-9)

The Princess Deception by Nell Stark. When journalist Missy Duke realizes Prince Sebastian is really his twin sister Viola in disguise, she plays along, but when sparks flare between them, will the double deception doom their fairy-tale romance? (978-1-62639-979-2)

The Smell of Rain by Cameron MacElvee. Reyha Arslan, a wise and elegant woman with a tragic past, shows Chrys that there's still beauty to embrace and reason to hope despite the world's cruelty. (978-1-63555-166-2)

The Talebearer by Sheri Lewis Wohl. Liz's visions show her the faces of the lost and the killers who took their lives. As one by one, the murdered are found, a stranger works to stop Liz before the serial killer is brought to justice. (978-1-635550-126-6)

White Wings Weeping by Lesley Davis. The world is full of discord and hatred, but how much of it is just human nature when an evil with sinister intent is invading people's hearts? (978-1-63555-191-4)